TOMB
~OF~
ANCIENTS

TOMB
~ OF ~
ANCIENTS

A HOUSE OF FURIES NOVEL

MADELEINE ROUX

HARPER TEEN
An Imprint of HarperCollinsPublishers

Library of Congress Control Number: 2018961751
ISBN 978-0-06-249873-1 (trade bdg.) — ISBN 978-0-06-294200-5 (int.)

Typography by Erin Fitzsimmons and Catherine San Juan
19 20 21 22 23   PC   10 9 8 7 6 5 4 3 2 1

First Edition

For Andrew, Kate, and Iris, who followed this journey to the end.

For my family, friends, and Smidgen.

For A. S. Byatt, whose work deeply influenced this book and all the books to come.

You see what power is—

holding someone else's fear in your hand

and showing it to them!

—AMY TAN

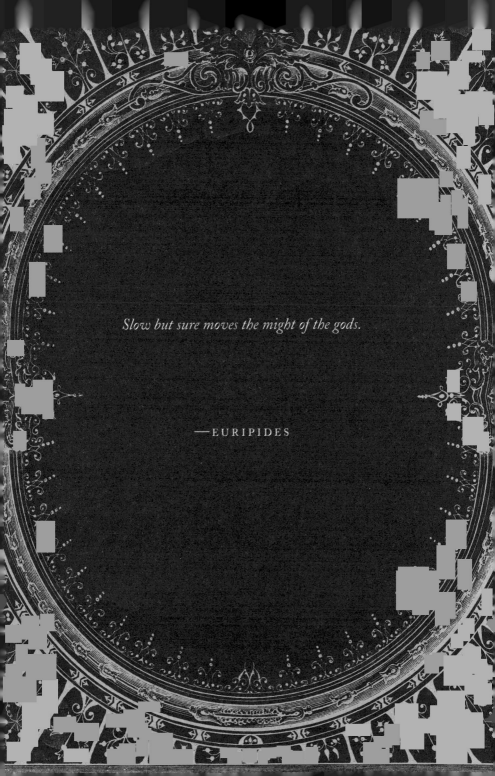

Slow but sure moves the might of the gods.

—EURIPIDES

Prologue

t was becoming less and less obvious where I stopped and he began. My father's dreams had become my own, and like his dark heart, they were ever terrible and troubling. I dreaded sleep yet fell into it with ease, a deep and dreamy slumber consuming me the moment my head touched the pillow. At times, in these dreams, I wandered the past—my past and his—watching as an observer, as an outsider judging my own choices and his.

But on that night, I explored a seemingly endless hall, high and arched as a cathedral, the walls and floor made of a black, twinkling glass. And while there was no explanation for it, I knew this place, and my presence in it, to be real. Though I slid through it in my dream, it felt as solid and true as the bones in my body and the blood in my veins. A real, true place, hidden somewhere, a church of starlight and mystery, with a tremendous secret churning like the determined and bloody chambers of a heart.

When I walked in that hall, I walked with my father's footsteps, his soul's presence in my body, his voice never far from my thoughts, as if he were there beside me, smirking, a question on his lips.

Are you lost, child?

I did not feel lost in that dream—in that strange, endless corridor. There was something at the end of the hall waiting for me, an answer, or perhaps an ending. I moved toward it with purpose and a trembling in my hands, for no ending came easily and no answer was ever given without a price.

Chapter One

London
Autumn, 1810

I was not strictly to blame for what happened at the Thrampton ball, though all those who witnessed the aftermath might claim otherwise. It would be hard to argue with their logic, considering I emerged from the house covered head to foot in blood, a small, dull knife still clutched in one hand. For a moment, it had been a sword, at times a shield; it became whatever tool of defense I needed it to be, shifting from honed to blunt at my will, bent by my Changeling powers—now more potent than ever.

For I harbored a god spirit in my body. It had been the thing used to resurrect me, and that was how all this trouble began in the first place. That was how a perfectly charming ballroom became an abattoir, a scene of horror and gore, guts in the punch bowl, screams of anguish splattered across the fine cucumber sandwiches.

I had not attended the Thrampton ball expecting to be ambushed, though there had been signs that something in London was terribly amiss.

The evening of the ball, I looked down at the stoop, littered with dozens of dead spiders, and instinctively reached behind me for the door. There was no mistaking what this meant—somebody with ill intent was watching the house, observing it—and us—closely, and now they were leaving a calling card. Not the polite, sensible sort of card like the one I had left with my long-lost half sister a few weeks prior. No, this was not a kind overture, but a warning. I wondered if it had to do with Mary. When we first arrived in London, she had been using her Dark Fae powers to shield our presence and the house. It was a precaution born of my anxious sense that we would never make a clean getaway from Coldthistle House. Too many dark events had transpired there, and she helpfully agreed to use the lightest shielding she could manage, a sort of mirage that would make us bleed into the neighborhood like a couple of boring, native residents.

But after weeks of all quiet, I had told her the protection was no longer necessary. How wrong I had been.

Toeing aside a few of the dead spiders, I flicked my eyes up to the gated perimeter of the lawn, seeking anything ominous that did not belong. But the fog was thick, and all those who were out late on the town were concealed by heavy black coats or gliding along in carriages, the mist making those carriages look as if they were pulled by nothing at all. By ghosts. I went back inside with heavy steps.

London was not at all what I'd expected.

For all its terror and strangeness, there had been a kind of peace at Coldthistle House. I would wake to near silence or the soft bustle of the staff and guests rousing, and I would sleep to the rumbling snores of Bartholomew the dog, or Poppy's voice as she sang herself odd lullabies, coaxing us both into dreams.

There was never peace in London, a fact I did not mind, as the traffic of the horses, cries of stray cats, and merry singing of the drunks wandering home at night made for distracting company. The noise kept me from delving too deeply into my thoughts and fears. It kept me from pursuing the growing number of voices in my head, those that had come almost the moment after my friend and former colleague Chijioke diverted my father's godlike spirit into my body, saving me from death.

Aye, the differences, the changes, did not bother me until the dead things began arriving on my doorstep.

The first had come the week before, a small and dusty bird wrapped in a handkerchief. Mary had been the one to discover it, shrieking as she opened the door to retrieve our wood and fuel delivery. The package had come, but the bird was on top of it, its coal-black legs curled up, its toes splayed horribly, part of the beak missing as if snapped away, a silver spoon impaled through its breast.

The second unwelcome surprise had come only two days later, while we entertained our neighbors, Mr. Kinton and his daughters. We had been enjoying a spirited round of whist, and then there was a knock at the door, and Khent excused himself to help our servant, Agnes, answer. They were gone for too long, prompting me also to take my leave from the game and join them in the front hall. Another strange thing had turned up—this time it was a child's toy in the shape of a shaggy black dog, its head torn off and left with the body. Khent and I had shared a glance that Agnes couldn't possibly understand.

I had a feeling we would share it again tonight when I retreated back into the house. But inside I found neither Khent nor Agnes, but Mary, her curling, reddish-brown hair braided neatly up, away from her ears and in a crown over her head. She wore a fine white gown and a green shawl draped over her shoulders. She rushed toward me, reading at once the pale fury on my face—I had only gone out to get a breath of air, nervous to attend my first social dance in the Ton.

"It's happened again, hasn't it?" she asked, her pallor matching mine.

Khent emerged from the shadows near the staircase, dressed for the dance in a becoming black suit and cloaked coat that hid his many tattoos and scars.

"What was it this time?" His low voice trembled with disgust.

"Spiders." My eyes slid between the two of them, and I walked to the staircase, leaning on the banister. I suddenly felt faint, and the whispering voices in my head rose like a restless tide. "A bird with the spoon, a dead dog, spiders . . . These aren't random warnings, they're messages from someone who knows our business here."

"I shouldn't have stopped shielding us, it must have been doing some good after all. Perhaps we shouldn't attend the ball," Mary said, biting her lip. "We could be in danger."

"Then we would be safer away from this house," I suggested. The hall glowed pleasantly with the sconces lit for the evening, a lingering scent of roast and baked bread remaining from our supper. Agnes and our housekeeper, Silvia, chatted in the kitchen, their work done for the day.

"I will fetch a broom," I added. "The spiders will frighten them."

"They have a right to know something is amiss," Mary replied, following me as I went to a small cupboard in the hall pantry. "Someone is trying to frighten you. Us."

"I know that, and I *will* tell them, Mary, just . . . in a manner that doesn't involve them stepping all over a pile of dead spiders."

I had snapped at her. She recoiled and slipped back toward the foyer, hugging herself tightly with the shawl. It had been happening more lately, my temper fraying, the endless battle to quiet the voices in my head turning me into an exhausted meanie.

"That was unfair, Mary, I apologize. I'm simply upset." And exhausted. And overwhelmed. I found the broom, carrying it quickly to the door and outside, glancing around again for signs of life on our property as I brushed the tiny black bodies into the hedges.

"As you should be," Khent grunted. His English had improved so much over our travels and subsequent move to London that he had only a trace of an accent. His penmanship still needed considerable attention, but that was far less of a priority. "From now on I will sleep outside. They will not feel so bold and clever when I catch them red-handed."

"That's absurd," I said, closing the door again and hiding away from the chilly fog. "We can take turns, can we not? Keeping some kind of watch."

"It almost makes me miss the Residents," Mary whispered, referring to the shadowy monster creatures that roamed our old home. They had kept a constant vigil, though I had from time to time managed to evade them. "I'm sure Mrs. Haylam would know some magicks to keep us safer—wards or something."

"We don't need wards," Khent replied, taking the broom from me and returning it to the cupboard. "We have . . ." He cleared his throat, checking over his shoulder to make certain Agnes and Silvia were not near enough to overhear. "Me. We have my nose. You've been kind enough to let me stay in this house, shelter me. Let me do something in return. Besides, you are . . ."

He was staring at me so intently, it almost made my skin itch. His unusual eyes pulsed with purple light, a side effect of his condition, the ability to shift into a jackal-like giant with razor claws and fangs. Then it dawned on me what he meant— me. My voices. My problem.

"Finish your thought, if you please."

"You should not take offense, *eyachou*. You have the voice of a mad god in you; that would test even the strongest Fae."

Mary took a step back from our bickering, still hugging herself.

"You know I hate it when you call me that." My temper was causing more of this, too, more fights, more disagreements. It burned to know that both Mary and Khent could see me struggling. I was supposed to be the head of the house, the one who had inherited the fortune that paid for our newer, shinier lives in London, a caretaker and someone to be depended upon. But it was becoming clear that my hidden fight was no longer so hidden.

I pinched the bridge of my nose and took a deep breath, shoving the voices away, trying to bundle them and lock them up tight. But it was like trying to pick up water, and one or two sly whispers always slithered free.

They question you. They dare question you?

The voices, quite obviously, were rarely friendly.

If I wanted my companions to consider me capable, then it was time to act like a leader. I pulled back my shoulders and calmly looked at them each in turn, folding my hands in front of my waist.

"We will attend the ball this evening, so as not to alarm Agnes and Silvia. Tonight, Khent will take the watch on the property, but tomorrow we will discuss a more permanent solution. In the morning, I will let our staff know that something is amiss and question them to see if perhaps they've noticed anything strange lately. Mary, maybe you would be so good as to write Chijioke? I'm sure he could either make suggestions of his own or talk to Mrs. Haylam."

Mary's eyes lit up at that. I had been surprised when she agreed to stay with me in London and not return to Coldthistle House. She had obviously made the decision with some regret, having discovered a kindling feeling for the groundskeeper of the boarding house. Their frequent correspondence since then had not slipped my notice.

"Diversion then," Khent said, giving me a toothy smile. "And libations!"

"One or two," I warned the Egyptian gently. "I shall remind you that this is not one of Seti's feasts." Khent had told me all manner of incredible stories about kings and queens whose names were as beautiful as they were unusual. I wondered if even half the tales were true, but he recalled them with such conviction and detail that I decided to believe. And anyway, it felt like a secret between us, these stories of ancient grandeur that he had witnessed firsthand. I was the only person lucky enough to hear these tales, their truth lost to time and, according to Khent, the persistent sandy winds of the desert. I attempted to read Terrasson's *The Life of Sethos* with him, but he insisted the inaccuracies were too much to bear.

He snorted and winked, and then held out his arm for me

to take. "His parties were tame compared to those of Ramesses. Have I ever told you about the time I ate two scorpions on a dare from His Radiance?"

Taking the proffered arm, I stepped with him out into the misty chill. "I do not think there will be scorpions to swallow at Lady Thrampton's ball."

"Vipers?"

"Nary a one," I said with a laugh. A few spider corpses remained on the stoop, but I tried not to look at them. A cold shiver slid down my spine.

Khent made a face, helping me down the short stairs in my dark crimson silk gown. Mary had been wise to bring a shawl, and now I was wishing for one of my own.

"Are we going to a celebration or a funeral?" Khent groused. "Damned English."

He would hear no rebuttals from two Irish lasses. We reached the gate at the edge of the lawn, and I grinned up at Khent, who seemed distracted by thoughts of grander, wilder fetes. With his rapidly expanding English vocabulary and friendly demeanor, I sometimes forgot that he had lived a lifetime ago and spent hundreds of years in frozen isolation, imprisoned by my father—by the cruel god now taking up residence in my head.

Turning down the lane toward our destination, he noticed my staring. Mary giggled softly behind us, but I ignored it. There was that shoulder-pinching sensation of being watched as we went, but I ignored that, too, chalking it up to the strangeness of living once more in the city and not in the secluded country fashion.

"What is it?" he asked, smirking. "That look makes me nervous, *huatyeh*."

Shrugging, I finally peeled my eyes away. "I'm simply glad you're free. And here. That we're all here."

The thick fog seemed to muffle and swallow our words. That feeling of being watched never left me, and as it persisted, a heavy dread settled over me. I had come so far, all the way to London, and made a new life for myself, one I had perhaps always wanted and dreamed of, but even now I was not safe. Even now, far, far away from Coldthistle House and its dark mysteries, I was hunted.

A group of women in white dresses so bright they cut through the fog huddled on the church steps across the road from us. I had noticed these women before on walks through Mayfair. Recently their numbers had grown, more clusters of white-garbed chanters appearing on street corners, shivering together like sheep on the moors as they braved rain and cold to sing or shout at passersby.

I couldn't help watching them now as we passed. Perhaps it was the fashionable thing to take a phaeton to the ball, but I preferred to walk and so did my compatriots. Khent craved the darkness and the fresh air on his face. Mary had been confined for a long time, too, and she enjoyed the exercise. Neither of them seemed to pay any mind to the chanters, but I did, squinting into the mist, listening to their shrill voices rise above the steady *clip-clop* of traffic.

"The shepherd guides you in love! Join the fold, join our flock—the shepherd, you are lost without him! You are lost!" Then they began to sing in unison, a childlike song about the safe embrace of the shepherd.

His arms keep out the wind; he forgives all who sinned . . .

That steel-edged shiver returned and so, too, did one of the voices in my head. I caught eyes with one of the chanters as she raised her voice to boom at us from across the road.

Are you lost, child?

The sound of evening hymns ought to bring comfort, but my stomach squirmed as if filled with snakes. Something was wrong, and either my own instincts or those of the soul in my head felt the danger keenly. I began to walk faster, as if I could outrun the man in my head and the strange women all in white, who watched, vigilant, as we disappeared into the dusk.

Chapter Two

A spider clung to the hem of my gown like a grotesque little bead as we were announced at the ball. I grimaced at it as I made my curtsy, presenting myself to the hosts. It was a tradition I detested, but Khent seemed oddly at home. Perhaps this pomp and grandiosity scratched some long dormant itch from his days among Egyptian royalty. Whatever the case, he swept a bow that did not go unnoticed. Lady Thrampton was a wealthy widow, tall and willowy, with penetrating brown eyes and a narrow chin. She was dressed in a white muslin frock, her necklace studded with fat emeralds. She fanned herself more vigorously as Khent, his black hair smoothed back from his wide forehead, his jaw recently free of the bristly whiskers that had sprouted there like weeds, gave off an eminently courtly style.

Sometimes it was quite easy to forget that he was Dark Fae like me, and that he could transform into a massive, shaggy jackal at a moment's notice.

Mary, however, reflected my nervousness. She made a wobbly curtsy, nearly dropping her shawl as she did so. It was my first ball, and a bundle of nerves gathered in my chest, a cruel reminder that I had been born in obscurity, poverty, and that my name—Louisa Ditton—meant nothing to the sleek aristocracy gliding across the parquet.

"Miss Louisa, I was so very pleased to discover that you and your . . . *charming* family would be joining us this evening." With pinched, rouged lips, Lady Thrampton stumbled over the word *charming*. She obviously meant *bizarre*. No group of people could look less alike than we three. "Miss Black spoke so sweetly of you, and I understand you recently resided in Yorkshire?"

I felt the urge to fiddle with my skirts but forced my hands into a tidy bundle at my waist, trying to appear prim. "Indeed!" *Good start, a little too enthusiastic.* "We decided to abandon country life for something more exciting. There are only so many birds one can shoot before it all becomes a dull affair."

Khent quietly cleared his throat.

"And you are unmarried?" Her lip curled at this.

Mary fidgeted at my side. I glanced at her, but she offered no help, her eyes huge with terror, as if this rich woman were a bear rearing up on hind legs and not a frail dowager. "I have . . . only just come into my inheritance. The business of matrimony can perhaps wait until I am more comfortably settled."

"An inheritance!" And now Lady Thrampton's eyes, glossy as glass buttons, sparkled. "How intriguing. You will have to tell me more, dear, after you sample the punch and enjoy a dance or two. You are most welcome in my home, of course."

Of course.

But there was a strain in her voice as she said it. We made our polite curtsies again and turned toward the arched entrance. To the left, a wide, shallow set of marble stairs led down into the magnificent foyer. I had little experience with great houses, Coldthistle House notwithstanding, but Lady Thrampton's was the subject of considerable gossip among the "glamorous elite." She favored bold chintz and exotic carpets, the foyer filled with stone pedestals, atop which stood statuettes and vases. Her wealth was on display for all to see, and I had no illusions that it was only my own recent and large inheritance that allowed me to mingle in her company.

If she knew my true origins, she would toss me out into the gutter like a used handkerchief.

"Miss Louisa Ditton, Miss Mary Ditton, and Mr. Kent Ditton!" Our names were all but shouted over our heads as we descended into the hall, a cane striking the floor afterward, making me jump.

"This jacket itches," Khent informed me, tugging at his collar. "I do not like how that woman gawks at you. How long must we stay?"

"You seemed right at home making an impression on Lady Thrampton," I teased.

"Charming a ridiculous person and tolerating this suit are not the same."

"At least until I've spoken with Justine Black," I told him in a low voice. Lady Thrampton was not the only gawker. Our presence was sure to drum up gossip—three mismatched strangers to Mayfair, swooping into society with few posses-sions, no connections, a mystery inheritance, and a pink spider in a cage, which had also been passed down to me from my strange father. We were bound to set tongues wagging, and the company at the ball did not even attempt to hide their curiosity or, of course, their disdain.

"Try to enjoy yourselves," I told them both with a tight smile. "After all, it's quite diverting, all of them staring at us because they suspect we're really poor or grifters when the truth is so much more horrifying."

"They would not act so superior if they knew," Khent said with a growling chuckle. "Is a demonstration in order?"

"No. Absolutely not." But he was only poking at me, and both he and Mary laughed. Ordinarily it would not bother me, and I might have shared in their merriment, but the beastly voice in my head woke and snarled and snapped. He did not like to be laughed at, my father, and his displeasure spread like poison in me.

I squeezed my hands into tight fists, feeling nauseated from fighting back the voice in my head. Something had to change. When we reached out to Chijioke about the strange happenings at our house, I needed also to inquire about how to eliminate the dark influence that day by day tried to overpower me. I was grateful, naturally, that Chijioke had saved my life, and I understood the desperation of that moment—my life leaking from my body, shot to death, and a conveniently nearby spirit that might bring me back. But still, it felt like another curse had been heaped upon me. I could more or less control my Changeling powers now, but this was something entirely different.

That I could not control it and that it so obviously longed to control *me* filled my heart with constant dread.

But the candles twinkled all around us, and couples in formal black jackets and regal gowns with puffed sleeves and dainty embroidery swirled about the floor, as pretty and perfect as dolls. Mary took great delight in knowing all about the latest styles in London, and she had done her best to clothe us so as not to be an embarrassment. Sadly, she could do nothing for my almost unnaturally pale skin and limp black hair. What's more, my fitful dreams had left me with bruise-like marks under my eyes and a hollowness in my cheeks. No, I would not be finding any eager suitors at the ball, though such matters were far from my mind.

"What does Justine look like again?" Mary asked.

Khent had spotted the lengthy table with refreshments and nudged us both in that direction. I allowed it, running my eyes lightly over every passing face, trying to find a woman who resembled both myself and my father, the so-called Croydon Frost.

"We met just the once," I explained. "I called on her unexpectedly, and she had to leave for an engagement. Most of my experience with her is through correspondence. But she is very pretty, tall and graceful, with black hair and expressive brown eyes."

"It was kind of her to listen to you," Mary replied. "After all, it's all a bit baffling, mm?"

"Messy and humiliating, you mean."

"N-No!" She looked taken aback. "You can hardly choose your parentage."

I nodded, distracted. In my father's papers I had discovered that he had children all over the place, and Justine was one of them. My half sister. She was one of the few, like me, who had survived his deadly schemes. I had written to several other survivors, but Justine was the only one who actually responded. Her letter had been meandering and careful, but it became clear she would be willing to pursue a friendship and to hear more of our odd father.

Though your story is, quite frankly, rude and implausible, some part of me knows it is true. You will forgive me for saying so, but I am glad at least that a measure of good may come from his bad deeds. So much time has passed, and we may never truly be sisters, but I send this letter with affection and a hope that we may know one another better.

At last, near one of the banks of windows at the far end of the ballroom, I spied my half sister.

"There," I said, nodding subtly. "Follow me."

Khent demurred, gazing longingly at a tray heaped with jam tarts.

I smiled and took Mary by the hand, pulling her along. A preemptive warning couldn't hurt, given I had seen how voraciously he ate at the house. "It isn't polite to eat them all."

He took that as his cue and hurried away toward the food. While I kept my sights on Justine, Mary's eyes wandered, her lips parted in wonder as she drank in all the many splendid gowns and slippers. It didn't affect me the way I might've expected once. No part of this new life in London had been what I wanted. My father's inheritance ought to have been a reward for a life of hardship, and all I'd thought I desired was the comfort of a warm home, plentiful food, and my friends. We might visit various parts of the country. Or see Paris! But nothing had yet brought me joy, and so far, even this ball felt like work. I had come seeking Justine, hoping to solidify a friendship, something to anchor me in London.

I told myself, as I waded through the warm, fragrant crowd, that this was my own doing—that my desperation to know Justine Black had nothing to do with the hungry spirit in my head.

"Are you quite well?" Mary asked.

I glanced at her with a soft grunt. "Aye, why do you ask?"

"You're practically crushing my hand, Louisa. Have a care."

She was right. Her poor little hand had gone red. "Maybe I should call Khent back," I whispered, letting go of her. For a moment I paused, silk, music, and sound swirling all around us, almost dizzying. I swayed on my feet, feeling the deep ocean crush of numbness that always preceded an episode. Did my father's spirit sense that one of his other daughters was close? What would he even want me to do with her?

"I do not think Justine will harm you," Mary offered helpfully. "You said your correspondence was friendly!"

I sighed and nodded, forcing my eyes open. The whole ballroom felt suddenly too bright. "It isn't her I'm worried about, Mary."

An image of one of the last guests I served at Coldthistle House, Amelia, flashed before my eyes. My father had drained her of her essence to preserve his own life, leaving her as dry and brittle as a bleached bone. So far, I had experienced no temptations of that variety, but it did not seem outside the realm of possibility that along with my father's temper I may have also received his terrible powers.

At the edge of the crowd, we reached Justine, who stood swaying prettily to the music, her bright blue skirt swishing from side to side. It was for me like looking into a kindly mirror, and for her probably more like a demented one. She was utterly lovely, with soft pink cheeks and my father's narrow jaw. Her dark, shining hair was bouncy and curled, lustrous where mine had the quality of old soot.

"Louisa?" Her eyes widened in surprise, but then she smiled. "Louisa! It is so good to see you once more!"

Justine darted forward, taking me by both hands and spinning me. The woman with her, older and more freckled, with gaudy lips and many twinkling gold necklaces, sniffed as if smelling something rotten.

"This is my guardian, Mrs. Langford." Justine made the introduction tidily. I presented Mary and then apologized, explaining that the third in our party had been waylaid by the desserts.

"Oh, that is completely justified," Justine told us, taking out a perfumed fan and flouncing it at my chin. "Lady Thrampton has one of the best cooks in London. I myself am partial to the marzipan."

"Perhaps fewer marzipans this time, Justine," Mrs. Langford drawled, eyeing first me and then Justine up and down.

"Hush, Mrs. Langford, I shall eat as many as I please. Now, you will excuse us, Louisa and I have so much to talk about. It is all gossip and scandalous in the extreme."

She winked at her guardian, who snapped open her own fan and turned away, gliding like a ghost toward the lemon ices. I was not sorry to see her go, though the forcefulness of Justine's company knocked me off-balance. It was welcoming, of course, but a shock. Before I could say even one word, she had taken both Mary and me by the arm and jerked us in the opposite direction of her guardian, plunging us back into the swelter of giggling, flirting guests.

"That was a joke for her benefit, you see, as I am always perfectly behaved, but I do so hope there *is* some truth to what I said. From your letters, it sounds like you lead such an interesting life. So much excitement! I feel I do nothing but work at my samplers and go to tea." She heaved a dramatic sigh. I thought of all the cruel things my father had said about his human daughters. How they were unimportant. How their lives were petty and brief. My heart throbbed at that memory, for nothing could be further from the truth—Justine was kind and vibrant, everything her neglectful father was not.

"Yorkshire was certainly eventful," Mary said wryly.

"I like the sound of that. You must tell me exactly how you discovered our connection, Louisa. I have a keen eye for deception, you know. There is something you aren't telling me about this whole thing, about our father . . ."

At first I felt certain it was just the heat in the room making my head spin. Everyone around us seemed to be clad in such brilliant white silk that it amplified the brightness in the room, making my head hurt. But it was only getting worse, a buzz at the base of my skull growing until I could hardly hear what Justine was saying. We drew up to the edge of the crowd again, this time on the wall farthest from the desserts. The room spun, the floor going soft, and I stumbled a few steps.

Mary was there in front of me in an instant, holding me steady. I blinked hard, her brown hair blurring until it bled into the floor.

Well done, child, you have brought me to one of my daughters.

That was what the buzzing had been about—my father's voice, his influence, growing until it blotted out my own thoughts. It was like all the rage of a thunderstorm concentrated just in my brain, and it took my breath away.

Consume her. You can. You must. We will.

"No," I heard myself say. My knees buckled. The pain was too much—I ripped my eyes open only to find I could see nothing at all, just a wall of crimson. Red red hatred. I felt my fingers curl as if to turn into claws, sharp and aching to tear.

Chapter
Three

leep came upon me suddenly, unexpectedly, as if descending all at once to keep me from behaving like a monster. How could I be waking and then so swiftly asleep? But there I was, standing once more in a great glass hall, the walls turning black as the red of my vision faded away, like a scarlet sunset giving way to night. And the stars came out, the same stars I had seen in this vision before. They dazzled. The ball and its overwhelming heat seemed a thousand miles away, below me, as if I really did float in the sky.

My head tilted back, I wandered down the black and shining path, watching as the twinkling lights above me began to move and dance. They remade themselves into shapes, constellations, four distinct patterns of stars arcing above me. The first shape resembled a stag, the second a serpent, and the third a ram; the fourth and final constellation was unmistakably a spider. Their forms complete, they began a battle of a sort, the stag rearing up before colliding into the others, obliterating the serpent and the ram, scattering the stars like beads plucked from a gown. Only the spider remained, and it looked as if the stag, growing larger, would trample it, too. Yet just before impact, the spider's shape changed, and it became a human figure. A woman.

The woman held up one hand, and the stag was halted, then

destroyed, and another dozen stars were thrown back into the heavens.

The sky lit up, blazing like a hearth, hundreds of different constellations pulsing with silvery light. It was impossible to count them all or remember the figures, and just as quickly as they had appeared, they were gone, and the sky turned flat, glassy black.

Then a heavy hand fell on my shoulder. My stomach crumbled.

I turned with a gasp, finding myself face-to-face with the thin, pale, skull-like face of my father. Father. His eyes blazed red with pinpoints of ebony, his shoulders draped in a cloak of tattered leaves that seethed and shivered as if full of whispers. Mist shrouded his neck and torso, and all of him smelled of rot.

"That was not for you to see." The thunder of his voice returned, filling my head to bursting. I winced and tried to fall back, but he held me fast. "That was not for you to take. You will remove yourself, child, *you will remove yourself from my head.*"

It was too loud—my skull was going to split. It burned where his hand touched my shoulder. I screamed out, flailed, and then in a twist of red and silver smoke, he was gone.

"No! You get out of mine!"

I came awake with a shout, lashing out with my arms, sitting up and finding myself nose-to-nose with a wide-eyed Mary.

Khent paced next to the small fainting sofa I had been laid upon. We were far from the ball and alone, isolated in a library somewhere in the mansion. A thin shawl had been draped over my waist, and a cold cloth fell with a damp *splat* from my forehead and into my lap.

"How long was I asleep?" I whispered.

"Not long," Khent answered. A bit of jam stained his shirt sleeve. Lines of worry eased from his brow as he came toward me, kneeling. "Moments. Are you well?"

"Obviously not," I said.

He and Mary shared a look of alarm, but I waved them off, taking the cloth and pressing it lightly to my feverish head.

"I have not been . . . completely upfront about what is happening to me." I dodged their prying eyes, concentrating on the embroidered shawl on my legs, trying to trace one of the paisley patterns with my fingertip. "The spirit inside me is banging on the door, so to speak, and the hinges are beginning to creak."

"Oh Lord," Mary breathed, crossing herself out of habit. "I thought it might be something like that. So you hear his voice, then?"

I nodded and pulled at one of the threads in the shawl; it came loose, and I slowly wound it around my finger. "More than that. I sense his will. I sense his need to . . . control me. Just now, I think he wanted me to suck the life out of Justine, in the same way he did to Amelia."

Khent swore under his breath in his native tongue.

"Where is she?" I asked, suddenly frantic. I reached for their hands, squeezing. "Good God, don't tell me—"

"She is very much alive," Khent assured me with a smirk. "Concerned—and talkative—but alive. She went to find a carriage to take us home."

"We should keep her away from me," I said, sullen. "Just to be sure."

"She will not like that at all. I thought she was going to faint when you collapsed," Mary added. "But we will make some excuse, and hopefully we can avoid being seen on the way out. Are you strong enough to stand?"

"I'm sure our host is delighted," I muttered and nodded. "More gossip." Releasing their hands, I swung my legs around to stand, placing the cloth on a tray beside the sofa. "I wish I could tell her the truth. All of it. These damn secrets are more trouble than they're worth, but the poor thing would never believe it all—"

"I would never believe what?"

All three of us froze, then looked to find Justine watching us from the open door. I gazed around at the narrow, cozy library, the walls covered floor to ceiling in well-maintained and dusted volumes. Justine was holding a small wine decanter and took a few bold steps into the room, setting her jaw.

"And I resent that, being called 'poor thing'—I am capable of understanding a great deal. So what are all these strange and terrible secrets?"

"*Ey*, now is not the time for—"

But Justine interrupted Khent, shaking her head and striding toward us. "Don't do that. I will not be discarded so easily. Am I not your sister?"

"Half sister," I corrected her gently, standing.

Justine met me halfway, then went to a decorative table near the sofa, where a neat set of brandy cups had been set out. Later, the men attending the ball might retire to that library to enjoy a cigar, but Justine made use of the serving set, retrieving two small crystal cups. She poured us both a bit of wine and handed me a glass, then pushed her own against it.

"To the truth," she said. "And to courage, which means I must ask: Was our father a criminal?"

Behind us, Khent vented a high whistle.

"In a sense . . ." I drank the wine, hoping the burn of it down my throat would indeed inspire courage. "How to even begin?"

Should I even begin?

But Justine's huge brown eyes were imploring, and when I looked at her, at what I might have been had I been born to kinder circumstances, I couldn't help but *want* to trust her. Had I not come with the express purpose of trying to forge a sisterly connection? If that connection mattered, then so did protecting her. I trailed away from her, back toward the sofa.

"'Tis so bad you cannot even meet my eye?"

"Mary," I murmured, ignoring Justine for the moment. "If anything goes wrong . . . can you shield her from me?"

With a slight nod, Mary crossed to stand between us. When I reached a safe distance, I turned back and spun the cup with both hands nervously. Justine fidgeted and then quickly poured herself another glass.

"I suppose you believe in God?"

Her eyes blew wider at that. "Oh! What an unusual question. Yes, of course I do."

"That will make this difficult."

"Good heavens, can it really be so awful?" Justine yelped. "Then he was not a godly person?"

I almost had to laugh at that. "He was tremendously powerful, like something out of a fairy story. He could command beasts and insects, and he ruled over a kingdom of fantastical creatures." And there I glanced first at Mary and then Khent. "Wonderful creatures. And he could change his form at will, becoming anyone or anything."

Is that how you describe me? Pathetic.

Cringing, I shook my head and willed him to be silent. The threat of another headache pulsed at the base of my neck, and I wondered if that was his attempt to keep me from sharing the truth with Justine. What did it matter now? He was locked away in my head, and she was his daughter, which gave her a right to the full story.

Justine lingered over that information for a long moment, unblinking. She had gone dangerously pale. "Surely you jest! How could such a thing be true?"

"It's true, Justine. I did not come all this way to tell you lies."

"I do dearly want to trust you, half sister, but f-fairy tales," she stammered, shaking her head. She went quiet again, then slowly said, "I . . . believe my governess told me stories of such things. Little oddlings that scurried through the woods, stealing babies and shiny things, turning into tomcats or birds to fool people."

"Just so," I told her. "But all those wild tales for children are true. I'm one of those things, too. I can change my own visage." The details of how did not seem relevant, and Justine already looked very pale.

"You? *You*. Then does that mean I can . . ."

"I'm afraid not," I interrupted. "At least, I don't think so. Our father hunted around for all of his children, his daughters, hoping that some of us would inherit his powers, hoping that he could consume us and our power to sustain his life for . . . well, for eternity, I suppose. He had grown weak over the ages." With a flurry of breaths, I tossed up my hands. "Forgive me, there is so much more. Wars and grudges. Other godlike beings all mixed up with one another."

She twined one finger around a black curl near her ear and looked at me askance.

"This all sounds like an elaborate joke."

"I realize that," I said.

"And yet you all look so deadly serious, it makes me want to believe you."

I took Mary's shawl from the sofa and handed it back to her, then nodded toward the door leading out from the library. "There is no need to believe me, Justine. You asked for the full truth, and I've tried to give it. All I can do is offer what I know. What you choose to do after that is up to you." Mary wrapped the shawl tightly around herself, walking next to me as we gave Justine a wide margin on our way to the door. "This is not a trick or a joke. I wanted you to have the truth because we're blood."

Khent met us as we passed Justine, and she put up a trembling hand.

"Wait," she murmured. "Do not leave just now. I . . . Will you continue?" She turned to us with those huge, glossy eyes and gave us a wobbly smile. "Please. I can't promise I'll believe you, but I can promise to listen."

"*Listen.*" Khent lifted his hand, too, but pressed it to his lips, silencing us. His purple eyes narrowed to slits, and I could see his ears perk. Our glances crossed, and I felt a cold shiver pass between us. "*Ewhey charou—hur seh eshest? Chapep.*"

Listen. Not a sound. Why so quiet? Strange.

He only spoke to me in that language for secrecy. Something was the matter, and his keen, canine-accentuated senses had caught it. And he was right—the ballroom had gone completely silent. Before, the steady hum of chatter and occasional bright peal of laughter could be heard, but now? Silence. No clinking of punch cups, no shuffling dance feet, no merry string quartet.

"It's awfully quiet," Mary murmured, noticing the eerie silence, too.

"How very odd—" Justine began.

"No," I told Justine. "Something is wrong. It should not be that quiet at a ball."

Her eyes widened with fright. Her voice became a whisper. "Mrs. Langford! I hope nothing has happened to her. We must investigate."

"*I* will look," Khent told us, removing his restrictive jacket and letting it fall to the floor. He rolled up his shirtsleeves quickly, revealing a crosshatch of scars and faded tattoos. "*You* will stay."

There was a sudden crash and grunt of pain from the direction of the ballroom. The chill in my spine spread quickly, unnaturally, and I realized with a gasp that this was not just fear inside me but a warning. I had felt this specific brand of uneasy iciness before, at Coldthistle House, when the shepherd's Adjudicators had begun falling from the sky.

"I think this sad English party just became much more interesting," Khent whispered, before dashing around the door and leaping into the hall.

Chapter Four

harp, unforgiving ice replaced the blood in my veins as the house shook, rattled as if thunder exploded overhead. That was enough. With one slippered foot already out in the corridor, I turned to Mary and Justine.

"Protect her, Mary," I said sternly. "Hopefully I will return in a moment."

"I should come, too," Mary insisted, loosening her shawl. "Three is better than two."

"Undoubtedly, but Justine needs you just now. I will be fine. Remember? There's a monster lurking inside me."

That did not seem to soothe her, but she remained, ushering Justine back into the library and closing the doors. That at least made me feel a little better—Mary's ability to use her magic as a kind of shield had astounded me at Coldthistle, and I trusted her to keep the innocent Justine safe from whatever was happening in the ballroom. My stomach roiled as I ran toward the commotion, an array of terrible and violent possibilities springing to mind. Foremost, of course, was the idea that those warnings on our doorstep had not been idle threats. Even before I had left Coldthistle, Mr. Morningside himself had warned me that anonymity was a ridiculous notion for one such as me.

"Pretend you can run all you like, girl, but ancient wheels have a way of turning, and old, ugly wounds have a way of opening up again."

I could only wonder for that brief moment before I reached the ballroom which old wound exactly had split.

There was little time to worry as I raced through Lady Thrampton's gilded halls; I soon found the ballroom. Its tall, grand doors were shut, and a few confused guests milled about outside, their voices rising with confusion and squeaky complaint. The evening had been intolerably ruined. Such a waste! This was all very shocking to them, of course, their soft, rich hands having known nothing more vexing than a late tea.

When I was nearly to the doors, they blasted open with a noisy gust. Dust and a woman's nosegay flew at me with enough force to knock the breath from my lungs. The guests screamed and scattered, their slippers, fans, and punch cups forgotten in their haste to flee. But not all who had been invited left, for I discovered a few lingering in the ballroom. Those remaining were dressed in stark white, their backs to the walls as they watched the conflict unfolding in the center of the room, just under an immense crystal chandelier.

A fine layer of plaster dust, ivory as snow, had fallen around the two figures circling each other. The ceiling above had been cracked by the force of whatever had caused that initial noise. That horrid frost in my veins had thickened for a reason—one of the shepherd's Adjudicators had come, dropping from the heavens and landing like an anchor on the parquet. The wood where she had fallen was splintered, almost ground to shavings.

"Sparrow," I said softly, drawing to a stop.

Her yellow hair had been cropped short, and she had abandoned her gray suit for what looked like a set of ancient leather armor. A clean white bandage was wrapped around her throat, and a brace hugged her arm, remnants of her encounter with Father at Coldthistle House. For all the wounds she had suffered at his hands, she now looked capable. And furious.

"Ah! The prodigal daughter is here." She darted toward Khent with unnatural speed, shoving him out of the way with her hip. "I knew this flea-bitten mutt was lying. I'm sure he couldn't help it; he's barely more than a dog. Does he come to you with a whistle?"

I found myself striding toward her. Ordinarily, the sight of her—tall, golden, and immensely strong—would make me think twice about an open confrontation. The only thing that gave me pause now was the number of innocent onlookers in the ballroom.

"I wouldn't if I were you," I told her. Off to Sparrow's side, Khent bristled, and it did not take a keen eye to notice the way the muscles in his forearms strained against his skin, the beastly form below bursting to get out.

"We snuffed out his kind ages ago," Sparrow said, shooting him a glare. "Shame we missed one."

The sound Khent made put my hairs on end. It was not a growl a man could make. Any moment now, he would explode into his other form, a doglike creature, eight feet tall and with razor-sharp claws. The noble ladies in the corner might actually die from the shock of it.

"Don't!" I cried out. "She wants to provoke you. She wants to provoke us both. We have to be better than her."

"Unlikely," she said, rolling her bright blue eyes. "A cur and a chambermaid."

Sparrow drew herself up to her full height, letting her human form melt away like candle wax, revealing the blazing, golden body beneath. Her facial features became difficult to divine, her skin and bones turning into molten gold. One arm, the uninjured one, flashed as it turned into a long, pointed lance.

I expected to hear gasps from the remaining guests, but none came. My jaw set, the cold dread in my belly no longer just from Sparrow. Her presence was frightening, yes, but more was amiss. Khent seemed to notice, too, glancing around in every direction, and as he did so, the men and women waiting near the walls began to close in around us. How could it be? Why were they not afraid of her?

Sparrow laughed in the face of our confusion, as haughty and irritating as ever.

"Did you think it would all just go away?" she taunted, waving the golden lance her arm had become. "You swallowed the soul of the Dark Father. The book—all that pathetic Fae knowledge? It's in you. Did you not receive my warnings, love? I thought the spiders were a nice touch, considering you're mere moments away from being a sad, dead little insect, too."

She charged, her golden skin so fantastically shiny it hurt my eyes to look at her. But I had to defend myself. I stumbled back but found that a row of guests was walking slowly to meet me. Their faces were all similar masks of fearlessness; one mustachioed gentleman even smirked. I felt the heat of Sparrow's body as she raced toward me, but I dodged at the last second, hurling myself out of the way. She skidded to a stop, then spun gracefully, a flicker of wings sprouting from her back before they were gone, before ultimately landing in a defensive position, lance lowered across her body. The point of that weapon, glittering with lethality, had almost punctured the mustachioed man's side.

"Stop this!" I shouted. "You're going to kill someone!"

Sparrow laughed again and shot herself like an arrow toward me. "That's the idea, darling!"

She was mad—madder than usual—and as she charged at me like a weapon made flesh, I heard the men and women surrounding us begin to chant. God, they were all the shepherd's chanters, no different from the bizarre crowds I had noticed spreading across London like a pale rash.

The shepherd will guide, the shepherd provides, for him we will live and for him we will die. . . .

They chanted it over and over again, low and rumbling, but growing louder. Sparrow bobbed her head along to the beat of their slow singing, raising her lance as if to conduct them with a baton.

I clenched my jaw, forcing myself to remember that they might have any number of reasons for following the shepherd. Perhaps they truly were lost and needed something to believe in to steady their hearts and give succor. Or maybe Adjudicators like Sparrow had found a way to convert them against their will. I did not know enough, and I had no proof that these humans deserved to be harmed.

"I will not hurt them," I told Sparrow, but she did not slow her pursuit. Her lance punched toward me, close, so close the blade's end ripped the shoulder of my gown. The contact startled me, and I fell to the side, rolling to avoid her weapon as it came down again, the lance burying deep into the floor. Sparrow struggled to extract it, and I used that time to roll back to my feet and join Khent at the opposite end of the ever-tightening oval. The chanting was almost hypnotic, but I forced myself to focus.

"Ideas?" he hissed. "Because they certainly will hurt *us*."

His arms keep out the wind, he forgives all who sinned . . .

"Let me think," I whispered back. But we both knew there was no time for thinking or for hesitating. A familiar tightness in my skull meant that Sparrow and her ring of believers were not our only problems. Like Khent, Father was ready to retaliate.

The chanting persisted, but one of the guests behind me darted forward, grabbing at my arms and trying to hold me. I wrestled against them, screaming, thrashing, but Sparrow took the opportunity to throw herself toward me, spear raised high.

"Do it," I told Khent.

He needed no further instruction. As I fought against the human pinning my arms, I heard his fine shirt tear to pieces, his beastly form pushing through his skin. That startled Sparrow, but only for an instant, one I took advantage of, letting my mind spin with possible defenses. I no longer had my beloved little spoon, but the memory of it did give me an idea. Metal. Armor. Closing my eyes hard, I went silent, all of my thoughts bent toward altering the state of my gown. The desperation of the moment must have helped, for at once I felt the silk shift and grow heavy, and Sparrow's spear scraped against a sturdy breastplate. Sparks flew up in front of my face from the impact, red and gold showering me in glittering heat. I heard the man holding my arms gasp in surprise, and I slammed down my foot on his, no longer clad in a soft leather slipper but in steel.

Twisting away from them both, I watched the crowd around us scatter toward the walls, but Sparrow remained undeterred. She spun her spear once and then leveled it across her middle, her sapphire eyes darting between the hulking form of Khent and me in my armor.

"Friends," she called, raising her spear arm to rally them. "Followers of our great shepherd, do not be afraid! Tear the fear from your hearts as weeds from a garden. To me! With whatever you can find, to me!"

We watched as the guests—the followers—in their draped finery and beautiful suits masked by white cloaks, scrambled to find serving knives and utensils. Bottles abandoned by bewildered butlers were taken up and smashed, the sharp, wet ends glinting in the chandelier light. And then they did as Sparrow demanded, rushing toward us, screaming, their monotonous chanting abandoned for shrieks.

Too late I felt Father's presence surge in me. Perhaps it was my own fear, which I had not even attempted to tear from my heart, that allowed his coming. Or maybe I had longed for this moment since surviving Sparrow's torment at Coldthistle

House. Whether it was my own weakness or desire for revenge, I could not say, but I heard a sound like heavy cloth tearing inside me. The armor stung, for the boundaries of my body expanded rapidly, twisting and reshaping, until my legs were longer and stronger, dark leafy vines twining around my arms as my fingers elongated and sharpened into black claws.

Whatever I had become, it gave Sparrow pause, but her gasp of surprise soon turned to a growl of determination. She and her followers fell upon us, a dozen or more hands slashing at us from every direction. I reached for a dull knife dropped by one of the guests and willed it into a sword, swinging it blindly to keep the shepherd's followers at bay. The sword did not stop them, and so I imagined the little knife becoming a massive shield, one large enough to push the humans away and create some space. Nothing seemed to frighten them. I only wanted them to stop, to retreat, but something in Sparrow's command had driven them mad.

I heard the meaty *thunk* of Khent knocking one of the guests away, his body tumbling end over end as if he were no more than a child's doll. Some of those knives and ragged bottles managed to aimlessly wound, and the floor around us became slick with blood, some of it mine, some of it Khent's, but most of it Sparrow's.

I reached for her. My head filled with crimson smoke; my vision narrowed only to her gold, glowing form and the spear that punched toward me. Without even meaning to, my arm stretched and stretched, unnatural and ugly, but useful in its strangeness. I grabbed her by the neck, saw the sudden terror in her eyes as I crushed against the bandages and then against more. Her spear slashed at my side, finding a gap in my armor, but I hardly felt the sting. More followers of the shepherd raced into the ballroom, but they were too late. Father's control had gripped me utterly, and his will dominated me as if I were merely a costume he had put on. I saw with his cruel eyes and struck with his cruel hand, slamming Sparrow down onto the floor, shaking the entire house once more. The chairs and tables around the edge of the room tumbled over, the entire ballroom in ruin. Candelabras spilled their candles onto the floor, small gouts of flame threatening to spread. A guest, thrown by Khent, sailed over my head. Roots as thick as a man thrust up from beneath, just as they had in the pavilion when we had all banded together against Father. Now those grasping black tendrils were on my side. Our side.

"The ceiling!" Khent growled out through his pointed teeth. *"Mahar!"*

Look.

Khent leapt back, slashing his way through the throng of guests, and I had the good sense to follow. I glanced toward the ceiling, the great shuddering and shaking of the house cracking the ornate plaster. The chandelier swayed, creaking dangerously on loosening brackets. The final push it needed came as Mary and Justine threw open the ballroom doors. Their faces dropped in twin shock and horror, but Mary stepped forward, flinging her arms across Justine as the chandelier's bolts gave, its gold and silver baubles plunging downward, candle wax splattering us as it fell. A faint ripple encased the two girls, Mary's shielding magic emerging like a wave from her arms.

I wanted to look away, but Father would not allow it. Khent cringed at my side as the chandelier smashed into the mess of roots and wood splinters and Sparrow below. She gave a weak, startled cry, but then came a long, eerie silence. I watched a candle pool into the ruined floor and reached for my side. It had begun to ache badly, and my hand came away drenched in blood.

At last, I felt Father's influence lessening, and I turned away, fully realizing then what I had done. Sparrow had attacked us, yes, but now she was grievously wounded. No, I thought with a shudder, dead. There were other bodies, too, and it turned my stomach to see them. My legs went weak, and I stumbled away, finding myself leaning against the buffet table, once beautiful and festive, now splashed with blood. Heaving, I chanced to see my reflection in a silver tray. What I saw there stole my breath away—smoking red eyes, charred skull face, a crown of twisting antlers . . .

A monster. *A monster.* My own face began to emerge, the beast I had become receding until the reflection showed nothing but a scared girl, her face smeared with blood, a dull supper knife clutched in one shaking hand.

Chapter Five

he crash of the chandelier and Sparrow's demise seemed to shake the followers from their mania. Those who could run from us did, streaming out of the ballroom, the white trains of their gowns flowing behind them like flags of surrender.

My stomach remained in knots. Khent breathed hard beside me, his dark gray fur matted with all manner of gore. His clever canine eyes, a vibrant purple, followed as I walked slowly from the table toward Mary and Justine.

I could not bring myself to look at the chandelier. At Sparrow. She had been a miserable thorn in my side since the moment of our meeting, but I refused to believe that she deserved such an end.

"Goodness gracious, Louisa, what a disaster! Are you all right?" Mary breathed, closing the distance and throwing her arms around me. "We heard such awful noises. . . ."

"We need to find somewhere safe to go," I replied, disentangling quickly and marching for the door. Justine was frozen there, her hands covering her mouth. "Where is your guardian, Justine?"

"S-She must be in the house somewhere," Justine managed to stammer. "I did not see her among the crowd, and surely she is not among the . . . the . . ."

"We must find her," I said. Though I sounded clearheaded, I felt anything but. Muffled voices came from beyond the foyer and out the doors. Brushing past Justine, I motioned to Mary and Khent—now returned to his human form and wearing very tattered clothing—and then hurried toward the commotion.

We found Justine's guardian, Mrs. Langford, fanning herself in a sweaty panic on the lawn of the house, joined by the guests who had fled immediately and those who had survived the battle with us. The survivors looked dazed, bloodied, their fight gone out of them now that their leader, Sparrow, lay dead under a chandelier. They all appeared to be looking at something on the far side of the lawn, and we moved through the crowd with no trouble—nobody who did notice me wanted to be near the girl with the bloodstained gown and knife. An older woman in an orange satin dress swooned and collapsed on the grass when I passed.

We found a lone man standing at the head of the crowd. He was young, hardly older than myself, and he had a ruddy complexion and bright ginger hair. His suit was very simple, patched in places, and a pale bandage was draped around his eyes, as if they were wounded. Even so, he appeared to see us plainly, and he shook his head at our approach.

The young man took the measure of the crowd as a strong little hand grabbed my elbow.

"Louisa! My God, Louisa, you were telling the truth!"

It was Justine, her hair a snarl, her pretty eyes wide with

fright. I turned to her fully, not knowing what to say or how to explain what she had just witnessed. In her, I had hoped to find a friend, some semblance of normalcy, but now, seeing what the truth had done to her, I regretted ever coming to the ball. Her hands shook so badly that I felt moved to cover them with one of my own and press. Father roared inside me, still heated from the battle, and he no doubt wanted more. More, of course, being the consumption of this daughter, despite her lack of Fae power.

I had to remove myself from Justine and soon, before he could harm her through me. She wept, her chin tucked against her chest, and I sighed. The only difference between us was an accident of birth. Had things gone differently, she might be the one cursed with Father's spirit, and I the privileged, happy-go-lucky lady about town. Mere chance had protected her from Father's rampage, his path leading him to me before it ever reached Justine. And it cut at me, seeing her so undone. I decided perhaps it was better that I had been the one to shoulder the burden.

"It will take time for you to really understand," I said to her gently. "And—"

But I could say no more, as the young man at the head of the crowd now addressed me.

"I suppose this is your bloody mess?" He heaved a full-bodied sigh and swept the fringe off his forehead. He had more freckles even than Mary. "You *are* friends of Henry's, so it figures."

"We are not his friends. We—" I began, but he pushed me aside, opening his arms wide to the assembled guests, who shivered in the fog under flimsy shawls. Justine continued crying into her gown.

"Dear friends, you are all so weary and confused, allow me to help." He smiled a genuine smile and inhaled, and then a soft, yellow light emerged from his chest, growing out and out and then bathing the guests and followers as if a beam of sunlight had pierced the night and fallen gently on them all.

Their eyes glazed; their mouths dropped open a little. Even Justine appeared utterly entranced. Then, just as suddenly as the light had come, it disappeared. The young man removed his jacket and draped it over me, hiding the scratches and blood.

I let go of Justine's hands. They had stopped shaking. She looked at me now as if I were a stranger. It hurt, but I let it go, knowing how gravely the knowledge and the carnage had disturbed her.

"There now," he said to the crowd gently, gazing at them with a serene expression. "What a scandalously bad party that was. You must all scold Lady Thrampton for her mediocre punch and talk endlessly of the flat cello in the quartet. And Lady Thrampton? You must remove your household to the country for a while, to recover from the shame of this sad little fete."

Lady Thrampton, whom I had not seen among the followers but now realized had been one of the attackers slashing at us, lifted a bloodied hand to her lips and frowned.

"That should give me time to clean up your misadventure," he said, then he gave a short, casual bow. "Dalton Spicer, the fool stupid enough to help you out this evening."

"Spicer," I repeated, following him toward the gates that led away from the estate. It was my turn to feel as if I were in a haze. The crowd mingled for a moment behind us and then gradually began drifting away. Justine had found her guardian, but I had to wonder just how much of the evening she would remember. Our discussion in the library, for example . . . She would remember none of it, if fate were kind.

"I know that name," I added. "Why does it sound familiar?"

"Because I'm an old chum of Henry's," he said lightly. "And an Adjudicator. The missing tine on the Sparrow and Finch trident."

At that, I froze, Khent and Mary flanking me. Dalton Spicer beckoned me along.

"There's no need for that. I'm not your enemy. I gave up judging and doing the shepherd's bidding a long time ago. Thus—" And here he pointed to the bandage covering his eyes. He tugged the covering away, revealing empty pits where eyes might have been. "We begin to go Sightless when we turn away from him."

He replaced the covering and strode right out of the gates, continuing briskly in the opposite direction of our home.

"Sightless?" I asked.

"I could not Judge you if I wanted to. My talents now

are limited . . . and growing lesser by the day. It's worth it, though. I'd rather slowly turn into a hedgehog than become like Sparrow."

He fell silent, and so did I, both of us appreciating the weight of her passing. It felt impossible that someone as powerful and magical as she could just be *gone*. And gone because of me.

"I wish you could've known her in a better time," Dalton told us, as if reading my dark thoughts. "She changed after I left. If I had known my going would make her so angry, so cruel, I might have done things differently. Many things. But that and your relationship to Henry are discussions for another time. Right now we need to take you all to a safe house."

A modest carriage with two immaculate white horses waited down the street, well away from the revealing lamps and the crowded lawn of Lady Thrampton's estate. He guided us to it with purpose, but I hesitated when we reached the door and he opened it. I noticed no driver.

"Wait," I said. "I appreciate your intervention, I think, but this is all rather sudden."

Khent nodded. "Mm. How can we trust you? You're one of them. I do not like it."

He was right. Dalton gave me that icy sensation in my veins, though it was far less noticeable than the way Sparrow and Finch made me feel. I studied the young man closely, but his face was unreadable.

"Sparrow and her followers know where we live," Mary

pointed out. "They were leaving dead things outside the door to warn us. I don't like this, either, but I think we should avoid the house for now."

"At last," Dalton snorted. "Sense. Look, I don't need you to trust me yet, but I do need you to listen. Those followers will not remain confused forever. Sparrow was no doubt using them to her own ends, and with her gone, someone else will come to take her place and control them. Their sense will return and so will their loyalty, and their first inclination will be to follow whomever is sent, Finch most likely, or another of the shepherd's minions. I bought you time, but only a little."

I fidgeted with the knife in my hands, passing it back and forth under the coat. "But all of our things! Agnes and Silvia will be concerned if we disappear completely. We shouldn't let them stay in that house if it's dangerous."

"I will go," Khent said with a decisive nod. "Agnes and Silvia can be dismissed, and I will gather what I can of our things in the phaeton. Where do I meet you?"

His forwardness seemed to please Dalton, who gave an approving grin and then jerked his head toward the carriage. "Deptford. It is not far. There's a little church there for St. Nicholas. You'll know it by the skull and bones on the gates outside."

That sounded ominous. But Khent simply touched both Mary and me on the shoulder, waiting for our responses.

"Of course, of course," I said hurriedly. "Go. I think tonight proved I can more than handle myself."

"I never doubted, *eyachou*." Then, more seriously, he said to Mary, "But you watch over her all the same."

"Aye. We will watch over each other," Mary told him. "I promise."

With that, Khent disappeared into the night. He was unbelievably fast when he wanted to be, and I wondered if perhaps he would transform into his other self in order to cut through the darkness at even greater speed. Dalton did not wait to watch him go but climbed into the carriage and hustled us in with an impatient sound.

"We should make Deptford before dawn. The less this city sees of you, the better."

The fog clinging to London's streets eased as we approached Deptford. I had never seen that part of town, and I let the orderly rows of homes and pockets of gardens distract me from the lingering unease in my heart. Mary, exhausted, fell asleep with her head on my shoulder. The carriage drove itself, the horses navigating through the city as if they had been trained for just that purpose.

"I remember your name now," I told Dalton Spicer softly, trying not to wake Mary. "At Coldthistle there was an old copy of Henry's book. The inscription was made out to you."

"I'm sure he's furious with me for leaving it behind."

His voice was tipped with regret.

"You two were close," I continued. "He spoke of you."

He shifted in the seat, leaning away from me and toward the window. "I won't pretend to be interested in what he had to say. But yes, we were friends for a time. He was part of what made me leave the shepherd's service in the beginning. He had all these grand ideas about fixing the state of things, ending the eternal bickering among the gods. It was all very radical and exciting. Now I see it for what it truly was," he murmured. "A lie."

"He's good at that," I replied drily. "Lying."

"We've arrived."

I could tell he was grateful for that, as he all but jumped from the carriage while it was moving. The jerky halt startled Mary, but I soothed her with a hand on her arm. Outside, in the still gloom of the night, an owl watched us from the top of a stone skull sculpture. Just as Dalton had said, two skull-and-bones pillars marked the entrance to the chapel, a macabre addition to an otherwise quaint place. The chapel itself loomed above the gates, pale and square, a spindly tree swaying on the right side of the lawn.

Dalton opened the door for us, and we climbed out into the cold. The carriage drove itself away, rounding a corner, the gentle *clip-clop* of hooves fading into the chill. I huddled down inside the borrowed coat, still holding tight to the dull blade. There was no telling if I would need it, but I had been unwise enough to trust one of the shepherd's folk before, and this time I would be prepared. Chijioke had warned me when the Upworlders first appeared that they would never be my friends, but I had stubbornly believed that the kinder ones, like Finch, would heed their consciences and not follow orders blindly. In the end, he had chosen the shepherd, horrified by what he had witnessed at Coldthistle House. Yet I believed Dalton Spicer, and my intuition told me he was a kind soul, or at least, well-meaning.

Father, however, had a different idea.

Murderer. Betrayer. Golden liar.

"That's enough of that, thanks very much," I muttered.

"Sorry?" Dalton turned toward me as we walked through the skull-marked gate.

"Nothing," I replied. "Are we to stay in the chapel?"

We moved across the lawn toward the door, but veered away at the last moment, skulking instead around the side of the building. I reached out and touched the cool stones, a shiver transferring from chapel to skin. Looking up, I gazed at the windows above but noted no candles and no watchful eyes.

"This has been a safe house for the wayward since . . . well, for a long, long time. Not just for my kind and your kind, but for humans, too. It has lasted through fires, through wars, through Tudors and Stuarts, through Williams and Georges . . ." Dalton vented a low laugh. "I suspect it will last long after Henry and the shepherd and you are forgotten."

It was strange to be clustered in with those two, but I did

not argue. Toward the back of the chapel, next to a handful of crumbling stone tomb markers, lay a heavy cellar door set apart from the main building. A haphazardly constructed stone arch was above it, engraved with symbols that meant nothing to me. Mary appeared just as confused by them. With the toe of his boot, Dalton tapped three times on the cellar door.

A woman's voice answered from within, oddly accented and melodious, even through wood.

"What is the reward of sin?" the voice asked.

"Death."

What sounded like six bolted locks were pulled open. The hinges shrieked, and then slowly the door slid open toward us. The spirit taking up lodging in my head resisted, but I pushed past him, knowing I would probably pay for my petulance with a headache later. I simply wanted to be out of the cold and to wear something clean, to drink a cup of tea and decide what we would do now as fugitives.

Almost as soon as we set foot on the steps down into the cellar, we were met by a surprising warmth. I had expected the moist coolness of rock, but the underground lair was fortified with ancient timbers, a felted carpet softening our steps as we descended. Large lamps repurposed from old barrels hung above us, close enough to reach out and touch. An herbal scent clung to the air—mint, lavender, and rosemary—as clean and fragrant as an apothecary's case.

At the bottom of the long, long staircase waited the woman

we had heard before. Dark-skinned and short, she wore an oversize man's shirt, nipped in at the waist with a sash, and a full, striped skirt. Her black hair was oiled and braided into a thick Dutch plait that hung over one shoulder.

"Fathom Lewis," she said, offering me a hand.

"I'm afraid my hands are . . . They're not in a fit state for shaking. Would you accept a curtsy?"

"If you insist," Fathom replied breezily. She, Mary, and I exchanged curtsies, which felt ridiculously formal, given the circumstances.

"Americans and their manners," Dalton sneered. "She's from something called Pennsylvania. God only knows what it's like there."

"It's actually nice," she told me with a smirk. That explained the unusual accent. "Dalton wouldn't like it—not enough snobs like him."

"Ha. Ha."

"He told me there might be trouble tonight," Fathom said, ignoring him. She strode off deeper into the safe house, and we followed just behind Dalton. "From the looks of it, he was right."

"Sparrow made her move," he explained. "I refused to believe she would strike so quickly. And with such violence. It didn't end well for her, or her followers."

The cellar opened up into a larger chamber, the walls covered in mismatched bookcases, each overflowing with papers, trinket boxes, and curiosities. The room reminded me a little of the library Henry had allowed me to use while I translated Bennu's journal for him, only the objects here did not appear nearly as valuable. Still, the memory filled me with a momentary nostalgia. That I remembered any bit of Coldthistle House fondly was astonishing, and the house and memory felt impossibly far away. I had not been safe then, but surely it was not as bad as all this.

Fathom disappeared into a side passage, then joined us again with a tray laden with cups and, thank heavens, a teapot. She set an ancient and rickety table for four while Mary collapsed gratefully onto one of the padded chairs.

"One more, please," Dalton instructed her. "We have a gentleman joining us. A royal son of Egypt by day, if I'm not mistaken, and a moon dog by night."

"An Abediew," I corrected, feeling offended on Khent's behalf. *Moon dog* didn't seem quite to capture what he was.

"My mistake. Yes, he's that, and he will be along shortly with their possessions. I don't think it's wise for them to return now that Sparrow has struck openly. Others will get ideas, and Finch will come looking for his sister."

I cringed. Finch. We may not have left things on good terms, but I knew Sparrow's death would send him into despair. They had been siblings, after all, if strange ones, and it gave me no pleasure to imagine his suffering, or what his retaliation might look like. I did not want to fight him, or anybody—I had only wanted to get away—but even escape and a normal life had been too much to ask for, it seemed.

"So are you . . . you know, one of us? A pixie or a demon or something?" I asked slowly. It was no use dwelling on Finch. If anything, I would do my best to avoid him and further confrontation.

Fathom shook her head. "Oh no, much worse than that. I'm a poetess."

"An *American* poet. Good Lord."

She and Dalton subsided into laughter, and I shared a glance with Mary, who shrugged and sipped her tea. They did not seem to be scheming against us or sharing furtive looks, and they had given us tea and a warm place to hide, but I still held on to my doubts. Their laughter clawed at something in me. An Upworlder, nasty as she was, had just died. Many *people* had just died. How could they laugh? Did they not understand the weight of the pressure on my shoulders now, with the red evidence of that death drying all over me?

It was Father's power that answered, my head suddenly full of that crimson mist again, my own thoughts diminishing until I heard and felt nothing but the steady crescendo of a drumbeat. My hands tightened around the teacup until it cracked, a hot drip of tea on my hand surprising me enough to break the spell.

When I opened my eyes, all three of them were staring.

A fine dust of plaster drifted down to us from the ceiling. My anger must have shaken the entire cellar, too.

"Forgive me," I whispered, hoarse. "There is something not quite right with me."

Nobody spoke. Mary reached over and squeezed my hand.

"I suppose you haven't heard about the *thing* sharing my soul."

Dalton shook his head slowly, and I rubbed at nothing on the table with my thumb. For a moment, Fathom left, and when she returned, she handed me a warm, wet washcloth. I scrubbed at my hands and sucked in a shaky breath.

"I'll begin at the beginning," I said.

And so I told them; piece by piece, I told them, trusting strangers, laying bare the whole fantastical story, hoping there was a solution to the danger lurking in me, knowing that I was likely to be stuck with the curse of my father forever.

Chapter
Six

alton and Fathom listened. With saintly patience, they listened.

"Sparrow must've heard about that soul ferrier, Chijioke. That must be what set her off," Dalton said gravely when I had finished and described the process of having an ancient soul placed into my body.

"'Tis not his fault," Mary shot back. "He only did what he could to save Louisa!"

"Nobody is casting blame," he assured her, pouring us all more tea. My cup had sustained only a small crack, but they gave me a new one all the same. "But Finch would never keep that to himself. The shepherd must have been livid, and now he's grasping for power with these zealots of his. He fears whatever Henry has become, whatever he's been cooking up in that house."

His eyes darted swiftly to mine, and I frowned.

"If you mean to ask what his plan is, I have no idea," I said. "Mary?"

She bit down on her lip, her cheeks swishing from side to side as she thought. "We only ever did as he asked, eliminating the bad people that came to stay at Coldthistle, and Chijioke helped him keep their souls in a menagerie of sorts. Birds, hundreds of them. He kept them all, I know that, but he never shared his reasons."

"How many birds?" It was Fathom who asked, leaning toward us across the narrow table.

"Hundreds," Mary answered. "I think . . . I think hundreds."

"Hundreds of trapped souls? Does that sound like an army to you? Because that sounds like an army to me." Fathom whistled and nudged Dalton.

"That's Henry all the way down, always thinking of himself and never what consequences might hurt everyone else. No bloody wonder the shepherd is desperate for followers." Dalton pushed away from the table and wordlessly retrieved a small decanter from a nearby shelf. It had been sitting next to a jar filled with what looked like pickled pig's feet. Whatever was in the decanter was added generously to his tea.

"I just want to stay out of all of this," I said, impatient for . . . something. Answers. Anything. Even if the answers were hard to hear. "Henry. The shepherd. It's their fight, not mine. All I want is to get this *monster* out of my head."

Dalton nodded, tapping his fingers thoughtfully on the side of his teacup. "That would be quite beyond me, but I know who might be able to help."

"Please do not say Henry."

He cleared his throat. "It's Henry."

"*Of course it is.*" I motioned to the decanter, and Dalton

hesitated before shrugging and pushing it across the table toward me.

"Louisa . . ." Mary looked sleepy, but she rubbed the tiredness from her eyes and sat up in her chair. "We intended to write Chijioke soon, aye? Is this really so different?"

"I had hoped to keep Mr. Morningside out of this," I said shortly. "You know I am not eager to return to Coldthistle."

In fact, I had hoped never to return. I'd told myself that if our new life in London proved impossible, then I would try any number of places before journeying back to Yorkshire. Even the First City, with all its ancient ghosts, appealed to me more. But now I watched Mary, noticing a small twitch in her arm. My eyes darted below the table, and I saw that she had taken the little carved fish Chijioke had made for her and was worrying it with her thumb.

"What makes you so sure Henry can assist me?" I asked Dalton, who stood yet again and went to rummage among the overstuffed bookshelves. If I was going to relent and return to Coldthistle, potentially walking headlong into a conflict between Henry and the shepherd, then I wanted a very good reason do it. I glanced at Mary, and while I could not be certain, of course, I could swear she looked the tiniest bit hopeful, a bright glint in her eyes.

"I keep reminding you to organize all that rubbish," Fathom muttered, stealing a nip from the decanter for herself.

"You might do it yourself, *poet*."

"*Poetess*, thanks very much."

"Ah! Here we are . . ." Something about Dalton's posture and mannerisms reminded me sharply of Mr. Morningside. I wondered just how close they had been, considering they appeared to stand and gesture in much the same way. They were even similar in build and height, though opposites in the hues of their eyes and hair. It was natural to imagine them as a pair, contrasting but compellingly similar.

Dalton returned to us with a handwritten diary, and I cringed, memories of a cramped wrist surfacing as I thought of furiously translating Bennu's journal for Mr. Morningside. Well, perhaps I did not have so much secret nostalgia for the library after all. This diary, however, appeared to be in English, and Dalton handed it to me carefully, as if it were made of spun sugar and not sturdy parchment. It was covered with dust, a musty scent rising from the well-worn and well-loved pages. The embossed leather cover was tied 'round with a bit of yarn, and it simply read: *1248–1247 BC.*

"You seem a bookish sort, so I doubt I need warn you that this is the only copy," Dalton said, his face tense as I took the diary in both hands and studied the cover. "When Henry and I traveled together, we discovered some remarkable things about where we had come from." He paused and swept his palm toward me, then Mary, and then back to himself. "Where all of us come from. Henry was obsessed with the Black Elbion—with all the books. He wanted to know how they had come to be. It was . . . a fixation. He searched tirelessly for the answers."

"And?" I prompted, admittedly excited about potentially learning more about the mysterious, godlike books. My own experience had found me bound to Coldthistle House after merely touching the Black Elbion, and my friend, Lee, was tied to it still by the housekeeper's dark will. She had used shadows and spells to return him to life, but it was only a shadow life, sustained by the book itself.

"Not one for surprises?" he teased.

"Mm. I'd love to hear your story in full, but I am somewhat anxious to be rid of the vicious god creature twisting my every thought and feeling," I said with equal tartness.

"Right. Well, I only mean to say that the beings who made the books of power can surely help you, if anyone can. Henry is convinced he knows where those beings are and how to infiltrate the place, but to my knowledge he refuses to do so. Or can't. It's all in there," Dalton explained, nodding toward the diary. "Maybe you can make more sense of what happened to us than I could. You said that your father somehow consumed the book for the Dark Fae, yes? The bindery where it came from could be of interest, then."

"And Henry knows where it is," I murmured. "He never told you?"

Dalton smiled, but it never touched his eyes. He turned his head away from me, resting for a long moment on the diary. It was dim in the cellar, but I could swear a sheen of tears filled his eyes. "You know him, don't you, Louisa? He's a man who covets his secrets. Even from . . ." Sighing, he wiped at his mouth and reached for the decanter. "Well. It doesn't matter. The diary is yours now. Read it closely. Still, I fear the solution to your problem resides in Coldthistle House."

Chapter Seven

Mary settled down to sleep not long after Dalton produced the diary. The cellar contained a labyrinthine series of narrow corridors, an improbable number of doors leading to storage, pantries, a toilet, and several cozy chambers with bunks and bedrolls. I had followed Fathom and Mary through this snaking tunnel, but I found when we reached the bunks that I had no desire to sleep. I was wide awake, the diary tucked under my arm too tempting to be abandoned for dreams.

I told Mary good night and waited briefly while she nestled down into a fluffy bedroll. Fathom was good enough to find me some old clothes to wear, as my gown was a tangle of threads and dried blood. The frock she gave me was oversize, but it would keep me warm enough, its velvety maroon sleeves fringed with expensive lace that had yellowed with age. Mary fell asleep almost at once, curled on her side, Chijioke's fish hidden in the palm she tucked under her cheek.

Fathom and Dalton had disappeared into one of the other rooms. As I crept back toward the main den, I listened to their muted voices and stopped outside their door.

"I need a bit of air," I told them through the door.

"Right. Tap on the cellar lid to be allowed back in. Be careful, Louisa. More than your shapeshifting friend is prowling London tonight."

That did not dissuade me. I traced my steps back through the safe house, then climbed the stairs up and up, shouldering open the heavy door and letting it back down with a quiet thump. At once, the predawn chill enveloped me, but I welcomed the shock of the air. The cellar felt suffocating, or perhaps that was something inside me, a growing fear that hourly intensified as my return to Coldthistle became certain.

All roads, it appeared, led back to Coldthistle. Over and

over again. I hated it. And I hated even more that it would prove Henry Morningside right. The self-righteous git would be overjoyed to know that I could not keep away, that I needed his help yet again. The moon, stunningly white, emerged from behind a long wisp of cloud, filling the churchyard with its light. I wandered a few steps from the cellar door and followed no clear path among the tall grass and gravestones. A high brick wall hemmed in the yard, pale placards placed there as markers for those who had passed.

I untied the piece of yarn around Dalton's diary and lifted the cover, then stopped myself. As of late, reading mysterious books had only gotten me into trouble. More than that, I worried that what I might find inside would change my feelings toward Mr. Morningside. I had no desire to know him better. I only needed his help, and a deeper understanding of his life was not required.

A light rain began to fall as a bank of clouds stretched across the full moon, though the moonlight hardly waned. I huddled close to one of the brick walls and under a tree, hoping to protect the diary but hesitant to go back inside. My shoulder touched the wall, and through the velvet fabric of my dress, I felt the cool resonance of stone. It was still bright enough to read the placard I had leaned against: NEAR THIS SPOT LIE THE MORTAL REMAINS OF CHRISTOPHER MARLOWE.

I found myself laughing, not at his demise but at the irony

of having once taken that man's pin from Mr. Morningside and used it to free myself from the binding magic of Coldthistle House. Now I had returned that pin, and yet still I would have to return to the place again. No pin nor overwhelming wish for freedom could keep me away, it seemed.

There was a faint rustling in the grass behind me, and I turned to find Khent skulking across the graveyard in my direction. His arms were laden with our possessions, and he wore a heavy pack on his back filled to overflowing with clothing and books. In his right hand, he carried a small cage. Mab, our pink-and-purple-colored spider, peeked out from behind the bars.

"You remembered her," I whispered, and he joined me under the cover of the tree. His hair was slick with rain, and he shook it out, much like a wet dog would do. "How did Agnes and Silvia take it?"

"Well enough," he said. "I told them you had been trampled to death by a horse and their services were no longer needed."

"Khent." I sighed, but then laughed again. "You might have been gentler."

He shrugged, apparently unbothered by the household's worth of goods strapped to his body. "They took some coin from me and left, is that not what you wanted? Why are you standing in the rain?"

"I just find the safe house a bit stifling. And I do not . . . I doubt I will sleep at all."

"No, no, you must rest. It was an exhausting day." He turned in a circle, glancing up and down. "Where am I taking these things?"

"That cellar door," I told him. "Here, let me show you."

Khent followed me through the steady drizzle to the door, and I tapped it three times, then gave the correct answer before the safe house door swung open. I gestured for him to go first and took the spider cage from him, holding it at arm's length as we descended. Something about the fat, fuzzy colorful tarantula had always bothered me; looking at it caused an itch in the back of my mind that often grew into a throb. It was simultaneously repellent and familiar.

Fathom greeted us warmly, a wool blanket draped over her shoulders, and she offered us more tea and food, but Khent refused her. He blinked heavily, anxious for bed.

"The bunks are this way," I explained, leading him through the labyrinth of halls.

"It is warm and dry here, *eyachou*. Why can you not sleep?"

I answered with a shrug, reluctant. When we reached the room where Mary slept, he carefully unburdened himself of the bags and trunks, but our companion did not so much as stir at the noise. I sat down heavily on the bunk across from where Mary rested, putting Mab's cage on a crate that had been repurposed into a table. A single candle lit the room, and I watched the pink and purple creature pace back and forth in its cage, agitated. Khent sat beside me, then fell backward, his legs hanging off the edge of the bunk while he used his open palms as a pillow.

"If you fear the shepherd's folk will find us, I will watch over this place," he said. "Or do you not trust our strange new friends? I smelled no magic upon the girl, only ink and kindness."

I wouldn't have called them friends. Yet. "They would have harmed us before you arrived if that was their intent. No, I do not fear them, but I do fear my nightmares."

Khent sat up, ducking to pull off the tattered remains of his shirt.

"What are you doing?" I asked, a hot flush filling my cheeks.

"I have nightmares, too," he explained, unaware of my embarrassment. He pointed to his right arm, and the crisscross of scars and markings there. They looked painful. Some had not healed well. "This was from the creature that bit me. And these?" He ran his finger along a line across his shoulder. "My father thought he could beat the curse out of me. He gave it everything he had. I was a nobleman's son, not a monster, and he would not accept that I had been bitten. No number of lashes took that back."

"And those markings?" I asked.

"These I asked for. These? They were my choice. At midnight on a full moon, I asked a priest of Anubis and a scribe to carve the ink into my flesh. I was not ashamed of my nature, and so I decided to tell it plainly to the world. My family was furious, but I knew I had lost them the moment that creature chose me.

They did not need to embrace me, they needed only accept me, but even that was asking too much. Thankfully, I had a new family, the one you and I share."

The rows of images on his arm were mottled with scars, but similar to the shorthand writing Bennu had used in his journals. They were somewhat difficult to read, but I could decipher a few characters.

Elder son, the one belonging to the Moon

"I'm so sorry," I said softly. "I can't imagine."

"Of course you can," he chuckled, his purple eyes half-lidded and sleepy. "To live is to be cursed, many times with things we cannot change. Scars and nightmares are what we share, *eyachou*. Do you think Mary dwells in ideal dreams? Her love is far away, maybe in danger. She was imprisoned by your father for months. No, Louisa, the nightmares come for us all."

I felt sheepish then, for having thought that I was the only one suffering when my eyes closed. There was no sympathy from my parents, or my grandparents, and certainly none at the horrid Pitney School.

"So few of my memories are comforting. Even as a child I knew nothing but neglect and scolding. My parents didn't want me, and my grandparents gave me away. Now I know my true father is even worse than the drunk I grew up trying to love," I told him with a sigh. "So what do I do?"

Khent leaned back again on the bunk, taking a blanket and

balling it up to use as a pillow. "You face the nightmare, *eyteht*. You kick it in the teeth."

I smiled at that and shook my head. For a brief while, I had thought perhaps my heart belonged to shy yet thoughtful Lee. Our fracturing had left me feeling raw, confused, but now I found comfort in Khent's forthrightness, even if it felt scary. And risky. Too risky, too vulnerable a thing for someone in my position.

"These pet names are becoming irksome."

He yawned. "I am never irksome."

"Indeed, if you would face your nightmares so boldly, you are not irksome, but *brave*. If only I had that courage. Instead I'm filled with trepidation."

His thumb poked into my back, just between my shoulders.

"*Eyem.*" *There.* "Now you may sleep. I've given you all my courage."

Somehow it worked, or else I could no longer stave off the impact of the day. Of the battle. I curled up on the cot and placed the diary under my pillow, blinking my last for the evening while Mab the spider danced in the candlelight.

It was not long before I woke into my dreams. 'Twas no mystery why I rarely felt fully awake—I lived one life during the day and another at night, leaving one world for another. There was no rest for me, not even at night. And now I found myself wandering the hall of stars again, this time surrounded by them completely, as if I walked through a tunnel made of sky.

The usual dread did not rise to meet me, though a dark mass like a tangle of shadow waited for me at the end of the hall. Above and around me, the stars shifted into their shapes, constellations forming and spinning slowly, a dazzling dance of twinkling lights. The shadow mass grew and grew, its core radiating with evil. *There* was the dread I had anticipated and feared; *there* was the nightmare reaching out toward me.

First blood, it whispered. *First blood.*

It was Father's voice, of course, the familiar dark thrum of it coiling around me like a rope. Suddenly it felt airless in the tunnel, and I gasped, reaching for my throat. My chest felt as if it might collapse from the pressure.

We have tasted blood now, their blood. *How does it feel?*

He had no form but the shadows, yet I felt him all around me, that cold, squeezing rope freezing me into place. My vision went red, and all I could see was Sparrow's limp body, her blood seeping out onto the shattered parquet floor. I had tried my best not to look at her in death, but Father had seen. Father had looked. Now I was forced to confront what I had done. No, no, what she had done. What we had all done.

"I didn't want to hurt her," I croaked.

Yes, you did. The first blood has been spilled, but now it will run free as a river.

I could see her vacant, icy eyes, a single bead of blood racing between them. They were staring into mine. Her mouth was open, a shard of chandelier crystal sticking through it, as glittering and sharp as her golden spear. The body beneath the glass and metal that had pierced it was twisted and odd, one open hand reaching toward me, the fingers at wrong angles. *Help me,* her permanent scream seemed to say, *help me.*

Regret is useless in war. Father's voice strangled me now, and no matter how hard I tried I could not tear my gaze away from Sparrow's dead eyes. *No more regret. Tear it out by the root. First blood,* more *blood. For what they did to our people:* More blood.

"I think not."

The shadows gripping me eased, and I heard a low, ancient gasp. Father had been taken by surprise. My vision was my own again, my breath, too, and I struggled to see who had come. It was a woman's voice that floated toward me, breaking up the shadows like a softly suffusing dawn.

I tumbled to the ground, released, then watched the mass of writhing black shadows coalesce into a form. Father. He towered over me in his shredded robes and with his skull-like face, his eyes glowing red and his antlers rising almost to the ceiling of stars.

"You have tormented this child long enough. She is not lost. Her feet have been on the path all along, only you seek to lead her astray." Twisting, I watched a tall, graceful figure glide toward us. She was dressed in magnificent magenta feathers, her skin dark, dark purple. Eight pink eyes blinked at me in unison, their lashes long and as fine as her bright gown with its countless feathers.

I knew her, yet my head burned when I looked at her.

Father's roar filled the space around us, the constellations vanishing for an instant as if frightened, but gradually they returned, and I felt the woman come close to me, the soft fringe of her dress brushing my hands. At once, I felt safer. Braver.

"I will protect her from you however I can, and so will my children. She is yours only by blood, but her heart is good. You bound me with spell and sage, blood and ink, wine and water, but cruelty can be undone by a willing one, and a willing one I have found."

"She will never be your servant." Father's words were almost lost among his snarls.

"No servant of mine, but a *friend*."

She stood in front of me, guarding me from Father, and while he thundered his protests and shook the stars, I could sense that his power was threatened by her presence. I scuttled toward her on my knees, taking hold of her skirt with both hands. She grinned down at me, beautiful and serene.

"I wish you would let me protect you in earnest, child," she murmured.

Father and his cloak of shadows were disappearing down the tunnel, though the glow of his red eyes could be seen for a long, long time. I shuddered.

"How?" I begged her. "How?"

"You will know me," she said. "You will know me by my name when you wake. *Mab.*"

That one word was like a hammer that broke the nightmare into pieces. I was enveloped in darkness, dreamless and still, that one name echoing on and on, carrying me to morning.

Chapter Eight

When I awoke, it was to eight tiny, curious eyes and a little hooked paw, raised as if to shake me out of sleep. A spider. My spider. My spider touching my face. Her leg brushed my nose, and I screamed, backing away on the bed frantically until I smashed into Khent. He shouted as he woke, throwing his hands in every direction at an imagined threat.

The curses that flew out of his mouth were creative even for him.

"I'm sorry! Oh! I'm sorry!" Mary shot forward, seemingly from nowhere. It was chaos. As my pulse evened, I realized that she had been out in the hall, and, from the pot of tea cradled carefully in her hands, that she had been finding us breakfast.

The spider watched me, unmoving, its furry leg still raised.

"I thought she must be so cooped up in there," Mary tumbled on, covering her mouth with both hands. "Perhaps it was foolish to open the cage . . ."

The unhealed bite on my hand began to itch, and I placed my other hand over it. "No, you were right to give her that freedom. She isn't a spider at all."

Mary stared at me, minding the teapot, then I saw her eyes travel slowly over my shoulder to Khent.

Pushing myself off the bed, I knelt in front of the cot, bringing my face level with the spider. It made no more attempt to touch me, but I could sense the intelligence hiding there.

"It was like having a word stuck on my tongue for months and months, but I know it now," I told them, ignoring their strained glances. "Her name is not Mab, but Mother. The soul of an ancient god cannot be killed, yes? But it can be concealed. Father trapped her in this form once he had the Dark Fae book. I saw her when I died, and I saw her just now in my dreams."

Mary came to kneel next to me, studying the creature as closely as I did, and Khent did the same from the bunk. How strange it must have been for Mother to have the three of us pressing our noses right up to her. She seemed to take it in stride, darting forward to touch her strangely soft, paw-like foot to my hand where it had been bitten.

"Aye, you bit me," I said, remembering how the spider had leapt from my father's shoulder to take a nibble when he was still trying to masquerade as a human at Coldthistle House. "You were trying to warn me, weren't you?"

The spider danced back and forth, still touching my hand.

"How extraordinary," Mary breathed. "And how wretched to be trapped like that for so long."

Khent chimed in, too, but his thoughts on Father and his methods were sharp enough to pierce steel; I was grateful that Mary could not understand him.

"But how to undo this?" I mused aloud.

"It must be buried in your mind somewhere, mm? If Father put her into this creature's body, then the memory of it simply needs to be found," Mary said. She leaned back on her heels and pursed her lips. "Ach, I'm sure that's easier said than done."

I stood and rummaged through the trunk Khent had recovered from our house, desperate to find ink and parchment. Vague remembrances of the dream lingered in my brain, and I needed to scratch them down before they disappeared. I came across a folded bit of paper and an old drawing charcoal. They would have to suffice.

"She said something about the curse in that nightmare," I told them as I scribbled. "He bound her with spell and sage, blood and ink, wine and water. I can only hope the same kind of ritual would undo all of this."

"Brilliant," Mary murmured. "What does it mean?"

"Perhaps Dalton or Fathom might know," I ventured, feeling hopeless. It seemed unlikely that Father would willingly part with the means to reverse his spell. Whenever I learned something he disliked, his anger emerged, and trying to help Mother would no doubt put him into a rage. My hands trembled at that. He was thirsty for more violence, and I feared the instrument of his will would again be my hands.

"I might know what?"

Dalton watched us from the open doorway, or perhaps watched was the wrong word, in light of the strip of fabric covering his damaged eyes. But his attention was fixed in our direction, and he sipped casually from a chipped teacup, dressed in a patchy white morning suit.

"It will probably sound a bit mad . . ."

"Then I am definitely interested," he said with a grin.

"This creature of ours was recovered from Father. She has the soul of an ancient Fae goddess trapped inside. The Mother, actually. Father's counterpart. It all came to me in a dream, but I only have a few clues."

"Which are?"

I recited the bit of Mother's speech that I remembered and stumbled upon my own memories as I did so. "It all sounds rather like what Mrs. Haylam does with her shadow binding, making a man of shadow, or preserving a person that way. Chijioke could bind an entire human soul in a small bird! Could it be similar magic?"

"This only makes me surer that I should write to Chijioke at once," Mary said, standing. "Could you assist me with that, Dalton?"

"Fathom can give you Wings, our owl. He's much faster than the post."

With that, Mary gave us all a quick, shy smile and dodged out of the room. I had no doubt she was very eager to write to Chijioke and have him receive the letter with magical haste.

"And I think you may be on to something, Louisa," Dalton added, joining us near the spider. His tea smelled rich with bergamot and lavender, and the scent made my stomach growl. "It will be difficult to find anyone with even a fraction of Mrs. Haylam's power in the city, but I may know someone across town. We need to gather horses at St. Albans anyway, and it will be along the way. Hello, what's this, then?"

He had taken the little square of parchment from me with the scribbled notes. Flipping it over, he found the letter I had taken ages ago from Henry, meant for the bookshop that had procured Bennu's journals. I had promised to deliver it when I reached London and never bothered to out of spite.

"This will be a spot of help," he said, running his thumb over the address. "It's been quite some time since I chatted with a shadow binder, but the chaps at Cadwallader's are the perfect place to start."

We made an odd sight, I'm sure, Mary and I in borrowed, old frocks that would not have looked out of place on a Covent Garden stage. Khent had also borrowed something suitable from Dalton, though luckily he could disguise the ill-fitting clothes with a heavy black shawled jacket, perfect for the persistent rain. Dalton hid under a hood, and Fathom weathered the wet in a sturdy leather coat that seemed fit for crossing the North Atlantic.

And, of course, Mab. *Mother.*

Now that my memories of her had returned, it felt uncivil to leave her behind in the safe house cellar, and so she accompanied us in her cage to Cadwallader's, which was not far, a short carriage ride to Greenwich, a stone's throw from the great, glass-domed Royal Observatory. The streets were all but empty as the rain poured down, but even with more threatening clouds hanging overhead, pockets of the shepherd's followers haunted corners, huddling under overhangs with their white clothes sodden and dripping. I could feel each of us in the carriage flinch whenever we passed another cluster of white chanters.

"Is it just me or are there many more of them today?" I whispered.

"We must be careful," Dalton told us as the carriage rocked from side to side. We had hired out a cab instead of taking the more conspicuous carriage with magicked white horses. "Cadwallader's is safe for us, but when we move along the streets, there will be eyes everywhere."

I pressed one knuckle to my lips, ducking down from the window. "Perhaps we should simply press on to Coldthistle."

"Wings will return soon with word," Dalton assured me, his face shadowed by his hood. "I should like to know the state of things there before charging in. Regardless, if we can truly free Mother and return her to power, having another ancient one on our side would be prudent. Sparrow will not be the last of our troubles."

"*Our* troubles," Mary corrected him, gesturing to herself, Khent, and me. "You're one of the Upworlders. Why should you worry?"

It needn't be said, I knew perfectly well that she wanted to return to Coldthistle and see with her own eyes that Chijioke and Poppy were safe.

"*Why?* Because we harbored you. Because I turned my back on the shepherd long ago. Because I did nothing to help Sparrow. Because I assist you still. The road to Coldthistle will be dangerous, and Mother could make our chances substantially better."

"Peace," I said softly, feeling the uncomfortable, fitful beginnings of a headache, one that I could easily attribute to Father. He relished this discontent, no doubt wishing I would tear Dalton to shreds then and there for his heritage. "Let us not argue. We will do what we can to help Mother and decide how to proceed when Wings returns."

But Dalton noticed me pinching and massaging my forehead. I had not made an attempt to hide my agitation.

"Are you well?" he asked.

"For now. The sooner we are away from those chanters, the better. I do not trust myself—Father—around them."

I had said nothing to anyone about Father's rising desire for blood, yet Dalton watched me closely. Studied me. I tried to give him a consoling smile, but even I knew it was thin and unconvincing. Any moment of peril might unleash Father again, and I said a silent prayer to whoever was listening that the afternoon would go forward smoothly.

The carriage rolled to a stop. Fathom went first, inspecting the alleyway for anything suspicious, but there was nothing. We paid the driver and ducked one by one under a low canvas awning. The streets ran with sludgy water, the scent of worms and urine making my stomach turn. Above us, the dome of the Observatory shimmered, slick and green as a washed onion. Dalton led us down a long, narrow passage of black stones, away from the Observatory, and into a kind of indoor market. The stalls were largely empty, wisped in cobwebs, caught raindrops winking in the light of lanterns. Gradually, the stalls became utterly decrepit, then off-puttingly so. It occurred to me that nobody would willingly walk this far down into the market, fearing ambush from thieves or worse.

At last we reached an unremarkable door, its knob dingy and rusted. The distinct chatter of mice could be heard through the walls.

"Charming," I heard Khent mutter under his breath.

"A little patience, please," Dalton replied.

The inside of Cadwallader's could not have been more different from the outside. It gleamed with row upon row of glass cases. Though a pleasant dustiness hung on the air, I could see not a speck of grime anywhere in the place. The carpets were comfortably trodden, patterned in ochre paisley. Black wood floors and oak paneling on the walls gave the place a cozy, secluded feel, like a grandmother's tearoom. Only here there was no tea, just books, of all shapes, sizes, and origins. Paper lanterns constructed from book pages blazed above us, strings of little paper shapes strung wall to wall like bunting.

"I could live here," I breathed, standing on the carpets and turning a slow circle. A staircase on either side of the wide room led up to a second floor, though I also glimpsed a passage up to a third.

"Out of curiosity," Dalton said, standing beside me with his hands in his pockets, "what exactly did Henry want you to do here?"

"Deliver this note," I said, taking the parchment out from under my cloak. "He wanted to know how Bennu's journal came to be here."

Dalton burst into laughter, adjusting the scrap of fabric over his eyes before it could fall. He had pushed back his hood, but it would have tumbled off his head from his sudden laughter. "No need. I brought it here. I figured it would wind up in Henry's library eventually."

"Did you want him to have it?"

"I did, yes." He shrugged. "But I had no desire to deliver it in person, and besides, he's horrible at accepting gifts. No, I knew that if his contacts stumbled upon a promising artifact, he would feel much cleverer and take it more seriously."

I gawked at him while the others began to explore the shop. "But how did you come to have it in the first place?"

"I went there, to the First City, looking for a way to make our past misdeeds right. What I found was the journal of a dead man." Here he lowered his voice, waiting until Khent drifted out of hearing range. "There was something about it, something strange, and I pried it from his skeletal arms because I knew in my soul it was the key. Poor sod. I'd been hunting the fellow for ages, but never managed to find him because of a damn translation error. I was told to find Bennu the Writer, not Bennu the *Runner*. Bloody embarrassing."

Dalton vented a laugh, but I didn't find it funny. "When I took it, one of his bones snapped. It was like a twig breaking in a graveyard, raising the dead. Things there began to wake up, the Dark Father began to wake up, and I fled. I brought the journal where I knew Henry could find it, one last favor, one last olive branch, and then I told myself that I was done. Out. No more. I would find a quiet place to hide and let the ages chip away at me until nothing but regret and memory remained."

"And how did that work out for you?" I sighed.

"Henry . . . My feelings for him have a way of bringing me back in." He sounded decidedly not thrilled about that bit. "One day I'll untie this invisible string from my finger, but apparently today is not that day. I can't face him alone, but I can help you. That's my olive branch this time."

I nodded, trying to take in all that he was saying and align it with what I knew from Khent and Mary. "The shepherd wanted to know where the book was. Our book. The book of the Dark Fae. But Father consumed it, so there was no way to really find it, was there?" I drifted deeper into the shop, overwhelmed by all there was to look at. A counter manned by a single person lay at the opposite end from the door.

"I had no way to translate that journal," Dalton explained. "But I had a feeling Henry would crack it. Anyway, if it really did hold the secret to where your book was hidden, I didn't want the shepherd to get his hands on it."

"But Henry you trust," I murmured.

"Yes." He sighed. "Occasionally. Well, no. But he has his moments."

I looked at the folded parchment in my hand. Some of the charcoal from my notes had rubbed off onto my palm, and I wiped it off on my frock. "So it's pointless to deliver this. But what do I tell Mr. Morningside, should our paths cross again?"

"Tell him the truth," Dalton said with a wry smile. "I only hope I'm there to see it. Ah! There's Niles."

"One man looks after all these books?" I asked. Mary and Khent had found a corner with a selection of novels, and Mary was reading him the titles, helping him with his English. Mother had been set in her cage on top of one of the stacks.

"Not always, but it looks rather slow today," Dalton said. "Everyone here is knowledgeable on the subject in question. There's a reason Henry relies on them to set aside anything dangerous or arcane that drops into their shop."

"And just anyone can come in here?"

"Certainly. Why not? They only go out of their way to

discourage . . . hobbyists. One has to possess a certain passion for the occult and unexplained to land here. You saw that alleyway, not many ladies stopping in for a copy of *Castle Rackrent*."

"Had I stumbled upon this place, I should never leave it," I said.

"Indeed," he said. "I share your fondness."

Fathom waited for us at the counter, leaning against it as if she were a regular. She had roused the one shopkeeper from his work, and he looked to us with enormous spectacles perched on his forehead. I had expected the man to introduce himself as Cadwallader, the owner, however there was something annoyingly familiar about his face.

"Niles! How are you? How's business?" Dalton clapped him on the shoulder, rattling the skinny older man.

"Hmph. Fine. Slow but steady. Who is this?" He collected his spectacles, observing me with eyes blown wide and blurry by the glass.

"May I present Louisa Ditton? She was until recently employed by Mr. Morningside at Coldthistle House."

The mention of Henry or the house adjusted the man's attitude toward me at once. He melted into a fawning smile, bowing so low he nearly hit his head on the countertop.

"What a delight," he said. "Simply a delight. Niles St. Giles, but please, no formalities here."

I snorted softly, my cheeks going red. "Niles St. Giles? No relation to Giles St. Giles of Derridon?"

His eyes grew bigger, if that were possible.

"Giles would be my brother, having chosen the noble profession of embalming and . . . whatnot." The whatnot, of course, referring to his predilection for helping Mr. Morningside do away with the souls and bodies of those that met their end at Coldthistle. "But of course it would make perfect sense that you two would be acquainted, sharing such a singular employer."

"What a very charitable description," I muttered.

"How is he—my brother? How is his cat?"

I smiled at the now-distant memory of sitting in Giles's salon, only just having escaped death at the hands of a mad doctor. Mary had spoken so fondly of his cat, and I had watched it laze like a giant furry lump by the hearth.

"Francis is well, last I saw him, but off the biscuits, apparently."

"Yes, Giles did have a dreadful habit of overfeeding his pets. A lesser sin, I think," Niles said with a hearty laugh. Now that I was looking for the comparison, I realized that he and Giles were all but twins—tall, lanky, and birdlike—with arms so narrow a stiff breeze could make them snap. "Now then, what brings you illustrious folk to my shop this afternoon?"

Dalton looked charmed by the man's effusion, though Fathom rolled her eyes liberally. I couldn't help feeling an immediate kinship with the man—any connection, any touch of familiarity in this rapidly darkening world, felt like a beacon in the shadows. Dalton mimicked Fathom's relaxed pose, leaning an elbow onto the case, which housed books so old they might have exploded into fine powder at the lightest touch.

"Given the clientele that moves through here, we thought you or Cadwallader may know of someone useful. A shadow binder, or someone with similar skills. We seem to have stumbled upon a powerful curse, one that we cannot lift ourselves."

Niles took this in as if he were simply hearing the latest dispatches from the Peninsular War. Grimacing, he nodded along to every single word, adjusting his spectacles with quick little fidgets. I put the letter that had been meant for the proprietor on the countertop, showing him the notes I had taken.

"Mmhm, mmhmm. Yes, very interesting. Fascinating. In fact, I know just the sort. Are you familiar with the Birch and Fox? The barkeep there is of *boundless* talent. Coaxed a nymph from a tree in Kensington Gardens not three weeks ago."

Niles beamed at us, pleased and clever, but Dalton shook his head, his brow furrowing over his bandaged eyes.

"We cannot make the journey, friend. The streets are rife with enemies. If time were not so short, I would explain better," he said. Then he nodded toward Fathom. "Could this barkeep be summoned? Fathom is less known to the Upworlders, and one woman on horseback is light and fast."

She pulled up the hood of her coat, already determined.

"Tell me what to look for," she said, sliding the parchment into her coat.

"Indeed, indeed," Niles chirped, disappearing below the counter to search through unseen shelves there. "I will make the arrangements. A curse lifted in Cadwallader's! How exciting. How simply *marvelous*."

Chapter Nine

1248, Constantinople

I had forgotten the hard, slicing winds of sand that sweep through the city in high summer. Where I was born was a temperate place, never too hot or too cold, and my whole self is melting in the relentless humidity. But Henry loves it. He loves everything, I think, or he masks his indifference with boundless enthusiasm so indistinguishable from the real thing that one is forced to believe it.

He is half-insane with a new obsession. The book Ara lugs around (she calls it the Black Elbion, which I'm sure is meant to offend me, but I refuse to be baited) is all Henry can talk about now. I hear him whispering about it in his sleep. She claims it came from the depths of the ocean, that its powers cannot be studied or understood. While they slept last night, I tried to read it, but the cover burned my fingers and the marks refuse to fade. Ara has not yet noticed the bandages, but she is sure to interrogate me once she does.

This fixation of Henry's is how we find ourselves in Constantinople. I would love this place were it not so unbearably hot. Ara makes us cover our faces with flimsy black shawls that wrap around our heads and pin to our tunics. She tells us that it will be easier to ask questions if we are concealed this way, dressed like the other citizens, our belts heavy with beads and metal, our eyes the only indication of our moods. We sipped a strong, sharp tea in the shade of the Ayasofya, and I could take only one or two sips of the stuff. How anyone could stand to drink something scalding hot on an already arid day is beyond me. No, I ignored my tea, looking instead at Henry, looking at him while he gazed at the splendor above us.

I think the best way to love something is through another person's eyes. He sees things I cannot, loves things with so much of his heart that I feel the echo of that passion and pain in my own. I know Ara caught me staring, and I weathered her sniggers with an air of humor I did not feel. Henry may adore this city, but I am a stranger here, and I feel the stirrings of ancient, unknown gods that frighten me. I long to be with my brother and sister and miss them constantly, and I am left to lie awake at night dreading what they will say when I return. Sparrow begged me not to leave, but I had an excuse, of course. The mission. This mysterious writer must be found, and the rumors of his comings and goings were so erratic that even this detour could be forgiven. Which brings me back to the books.

The books. There are more of them now, more than just ours and the thing hiding in Ara's pack. While the two of them sipped their tea, Ara berated Henry for leading us on this fool's errand.

"How many times must I tell you," she snapped at him. "The books appear when they wish to. Pluck this idea out of our head, Henry. There will be no answers at the end of your search."

She spoke with such authority. I noticed it, and naturally

Henry did, too. He stared at her for a long moment, his eyes reflecting the water-bright tiles beside us, steam rising steadily from his cup. "How do you know? How can you be so certain?"

Ara tugged at her sleeves nervously then, and I could not help noticing the markings on her arms. She was not a very old woman, but something had aged her so severely that deep lines were already carved into her forehead and chin, wisps of gray spreading through her dark hair. Yet she was a handsome woman, regal in her gathered linens the color of wheat.

"I only want to protect you from disappointment," she said, distant. "There are secrets in this world long buried and best forgotten."

She reached across the table with one sun-leathered hand and touched Henry's wrist. I looked away, embarrassed by the motherly gesture and feeling as if I were trespassing on a moment in which I did not belong.

Then Henry yanked his hand away, marveling up at the masterpiece that shaded us, the temple rising so tall we could not see its end point.

"Nothing will keep me from speaking to this Faraday person. I've already arranged the meeting, and besides, it's only a few questions. What's the harm in that?"

Ara had no time to answer, for Henry's pack had spilled over, a wriggling bundle of fur tumbling out onto the dusty stones of the road. He squealed with delight and picked up the pup, settling it in his lap with a fond little pat.

"I cannot believe you insisted on bringing that thing," Ara muttered, pulling her sleeves again.

"That thing is vital for any adventurer," Henry replied with a sneer, holding up the brownish ball of fur and kissing it on its black nose. It pawed at his chin and made playful growls. "For what is a man without his dog? Anyway, this sweet fellow can sense a man's true emotions. He will be of utmost importance this evening."

"What nonsense," I said, echoing Ara's displeasure. It was perhaps the one thing we agreed upon. I had always favored cats. Until this venture I had known Henry only to keep birds, but apparently his interests had blossomed.

"Tell me, Bartholomew, is Spicer pointlessly cross with me right now?"

The puppy gave a high, tiny howl, paddling air.

Henry shrieked with laughter, hugging the thing to his chest. "You see? He's perfect."

As are you, I thought, when you aren't unbearable.

"Bah. It's going to get huge," I murmured, crossing my arms over my chest and baking in the heat. "I won't be cleaning up after it."

"Not for centuries," Henry corrected, his knowledge of all things magicked and Fae unchallenged. Well, perhaps challenged only by Ara. "He will fit in my pack for years and years to come, and then I shall find some place for him to grow. Now, finish your tea, I want to explore the temple before dark."

Thunder shook Cadwallader's to its foundation as afternoon turned to dusk. Rain lashed the outer walls of the shop, though without windows it was nearly impossible to tell time in that place, the steadiness of the candles and lanterns never rising above a gentle glow. As the hours disappeared, so, too, did my patience. I couldn't help thinking that our time would be better spent on the road, leaving behind London and its perils. But Cadwallader's lay between Deptford and Dalton's man with the horses, offering us a chance to bring Mother along on the road and with her, greater defenses.

And when I glanced at the spider, Mab, in her cage, I remembered that there was more at stake than just what was trapped inside *me*. If this was the faster option, then she deserved to be freed at once.

The door to the shop crashed inward just as I was turning a page in Dalton's diary. I had found a secluded nook and tucked up with it while Khent prowled near the entrance and Mary chatted with Niles. All of us jumped to our feet as Fathom returned, a strange wind blowing in with her, ruffling pages and rattling shelves. Dalton had sent Fathom out on the errand, as one lone human navigating the city would be less noticeable. A salty, muddy smell filled the shop, a scent I knew well, a warning from the clouds that a vicious storm was on the move.

Candles flickered and faltered as a cloaked figure bustled in, a parcel held to her chest. I closed up the diary and joined the others, hurrying down the staircase to the counter. We gathered there, waiting for Fathom and the stranger to approach. I could see only the hands clutching the parcel, and they were white as bone.

"This is the barkeep?" Dalton asked, tapping his fingers on the glass counter. "From the Birch and Fox? So the rumors are true . . ."

"I understand your need for haste, but let us not make even one mistake." It was a woman, small and almost frail, and she removed her hood to reveal starkly pale hair and skin. Her small, cunning eyes were a watery spring green, but her lips and cheeks lacked all color. Snowy white hair had been bound up in a single black ribbon, a few wayward curls brushing against her chin. Most perplexing was the talisman around her neck, a starlike enameled brooch with a gem that never resolved into any one kind of stone. In the space of a breath it had become a ruby and then an amethyst.

"And you are?" Dalton said, glancing hopefully at Niles, who became instantly busy with something underneath the countertop.

"That is not important," she replied. Her voice, quiet but commanding, held the faintest hint of a dockside upbringing. Her dress surprised me, coarse, so unlike her fine porcelain hair and skin. "I know how to undo this curse. At least, in theory."

"Very comforting," Khent drawled, his eyes never leaving the woman's face.

Her age was impossible to determine, though her hands were weathered and strong.

The stranger fixed Khent with a withering stare. Then she unpacked her parcel, removing a bundle of leaves, a smooth piece of wood, a sharply pointed bone, a bowl, and a corked bottle. "The storm worsens. Our time is short. If you have questions, ask them now, but I would rather begin the spell—it may take all night."

Khent opened his mouth to snap back at her, but I stepped between them, lifting Mab's cage onto the glass, setting it next to the bottle she had just unpacked.

"I only want you to promise me that you will not hurt this creature. The being trapped inside it is . . . precious. Very precious. Do what you can, but please, this being is innocent," I said, looking into her shifting green eyes.

She tilted her head to the side and smiled at me as if I were a simple child. "You have a sentimental heart. My condolences, that will make this difficult indeed."

"S-Sorry?" I stammered. "How so?"

"Have any of you others seen the creature's true form?" she asked, still staring into my eyes.

Silence. I had expected that, but it chilled my blood nevertheless. Though we were surrounded by friendly folk and the anchoring comfort of so many books, I felt horribly alone then, sucked into a world where only I and this stranger existed, with her seeing directly into my heart. And my heart quaked. I did not at all like the look of that long bone implement. After all, I had not forgotten the notes.

Spell and sage, blood and ink, wine and water . . .

Blood. My hands had gone slick with perspiration, and I wiped them on my skirts, hoping the stranger didn't notice. But she did, of course, and raised one white eyebrow.

"It falls to you. I hope you are made of stronger stuff than a tender heart and sweaty palms," she warned, turning back to her array of instruments on the counter.

"Listen, you," I told her, annoyed. "The Devil was my tutor, and I say to you now: do not underestimate me, for he taught me well."

She only scoffed at that. "I'm terribly impressed. Now, it will not take long to prepare. That open area on the carpets will do. Surround it with eight candles, black if you have them. Put the creature in the middle and then kneel beside it."

Dalton and Niles fell at once to action, Niles vanishing into a back room while Dalton went to clear more space near the carpets under the paper lanterns. The storm shook the store again, and I rubbed my arms, taking slow, reluctant steps toward the middle of the shop. Mary and Khent appeared at my elbows, and though they said nothing, I sensed their trepidation, as it so clearly echoed mine.

"Oh, Louisa, perhaps it will be all over quickly," Mary said with a shiver in her voice. "Like one of Poppy's screams. Maybe I can even shield you—I'll ask her—though to say it true, I do not like the look of her."

Khent proved far less optimistic. "She smells of old beer and vomit. And craft—ancient, terrible craft. I don't trust her."

"What choice do I have? We cannot keep Mother trapped in there forever."

Selfishly, my fears had little to do with what pain or fright could accompany this ritual, but with how Father would react. Already I sensed a boiling inside me, a sensation like a teakettle growing hot to the touch, iron thrust in fire warming until it burned. This was his doing, after all, and though his exchange with Mother in my dreams—or simply in my mind—had intimidated him into silence, I knew that reprieve could not last. The sands were slipping through the glass, and only a few grains remained, my hands clutching into fists preemptively as if I had the means to stop a crashing wave with a small and whispered, "please."

Perhaps Father's displeasure was falling from the sky, the rush of rain against the bricks so noisy it sounded like the whole of London was sinking under water. I tried to ignore the deluge and the thunder, each random rumble making me jump.

What had Mother called me? A willing one? Aye, I was willing, but also I was so very afraid.

We needed allies. We needed help. I feared our escape from London would not be an easy one, and harder still whatever awaited us at Coldthistle. I remembered the feeling of safety and warmth I had felt in my dream when Mother came near, and it steeled my heart to think that I could carry that same feeling with me to confront Henry and ask for his help ridding Father from my mind. Or better still, perhaps Mother herself would know how to banish him without leaving me a soulless husk.

The mood became somber, that of a funeral procession. On the rich carpets I had so admired before, Dalton had placed Mab out of her cage. The fuzzy pink spider did not move, though it had turned to watch us approach. Niles breezed by us a moment later, mumbling to himself as he clumsily laid out the stubby black candles in a circle. Then we were all assembled, Fathom and Dalton standing nearest the entrance, Khent and Mary toward the counter, Niles huddling behind them. The stranger carefully flattened a burlap cloth next to Mab and put her instruments down upon it.

Lifting my skirts, I stepped over one of the candles, feeling its heat lick at my ankle as I joined Mab and the stranger.

"What are you?" I asked her, giddy with nerves.

She stood and faced me in her rough-spun barkeep's woolens and gave me a mild smile. "Most would call me a witch. I studied under the last true *Da'mbaeru* of London, who disappeared some years ago. She taught me her craft, though in my heart I sense she withheld much."

I lifted both brows at that and said nothing. In fact, I had a strong suspicion where that last *Da'mbaeru* had gone, and what her current occupation had become. Strange that they had both landed in positions of service. That this woman had known and been taught by Mrs. Haylam almost gave me solace. Almost.

"Nothing good comes of their arts," I said at last, thinking of Lee and the curse I had thrust upon him in death.

"We are not performing *their arts*," she replied tartly. "We are undoing them."

"That does not sound like Father's magicks," I mused aloud, and the stranger nodded.

"The manner of binding Fathom described is not known to me, but binding as a concept is the foundation of our work. Had you not given me the list of steps in the spell, I would not have agreed to come," she finished. Then she motioned to the spider and I knelt beside her.

"What can I expect?" My voice trembled now, and the heat of the candles circling us pressed in on me like eight too-warm hands.

"First, a chant," the stranger murmured. "Second, a burning of sage. Then I will ask for your palm and prick it with a needle and ink, which is a common appeasement to dark spirits. Finally? A baptism and a sacrament. There will be no turning back once we begin, do you understand?"

I had anticipated that from what I had witnessed so far among Unworlders and Upworlders—a dangerous pact once started must be seen through to completion.

The stranger cleared her throat once, crouched behind me, and placed her fingertips on my shoulders. I had enough time to glance at Khent and Mary, who were now all but hugging each other for comfort. Khent mouthed something to me, and it took me a moment to realize what he was saying.

"Courage."

Then the stranger spoke directly into my ear. Her voice had changed, becoming more liquid, more dangerous. "Close your eyes," she said. "And if you are willing, it will begin. Once the ritual starts, there will be no going back. You *must* endure."

I did as she asked, though I had no earthly idea if I was willing or not. That one word—*courage*—repeated itself over and over as I drew in a weak breath. The stranger began to sing, a low hum that wound its way up and down until it sounded like the keening of a widow deep in her grief. The cry entered me and slithered into my blood, and my flesh felt suddenly as if it were on fire. I wanted to snap my eyes open, but instead I gasped, taking more of the wailing into me, drinking down the piercing sound.

At once I was plunged into darkness deeper than what lay behind my eyelids. It was a pit from which there was no escape and which no light penetrated. My breaths became short and harried, and then a single candle began to glow in front of me, and my whole being shuddered with primal dread. *I* did not know what sat before me, but my bones and blood did. Whatever ancient intuition had been gifted to humans and animals came to life, trilling with warnings.

Courage, I reminded myself desperately.

A voice emerged from the poisonous dark.

"Oh, but you will need far more than courage here, Daughter of Trees."

Chapter
Ten

The place I landed did not have the hazy quality of a dream, yet I did not recognize it at all. Dream or otherworldly realm, I could not say. My eyes would never adjust to this dark, for it was no natural darkness, but the true dark of hell. There was a table between myself and the voice, and even the candle that burned upon it glowed with a hollow purple flame, illuminating nothing. Had I reached out with my hands, there would be no way to see them.

The man—no, *thing*—seated before me almost appeared as if its head floated in the blackness around us. Yet when it shifted, I saw that it wore a mantle of serous ebony sap, as if a thick black sand were being endlessly poured over its shoulders. Nothing made sense; I could not see my own body, yet I could see this entity before me. Long, white fingers emerged from somewhere inside the cloak and tented, though they were fingers only in the loosest sense, as each hand possessed three "fingers," each a writhing snakelike creature with an open sucking mouth. In the vast quiet, I could hear those horrid creatures teething softly on the air.

If indeed we breathed air here. I may as well have been taking in terror itself.

And the thing's head, oh, its head. I wished for nothing more than the ability to tear my eyes away, but my gaze remained ever fixed on its white, rising skull, the length of it too slender and unnatural, waxlike, with a slimy surface that made my hairs stand on end. It had two narrow slits for eyes, black, and a serpent's diamond nose. Its mouth never quite closed, lolling as if its jaw had been broken in a hundred places and never allowed to mend.

It leaned forward suddenly, carrying with it the smell I knew only to be death. Rot. It was studying me, examining me, peeling away flesh and bone so that I could easily see beneath, and I gasped again, my chest searing with pain, throbbing as if the thing had ripped open my rib cage to peer inside.

"Daughter of Trees, of Darkness," it purred, ever-moving mouth slopping from side to side, the reek of corpses, sickly sweet, pouring out. "Willing One, Changeling Child, Servant of the Devil, Companion to the Moon's Own Son, you come with a request."

It was not a question. The way it drew out the sibilance in *request* prodded at my spine.

"I do," I said, not knowing if there was some set exchange I was expected to know. "Who are you?"

Though the ancient strands of life in me knew the answer, I wanted to hear it spoken aloud. All of me shouted, *it is Evil Itself,* but I waited, my hands knotted and sweating. It pendulated, weighing my question, relishing it with what I assumed was a smirk.

"I . . . am a Binder. Eight are we. Eight we are who make the world. You know our work, little Unworlder. I sense its touch upon you." And here the Binder wriggled one of its eellike hands, showing me again the undulating mouths of its "fingers."

I felt a burn across my own fingertips and frowned, overburdened then by knowledge and fear.

"You make the books," I said. "The Black Elbion—I touched it once and it marked me."

"The mark was made forfeit by death, but still I know it upon you." The Binder looked . . . proud. Smug. That expression twisted its liquid mouth into a hideous shape. "Yet I do not make the books, Freedom Seeker. Eight are we, and only one binds the books. I bind *souls*."

"That's why I'm here," I said, trembling. It was best to hurry. I knew that nothing I said would surprise the Binder; it already understood me completely. "I came to unbind the Mother. Her soul is trapped inside a spider's body, put there by my father ages ago."

The Binder inhaled as if enjoying the bouquet of a fine wine, its slit-like nostrils flaring wide, revealing only moving black ink behind them. "Yes, I remember it well. Not a pact I took lightly. *Not* an easy binding to undo." It leaned farther across the table, and I nearly retched from the smell of it. "This will not go well for you, Fae Spawn."

"I—I'm willing," I stammered. Courage. I remembered the frisson of bravery I had felt when Khent pressed his thumb between my shoulder blades. "What must I do?"

It waggled a wormy finger in my direction, shaking its narrow white head. "The chanting has already begun. Now"— it inhaled again, its entire body twitching with delight—"now comes the ssssage."

I smelled it, too. The acrid tang of burning sage filled the air, a halo of smoke rising around us from the ground. It rose and rose until it began to choke me. The Binder remained unaffected, smiling ghoulishly as I coughed and patted my throat, my mouth raw from the hot sting of the smoke. I was breathing in fire, I realized, and it was scorching me down to my stomach. Then the flames came, erupting fast, circling me and leaping onto my gown. I struggled in vain to put out the fire, but there was nothing I could do. The skirt flamed with hungry red blossoms that climbed up my body, the pain in my legs so excruciating that they soon grew numb. Not numb, burned away. I could see bone then, and fluid muscle, and fat oozing from the fire, crackling and speeding the kill.

My screams must have been terrible, but I couldn't hear them above the pop and sizzle of the flames. I watched helplessly as the remainder of my dress caught, and the flesh of my fingers burned away, nothing but furnace-hot bones left behind to claw at the flesh of my neck that bubbled and ran like wax. The screams ended, they must have, for I no longer possessed a mouth, just a gaping wound that breathed endless fire, cooking me from without and within.

I felt a deep throbbing in my face and then sudden wetness, a jolt that came with a sound like rifle fire. My eyeballs popped.

It was all over. I had to be dead, for the pain was madness and the fire had consumed me utterly. And yet . . . And yet. My vision returned, and with it, the Binder. It was as if nothing at all had happened. The flames were gone and my throat had only the lightest taste of char upon it. But my relief was short-lived. When I looked across the table and saw the smile that awaited me, I knew beyond certainty that my trials had only just begun. "Are you still willing?"

With the heat of the fire having left so abruptly, I felt chilled and clammy, as if I were experiencing the warning signs of an impending illness. I hugged myself tightly and looked away from the Binder, knowing that this was some kind of test or game. This stranger had warned me that there was no going back, that once the ritual began it must be completed.

"Yes," I whispered. "I'm still willing. Is this what my father suffered? To do the binding?"

The Binder drew back, narrow eyes widening as if in surprise.

"After bleeding Mother to a state of death, he captured eight humans and carved the willingness into their chests, then burned them in a field of sage. The rain did not quench the embers for days. When they were ash, he mixed it with wine and feasted."

"So others suffered instead? How very like him." I shook my head.

"There is more than one way to gain the attention of a Binder," it said. "Yours is a tender heart. His is stone. Now give me your palm, bold fool. A sacrifice is required."

Had I not already sacrificed? And yet this was the step of the binding that I feared most. *Blood and ink.* The only way forward, I decided, was breath by breath. Nothing in this strange shadow land was real, even if the pain of the fire had been deeply felt. Even if my fear was undeniably real.

I reached my right hand across the small circular table between us, showing it to the Binder palm up. As I closed my eyes, the Binder ceased leaning in toward me. It was only when I opened them again that it moved. God, it was forcing me to watch whatever sinister thing it had in mind. I swallowed around a lump and sat straighter, determined to press on. Breath by breath. I simply needed to keep breathing and remember that this was a realm of tricks.

The Binder's left hand hovered over my palm, its three wriggling fingers lowering inch by dreadful inch. The little mouths opened and closed rapidly, faster and faster as they neared my skin, hungry. My stomach turned and I held back a cough, as if my own guts were filled with those twisting snakes. I could tell the Binder was not watching our hands but my face, enjoying every twitch of discomfort that tightened my lips.

The Binder's fingers found my palm, and at once the long tubes of them went rigid, attaching to my flesh. The sensation at first was mild, just a light tugging, as if someone were playfully pinching the meatier parts of my palm, but the pulling did not stop, and the pinching was no longer so playful. My eyes flew to the Binder's, and the calming breaths I had ordered myself to take were ragged and noisy.

"Shall I stop?" It was taunting me, all but giggling.

"No," I shouted. "No, I am *willing*."

"But are you truly willing? You are willing in the mind, but are you willing in the spirit? Let us see."

I hated its voice, eerie and cold, and I hated that it frightened me. Its fingers pulled and pulled, lifting now, though my hand, gripped strongly by some unseen force, stayed against the table. I watched with open-mouthed horror as the flesh of my palm grew taut, then I felt it begin to tear. The wound was small at first, but at once the blood came, filling in at the seams where my skin gave. Hot blood pooled, almost burning in contrast to the chill in the air and the Binder's fingers, which were oddly without temperature, as if the thing was neither warm enough to be living nor cold enough to be dead.

I gritted my teeth, but the pain of it was no illusion, no trick, my mind revolting at what my eyes beheld, a tremor starting in my core that moved quickly to my stomach. I know I must have vomited somewhere into the darkness around us. I know I shouted, but not for mercy, for I refused to be trapped in that void forever. I cursed the thing. I found ugly words I had never uttered aloud before. I screamed at it incoherently in a language that wasn't even my own, one I could not decipher if pressed, one that felt true and evil enough to punish it for skinning my palm right before my eyes. A raw, bloody flap came free, peeling away to reveal the slick, pink meat of my hand.

It was surprise, perhaps, that made the pain vanish for an instant. Blood poured from my hand, spilling in thick rivers onto the table. The Binder's fingers lingered, keeping the skin of my palm aloft so that we could both see what was beneath.

A word. A single word was somehow there, written on slick and shining sinew.

I was dizzy and faint, hoarse from screaming, but the sight of that word somehow gave me comfort. A test had been passed, one I did not know I had prepared for. The Binder sneered but released its cruel grip on my skin. I teetered back, eyes rolling from the blood I had lost, which spread all around us. My hand burned steadily, pinpricks of red light dancing in front of my eyes. The fiend in front of me spun and tilted. My mouth went bone dry; I was going to collapse.

Then I was falling, tumbling helplessly into the dark pit, the concentrated burning in my hand the only thing I could really feel or hold on to. Above me, high above me, I heard the Binder whispering:

Spell and sage, blood and ink, water and wine. These bindings are undone.

Chapter Eleven

s if stirring from a deep sleep, I distantly felt someone lifting me up. Cold, clean water trickled into my mouth, and I was forced to swallow it. Then came the taste of something bitter, and I went away again, not to the Binder's realm but to unbroken and welcome rest.

When I woke more fully, it was to the sensation of a cloth pressed to my forehead. Mary was there, staring down at me with wide, worried eyes.

"Oh, thank every star in the firmament!" she cried. "She's awake! Everyone! Louisa is awake!"

My head felt as if it had been stuffed on a pike, my neck stiff and sore. I tried to rouse myself, but, weakened, I flopped back down to the pillow. Blinking around, I did not recognize my surroundings, but the light, dusty smell on the air was familiar. They had placed me in a small bedroom, its chintzy, cozy manner reminding me of Giles St. Giles's home in Derridon. There were overstuffed chairs and fluffy carpets, with a fire in the hearth and two orange cats dozing in front of it.

"Where are they?" Mary fussed, standing and trotting to the open door.

In answer, raised voices rumbled through the floorboards, then a series of sharp cracks like fevered pounding on a door. I forced myself to sit up, ignoring the dizziness lingering in my head. My right palm hurt as soon as I touched the blankets, and I hissed, pulling it away to find I had not escaped the dark pit unscathed. Scarlet with irritation, black script had been carved into my hand. It was unreadable, a language neither I, nor apparently Father, spoke. But I knew, of course, what it must mean.

"How did I get this?" I asked as Mary ran back to the bed.

"Louisa, I will explain it all to you later. Something is amiss downstairs. Hurry!"

She was right. There were shouts now and more banging, and I let Mary throw the covers off me and pull me carefully out of the bed.

"Wait," I said, teetering. "The diary . . ."

"Dalton has it," she assured me. "Come on!"

My body felt as if I had been tumbled down a mountain, but I followed, leaning heavily against her shoulder as we left behind the cats, which appeared unbothered. We emerged onto a walkway above the shop, on the fourth floor, with all the many shelves and lanterns spread out below us. From that vantage, I could see Fathom and Khent braced against the front door, their backs pressed to it, their legs straining.

Dalton shouted across the floor to Niles, who had managed to find a number of pistols stashed underneath the counter. But as Mary dragged me along toward the stairs, all I could focus on was the woman lying in the middle of the store, curled on her side in a dark feathery dress, unmoving. *Mother.* There was no sign of the witch.

"Did it work? Or is she . . . Please tell me it worked," I murmured.

"We were afraid to move her, Louisa. She hasn't taken a single breath since the ritual. You were moaning and groaning, so we thought it safe to bring you to bed. Oh, but it's been hours and hours. I was afraid you would never recover."

My heart sank. The Binder had said the bonds were broken. Why was Mother unmoving? Had the ritual somehow killed her? Had I done something wrong?

With each step, I felt slightly stronger, and at last I could walk on my own, hurrying across the walkway. We skidded to a stop then, as Fathom shouted something incoherent and the door behind them contorted, sagging inward, then exploded in flames. It was madness to move toward the fire, but our friends were in danger, and I could not just stand there and watch.

"Come on, Mary." I tugged at her.

"You're still too weak," she insisted.

But I was already on the move. "We will find a way to be useful somehow."

"Torches!" I heard Khent thunder. "There are too many of them!"

Too many of them, and the moon would not be full again, if

it were indeed evening. I glanced frantically to Mary as torch-bearing followers of the shepherd streamed into the shop, swinging their lit truncheons in front of them as they went. Khent and Fathom fell back, and Niles and Dalton stood not far from Mother, in front of her on the carpets, taking aim and firing as best they could.

"Mary!" I cried. "Can you not do something?"

"I'm weak from the ball, but I will do what I can," she said, pursing her lips tightly and throwing her hands outward. Her shielding powers shimmered out from her chest as usual, though the glimmer seemed somehow dimmed. I dodged around her, taking the steps two and then three at a time, pelting across the shop floor in time to see the shelves nearest the door catch fire. It was all too soon—the taste of smoke filled my mouth again, and I fought a wave of nausea—this time it was real. This time my friends could be killed if the fire raged out of control.

Courage.

Mary's shield enveloped us, lessening the sting of the smoke and the heat of the flames, but already the fire was shooting along the walls, the old, brittle pages of the books the perfect but heartbreaking kindling. We may as well have been trying to stand against our attackers on a pile of dry twigs. Khent backed into the bubble, accepting a pistol from Niles, but knowing not what to do with it, he simply bludgeoned the nearest person in white, knocking the torch from their hand and stamping it out with his boot. Fathom quickly loaded the pistol she had taken from Niles, and proved an excellent shot, but there were simply too many targets.

And worse, more threatening than their swinging clubs, was the fire now creeping across the wood floor toward us.

"They must have followed me back from the tavern," Fathom muttered. I could hardly hear her over the melee and the crackle of flames.

"I never thought I would say this," Dalton said, firing blindly into the crush of bodies surging against us. "But now would be a good time for your father to come out and play."

I went rigid, staring at him. Hurt. But he was right. We were being overwhelmed, and I was not at all the marksman we needed. Mary's powers were faltering, the gossamer surface of her bubble fading out, more and more smoke curling in toward us. And the fire? There was no stopping it now—it ate and ate, hungry, gobbling up whole shelves, hemming us in on three sides with walls of climbing flames. Mary screamed as a beam not far above us cracked and swung free, then crashed down to the floor, glass cases showering us with shards. Her shield depleted completely, and I heard her footsteps as she abandoned the loft and joined us.

Khent took a bad blow to his forearm, stumbling back into me. I caught him by the shoulder and watched the blood seep through his shirt. I closed my eyes, letting the chaos and smoke fill me, letting the blood be all that I saw. *First blood. More blood.*

Father woke almost too eagerly. He had been waiting for this moment. My eyes glazed with red, and I felt the strange and wild stirring of his power as it overtook my own thoughts. I shook, not wanting to lose control, not wanting to unleash him again. There was no telling who would be caught in the ensuing carnage.

I could see nothing, but I heard the roar of the fire and the screams of righteous anger from the followers as they beat us back farther into the shop. We were losing ground, and I was out of time. But a light hand fell on my shoulder, soft and consoling, so consoling that I felt Father's influence over me loosen until it fell away completely. I looked up and to the left and found Mother gazing down at me, her mouth half lifted in a forlorn smile.

"No," she told me. "You must never let him out."

"But—"

She silenced me with a shake of her head. All eight of her delicate purple eyes closed, and the hem of her feathered dress fluttered from the gust of the fire. Pressing on my shoulder, she moved ahead, and then seemed to glide across the singed carpets toward the fray. She was defenseless and carried no weapon, and I scrambled after her. I could not let her die at the hands of these people, not after the ordeal I had undergone to save her. She was met with alarmed shouts from Khent, Dalton, and Fathom, who tried to coax her back toward safety, but she would not be deterred.

"Peace," I heard her say just above the din. Then louder, "*Peace.*"

All at once, as if put under a blanketing spell, the followers lowered their clubs and torches, mouths hanging open a little in wonder. She had captured their whole attention with two words, spoken as if in friendly conversation. Flinging her arms wide to them, she gazed around, seemingly unconcerned by the smoke or the fire eating its way toward her.

"I know your hearts," she said. "I know that when you wake tomorrow, tired and afraid, you will look back on this moment and feel only one thing. *Regret.* Turn away. Turn away from this violence and this hatred. Turn away from this place. Someone awaits you. Will you greet them with relief or with regret?"

A hush fell upon us all. The mob shifted, and then I could make out their individual faces. Men and women, old and young, their eyes open wide as if seeing us and one another for the first time. One club fell to the ground, and then another, and I watched a mismatched pair grab hands and turn toward the broken door. They were *leaving.* Retreating.

"This is our chance," Dalton said, gesturing for us to follow. "There's a back way out. Quickly. I had hoped to save the books, but we have no choice."

I let Mary and Khent go ahead of me, pushing them along, then watched Mother stay there on the burning carpets until the last follower of the shepherd dispersed. Then she turned and drifted along beside me, her hands clasped at her waist, feathery train trailing behind her, dragging through the charred remains of books and shelves.

"That . . ." I was astonished, almost at a loss for words. "How did you do that?"

She glanced down at me, a dimple running down one cheek. "It was only possible because they had no true hate in their hearts for us. I wanted to give them a chance. Peace is always preferable."

"Now I know why Father wanted you gone so much," I murmured, following the others behind the sales counter to a backroom and then a short door blocked by a bookcase. Niles nudged it aside and opened the door, letting in the blessed, rain-soaked air.

"He was not always as he is now," she told me with a mournful sigh. "But he watched too many of us die. When you lose your children, something changes inside you forever."

"They were your children, too," I pointed out.

"Their loss broke my heart," she said. "It scorched his to ash."

Chapter Twelve

1248. Constantinople

"You do not know where to eat, my friends. You do not know! Baki will show you. Baki knows every stall and butcher from Galata to the port. That tea shop by the temple serves piss. What were you thinking, Dark One?"

My Greek, far better than Henry's, was proving useful when dealing with Baki. I knew him only tangentially through Finch, who spoke highly of the man. Baki took up nearly the entire alley ahead of us, his immense belly popping out from under an embroidered vest and short tunic. His head and shoulders were covered with a fantastically striped shawl, though it did little to hide his horns and pointed ears.

"We're not here for the food," I told him with a snort.

"But we'll be sure to try the oxtail," Henry teased.

Baki rumbled with laughter, patting his stomach and turning to give us a wink. His eyes were mismatched, one blue and one a catlike yellow.

"Very good, my friends. I myself do not partake in cow flesh, but Baki will look the other way if you are so inclined. Maybe we can discuss your friend's quest for the writer over honeyed pudding tomorrow. There are rumors of some great battle at the Henge, and Baki is always ready to talk of battle!"

Leave it to Henry to make friends with another Upworlder faster than I could. The narrow passage we traveled down was lit only by the lanterns of homes above us. The neighborhood was one I couldn't name, somewhere to the southwest of the coliseum and garden-heavy estates of the wealthy. The walls here had once been painted but had been long since neglected. Rat eyes sparkled from every crevice, flies gathered over piles of refuse and rotting bones, their swarms thick enough to choke you.

Inside Henry's pack, the little hellhound pup whined. I sympathized. We let Baki go ahead while Ara took up the rear. Her indistinct grumbles joined the dog's whimpers.

"I don't like this," I heard her say. It was a phrase she must have uttered twenty times already that day.

"You try and stop him," I replied. "You know how he gets once he has a notion."

"Me?" Ara laughed, though her laughter never sounded innocent or merry. "You try. You know he worships you."

I rolled my eyes, watching Baki lift a drooping clothesline out of the way. The darkness here was dense and soupy, the walls pressing in more and more as we followed some path only Baki knew. I told myself we could trust him. Finch was a good judge of character, and Baki was one of ours. Under his shawl, down near his waist, I could see a small tail swishing against the fabric, barely concealed. He was a Re'em, strong as a team of oxen, with horns and teeth that could make quick work of flesh.

Perhaps only Goliath and Nephilim were stronger, or whatever Ara was, but she was not one of ours.

"We are close, my friends. Only whispers now, and only if you must."

The silence allowed me to hear the skittering of unseen rat claws and the occasional deep voice muted by plaster and brick. Deeper we went, as if navigating a jungle and not city streets. What I would've given to be back at that mediocre tea shop, sipping herbal brew and complaining about the heat. I had no stomach for these dark adventures, but Henry, whether because of his own dark nature or his curiosity, could not get enough of them.

One day I would learn to turn him down. One day . . .

"And you're sure this Faraday chap can help us? I'm spending a lot of coin on you, friend, it had better not be a waste," Henry hissed.

"I would take you to him for only the gift of that little doggy," Baki said, his pointed ears perking under his shawl. Under his tunic, his tail swished faster.

"Ha. Unlikely. That runt is worth more than any information you or this stranger might have," Henry replied. "And anyway, I've grown attached."

"Of course, of course. Now, friends, be silent, we are here."

I murmured a prayer of thanks to the shepherd, huddling close to Henry and Baki as the tall and round Re'em drew up short to a door hidden by a tattered burlap cover. He pushed the cover aside and knocked in a strange pattern, then waited. Something brushed by my ankle, and I gasped, nearly leaping into Henry's arms with fright.

"Steady on," he whispered. "Just a mouse."

"Mice are not cold and wet."

The door swung open, revealing a hovel with a low ceiling. A hunchbacked woman met us there, her hair white, her eyes white, her garb completely black. Nobody would call her appealing to look at, her mouth no more than a short slash above her chin.

"Ah, White Keeper, you are looking radiant this evening," Baki cooed.

White Keeper. That certainly fit. The rest of it? Henry and I exchanged a glance. She reached a crooked arm out from her black cloak, the wrinkly white skin covered in faded ink markings. Patting Baki's cheek, she puffed out a dry laugh.

"What do you need, my boy?" she asked in Greek. "I take it this is not a social call. How disappointing. You never come to see me unless you need something."

Baki shrugged and patted his stomach. "You and me, we catch up while these others pay their respects to Faraday, eh? Maybe you still have some supper on the stove . . ."

The old woman's eyes narrowed, and she turned a vicious sneer on us. "The master? Oh no. Oh no, no, no. You will not be *seeing him. Not tonight. He is in a foul mood and is as likely to throw you from the roof as he is to serve you tea. He has not been the same since returning from the salt."*

"Please, mistress," Henry pleaded, turning on the charm. He leaned languidly against the doorframe, giving her his most boyish grin, flipping the dark hair out of his eyes before lowering his cowl so she could see him completely. "We've traveled such a very long way. It would be a damn shame if it was all for naught."

He looked beyond her and into the hovel. The candle she carried illuminated a series of strange markings on the plaster walls. I was not meant to know them, but they turned my stomach to behold. All of them, strange stars and crude characters, were drawn in blood.

"I do not fear what lies within," Henry assured her. "And we will not be a bother to your master. We merely wish to ask a few questions."

The White Keeper stared at him for a long time, then shifted her gaze to me and finally to Ara, who fidgeted and muttered with boredom while the decision was made. Then the Keeper flicked her head once, and Baki held the fabric cover aside while we ducked inside.

The hovel smelled overwhelmingly of incense, a wild, purple smell that could have only one purpose: concealing the true stench of the place, the reek of old bones and human decay. The blood on the walls was fresh, though dried markings lurked below, the newer signs having been applied recently. They glittered in the candlelight, releasing a wet-coin smell that tightened the knot in my guts.

I confess, I wanted to flee. Henry followed the old woman with a bounce in his step, but I could not match his enthusiasm. Something was very wrong with this place, I felt it deeply, and it was not just my Upworlder aversion to the ways of Henry's people.

This was a place of evil.

There was almost nothing in the hovel, just a single spit for cooking and a few lumpy cushions. The floor was dusty with sand and dried flecks of blood, and all of us had to duck our heads to avoid the ceiling. The White Keeper led us down a passageway at the back of the house, clay stairs built into the ground, perhaps predating this neighborhood or even the city itself. The air ought to have grown colder as we went, but instead I found myself tugging at my cowl, fighting off the feverish heat that became almost intolerable as we descended.

"Why is it so bloody hot?" I muttered.

It was then that I noticed that Baki had stayed behind. At his height, he might not have even fit in the passage. Yet his absence filled me with unease. He knew these people better than we did. Why had he remained outside?

At last, the White Keeper stopped. The wide arch of a doorway lay ahead, carved into the pale rock below the city, a flimsy curtain swaying back and forth in front of it. The light of a hundred or more candles blazed on the other side. Something soft tickled against my toes, falling onto my sandal. I picked it up and turned it in front of the glowing curtain. A feather, long, brown, and sharply pointed.

"How peculiar," I whispered.

"The master is within," the White Keeper rasped at us. "Do not test his patience."

Then she was gone, leaving us in the stench and heat of that unholy den. I looked to Henry, but his eyes were wide with childlike pleasure, and he drifted toward the curtain. Had I wanted to, I could not have stopped him from gently pulling the fabric aside. Even Ara seemed fascinated, sidling up next to him, her breath coming short. Inside Henry's pack, the pup gave a low, sad howl.

That howl startled the creature. It had made a kind of small citadel for itself, a dark church of candles and straw. The floor was littered with feathers like the one I had found. The creature had great, tawny wings with hooked talons at the points. And it was a man of sorts, narrow of frame and muscular, wearing the torn and bloodstained tunic of a much larger adversary. Thick strands of black beads hung from around his neck, and his skin shone with fissures, haphazard cracks in the flesh, red-gold light blazing from within.

It hurt to look at him, and my stomach roared with pain.

"Šulmu, Gallû," Henry said, taking a step into the creature's *lair and bowing.* Greetings, Demon. *He sounded positively cheery.* "Faraday, I presume? Although by the looks of it, that isn't quite right, is it? More likely Faraz'ai, the name lost to time. Or Furcalor or Focalor . . . Let us settle upon that name. Focalor, Great Duke, the Abandoner, Leader of the Thirty Legions, and most importantly dead, last I heard anything of it. How did you come to be here, and what do you know of the books, of the binding?"

Faraday—or Focalor, as Henry had called him—swiveled to face us completely. His face might have been unbelievably handsome were it not for the cracks of light splitting it into strange shapes. He spread his gryphon wings wide and held out his hands to us, tears rolling down his cheeks. His right hand was missing two fingers; his other had lost the pinkie.

Focalor's voice was like pipe smoke, rich and intoxicating, a young singer's voice, but sad, a voice made only for dirges.

"Oh, yes, Dark One, I have gone to the white plains. I have gone to the salt to meet a Binder, and the journey took everything from me."

Four and then five days lurched by with no word from the owl, Wings. There were precious few distractions in the Deptford safe house, and we were left to do nothing but lick our wounds and wait. Niles had decided to join us, seeing as he was without employment now that Cadwallader's had burned down, and we agreed to take him with us to Coldthistle House. From there, he would continue on to Derridon to reunite with his brother.

Under ordinary circumstances, a delay of this length would not be troubling, but Dalton had assured us that the owl should have returned with word by now, if indeed there was word to send.

"Ach, Louisa, but something is mightily wrong."

Mary and I were allegedly playing whist, but in truth her full attention was in taking the carved wooden fish from Chijioke out of her pocket and fussing with it, thinking I did not know what she was doing underneath the table. The tension inside the cellar was suffocating. Fathom was worried we would be followed and found again, and so we were staying belowground as much as possible.

"Do you think they could be ignoring us on purpose?" I asked Mary. "Maybe they're cross with us for leaving."

I had won the last trick and it was Mary's turn, but she failed to notice. She shook her head, looking through her cards listlessly. "Chijioke wrote me all summer long. I would know if he was angry."

"What do you think we will find there?" I asked. I had told her little of Dalton's diary. What I had read so far seemed somewhat promising. Maybe Mr. Morningside had found his own way of summoning Binders, working from Focalor's experiences.

They had been following Mr. Morningside's fancy and chasing down the origin of the strange books, and now that I had met a Binder, I knew well they had great power, power enough even to remove Father from my spirit without killing me.

"It pains me to speculate," she murmured. "My heart aches whenever I allow myself to imagine . . ."

I watched her match a suit, and then I reached for a card on the stockpile, inhaling through my teeth when the edge of the card scraped the raw marking on my palm. Mary had taken me through exactly what had happened from her perspective during the ritual. In her eyes, I had gone nowhere, simply kneeling on the carpets with the stranger. Then, abruptly, I had started screaming, throwing myself on the ground and rolling, thrashing my arms. She hadn't understood why I'd had such a bizarre reaction to a bit of sage being burned. And I was speaking a horrid language, she said, hardly even sounding like myself, screaming things that made no sense to her or anyone in the room. They were black, evil words, she told me—there was no mistaking that.

It had grown worse when the stranger took my palm and began tapping ink into it with the bone needle. The stranger had spoken the same frightening tongue, and her eyes had rolled back in her head, the white flickering as she blindly scored the ink into my skin.

I flipped over my hand and regarded the inky lettering that remained there. It seemed to change each time I beheld it. A black and evil language. Even though I knew from the Binder that the marking meant "willing," it looked awfully sinister.

"Does it still pain you?" Mary asked gently. "I can fetch more balm."

"The ache is fading," I said. "Now if only the mark would fade, too."

"At least it worked. Though I have no idea what to think of *Mother*."

I shared her bafflement. Fathom and Dalton had scrounged up more mundane clothing for her as a disguise, and they'd given her a widow's black veil to hide her unusual hair, skin, and eyes when we were not concealed in the safe house. She kept largely to herself, reading voraciously, studying all the trinkets she could find here and spending long hours regarding us, as if trying to memorize our every gesture. All the stray insects that infiltrated the cellar flocked to her, buzzing at her feet like ready little servants.

"Louisa . . ."

Mary was watching me with her lip pulled between her teeth, her cheeks dyed dark pink.

"Yes?"

"Louisa, I think we should go to Coldthistle House as quickly as possible. I know the attack on Cadwallader's shook you, and I know you fear a trap, but I don't think we should wait any longer. This waiting is driving me mad," she said, scattering her cards to the table.

"I agree," I replied, to her surprise. And frustration.

"Really? Then why tarry? We should find a proper carriage straightaway—"

"We haven't gone because I'm afraid," I told her, interrupting her excited planning. "I know what it's like to meet a Binder now, and I'm not sure I can survive it again. It was awful enough lifting a curse from someone else, I can only imagine it will be much harder to undo magic done to *me*. I'm afraid of what it will cost. I'm afraid I won't be strong enough to endure it next time."

She frowned and nodded, then put her hand over mine, the uninjured one, and gave it a gentle pat. "I have seen you accomplish remarkable things, Louisa, and you are not alone. There's a reason I stayed with you instead of going back to Yorkshire already. You need my help, and Khent's, too. We are all so much stronger together, Louisa, and weakened when alone."

I tried to smile, but my doubts lingered. She didn't know what it was like to live this way. She didn't know how it was to be afraid of your own mind. Mary might have witnessed the ritual from afar, but she hadn't seen the Binder face-to-face and withstood its test.

"We will find a way to fix this, I promise you that, and our chances will only get better if we have Chijioke on our side, too. And Poppy!" She gave a short laugh. "And though you do not trust them, I believe in my heart Mr. Morningside and Mrs.

Haylam will help you if they can. Maybe with their help it will not be so bad this time."

I sighed, putting down my cards. "Perhaps you're right. Perhaps the not knowing is a prison rather than a shield."

It was decided. I only needed to convince Dalton, though that proved harder than I expected. He was reluctant to go without knowing the state of things at Coldthistle House, but we had waited long enough, and I appealed to his tenderness for Henry, which was deeper than I had assumed. In this regard, the diary proved a cunning tool.

"Why did you give me this?" I asked him as he took tea that same afternoon alone. Holding up the diary, I—perhaps childishly—waved it in his face. "What is the point of it all if you do not let Mr. Morningside help me? If Mother had done nothing, I might have torn those people in the shop limb from limb. The time for waiting is over."

He regarded me over the rim of his teacup for a long spell, then he glanced at my healing hand and closed his eyes, pursing his lips. "I know," he said. "Only I'm afraid."

"I'm afraid, too," I confessed. "But that's not enough anymore."

Fathom took charge of organizing our escape from London, though she was wary of leaving the safe house even to arrange the carriages. We decided to leave that evening, using the cover of dark to ride to St. Albans and then exchange carriages, riding northeast toward Malton. Dalton assured us he could acquire faster transport in St. Albans, shortening the normally lengthy trip to North Yorkshire with a bit of help from a holy man and his even holier stock of horses.

This was all explained to Mother, who absorbed the information silently, nodding, that permanent beatific smile growing a little upon realizing we were indeed going to Coldthistle House.

"Good," she replied. "I should like to see where Father was defeated."

I said nothing but turned away to hide my frustrations. He certainly did not *feel* defeated.

Chapter Thirteen

I dreamt of a black-and-silver hall, a corridor of stars that went on into eternity. A ram the size of a mountain reared onto its hind legs, towering above me and made of dazzling white globes in little clusters, while a serpent as long as the Thames uncoiled and showed its star-bright fangs in warning. It happened slowly, the clash of these two impossible animals unfolding over hours, and I had almost enough time to count the stars that made up their forms.

When fang touched muzzle, the star creatures came crashing down, falling at my feet and toppling me to the glassy ground. The ram and serpent shattered, broken apart, their radiance scattering around me, like a spilling of jewels or a fallen chandelier, crystals sharp and spinning. I lifted my arms, and they were stars, too, and soon I was floating, lifted, hovering high above it all, something beautifully remade. Something new.

"How can you sleep so much? Those horses and the rocking— so much commotion! *Nhugh*."

Yawning awake, I found myself staring at a cross seatmate. As planned, we had changed horses at St. Albans, a kindly man of middle age lending us two teams of sleek mares, their coats and tails yellow as buttercups. They pulled us across

England at alarming speed, and Khent was not wrong about the considerable clatter and crash of their hooves as they churned the roads beneath us. Even the mud seemed not to bother them, and the bad storms had driven most travelers off the paths, allowing us to make each stop well ahead of schedule.

Khent was bundled under a thick plaid blanket, never one for the damp and cold.

"I'm simply exhausted," I told him. Mary shared that feeling, apparently, dozing next to me, curled up on her side. Mother might have been asleep behind her dark veil, but it was difficult to say. Fathom drove our team of horses, while Dalton and Niles took turns driving a smaller, lighter carriage that we struggled to keep pace with.

"How is your hand?" he asked. "Do you need more of the draft?"

I showed him my palm, now almost completely healed, a few curls of dry black skin flaking off and falling to the floor. At the safe house, he had mixed me a concoction I had sampled before, when Giles St. Giles and Mary had tried to calm me after I'd been attacked on the road to Derridon. It was a magical tea, deliciously sweet, and it soothed the mind and encouraged healing.

"It only itches now," I told him. As it had before, the illegible markings on my hand seemed to shift. "What does it look like to you?"

The more he practiced his English, the more he used it with

me, though frequently he slipped in and out of languages, often reverting to his native tongue when he was at a loss for the word in English. "*Eyou-ra.*"

The language of hounds.

"But I know that is not possible," Khent added with a twist of a smirk. "There is no written way to communicate such things."

"So . . . like a howl? It looks like a howl to you?" I asked, matching his smile.

His lavender eyes, however, lost a bit of their sparkle. "Not . . . No. No, it looks like the sound of a wounded animal."

"Fitting," I muttered. "It looks like gibberish to me."

"You will forgive me for saying so, *eyteht*, but it unnerves me to see it. I wish I could forget the words you screamed that day, and the helplessness I felt while that woman poked and prodded you. Well I know that sting, but I asked for it—you did not." Then he gasped and covered his mouth with both hands, snorting. "Oh. But that pet name is irksome. I'll do better."

Sleepy, I leaned my head against my arm and the window, watching the rain-soaked countryside fly by. "Maybe it's growing on me."

His thick brows lifted at that, his head tilting in an indelibly hound-like manner. It was a question and a look of interest in one.

"When this is all over, I will take you to a party. A real party. With scorpions and music that does not put you to sleep. Just the two of us, mm?"

"No, Khent. My heart is as fractured as my mind. Who would want that?" I sighed.

He shrugged, apparently unoffended, snuggling down into his plaid woolens. "Someone who sees that even scars can be beautiful."

"Aren't we just maudlin," I teased, bracing as the carriage rocked sharply, something going hard under the wheel. No, not something on the road, the road itself. It was *shaking*. "What on earth . . ."

We had escaped London by night, unseen, and we had made four stops on the journey without event. But the thunder shaking the ground was nothing natural; it had the rhythmic, four-part cadence of a beast running at a gallop. The carriage jerked hard to the left, waking Mary, who tumbled against me with a shriek.

"What the hell is that!?" I heard Fathom scream through the window.

Khent reacted the quickest, shooting out of his seat and slamming down the window. Sticking his head outside, he twisted, then pulled himself back inside. Mother lifted her veil, her eight eyes blinking rapidly with sleep, before she peered outside, mildly, as if this were no surprise at all. Her lips tightened with disdain, the first time I had seen her look anything but contented.

"The shepherd does not want us to reach him," Mother

observed through clenched teeth. "And he has sent a terror to do his work."

The other carriage dropped back alongside us, and a rock hit the window next to Mother. Mary quickly lowered the window, just enough to hear Dalton as he shouted across at us, his hair wet with rain as we sped down the road, the carriages shaking and jumping.

"It's a Tarasque," he cried. "We might outrun it. Coldthistle is but six miles down the lane!"

"And then what?" Mary wailed, stricken. "We're leading that thing to our friends!"

"Mother! Can you not do something? Appeal to its . . . its . . ."

"It's coming closer!" Khent kicked open the carriage door. The horses up front whickered and bucked, gravel and rain spraying our feet. "I want to get a better look."

And with that, he climbed out and onto the roof, the heavy tread of his boots thumping above our heads an instant later. Mother shook her head, opening her hands to me with a soft sound of regret.

"I cannot harm this creature, child. It cannot hear reason as a human might, and bloodshed is not my way," she said.

"I can try to lead it away," Dalton screamed from the other carriage, banging on the door to get Niles's attention up front. "We're lighter and faster, perhaps we can be a distraction!"

"And then what!?" I heard Fathom shoot back from the driver's box.

She was right. Simply outrunning it was not enough. Eventually—soon, in fact—we would reach Coldthistle House, and with no word from Wings, we had no guarantee that its inhabitants were in a state to be of any use. My heart raced. I hadn't yet even seen the thing, but I could hear it shaking the ground as if a herd of giants pursued us across the moors.

"Mary," I said hurriedly, rummaging in the only bag I had taken into the carriage. "Can you shield us?"

"I'm still weakened, I fear," she replied with a whimper. "And I doubt I can stop something that bloody big!"

The creature chasing us let loose a high-pitched shriek, an unholy clamor that sounded as if the sky itself had been torn in two. The breath of it rattled the carriages, buffeting us forward a few meters. The carpet bag nearly leapt out of my hands from the constant and violent shaking. There was so little inside. Some bandages for my hand, a tawdry novel, Dalton's diary, and the dull supper knife I had taken from Lady Thrampton's ball . . . I picked up the knife and twisted it in my hand, an idea slowly but steadily forming.

I fumbled toward the window, sticking my head partly out and looking up, finding one of Khent's hands gripping the wood and canvas edge of the roof.

"*Yehu!* How is your arm?"

"Mended, silly one, you know that!" His face appeared

suddenly, bouncing back and forth as he struggled to stay flattened to the roof.

"No, I mean . . . can you aim? Can you throw?" I called.

His eyes lit up, his mouth falling open with eagerness. Perhaps it was unkind, but I could imagine a dog excited over a bone making just such an expression. "*Eyteht*, I once raced chariots with the god-king himself. I let him win, though he was lousy with a lance."

"Perfect!" I cried back, then softer to myself. "I think."

"Louisa, don't be ridiculous, you can't go out there." Mary scuttled across the bench to me, trying to grab my ankle, but the carriage shot forward again, and I dodged out of her grasp.

"Do you have a better idea? Trust me!" I ignored the flash of pain in my hand as I pushed open the carriage door and the wind whipped against me. The rain lashed harder than I expected, and I said a silent prayer that this would work and that I would accomplish it without losing my legs under the wheels.

"Pull me up!" I put the knife between my teeth and grabbed the roof's edge with both hands, trying to steady myself as the breathlessly fast pace and jumping wheels nearly rattled my bones free of my body. Khent swore, his strong hands closing over my wrists and yanking hard, my feet kicking free.

For a single, terrible, exhilarating, wonderful moment I was hanging there in the air, as weightless as a bird. I heard myself squeak with crazed relief as he hauled me up and onto the roof.

But it was harder to find purchase than I expected, and I was forced to lie completely flat, creating as little a target for the wind as I could.

"What are you doing!?" He was furious, his face a finger's breadth from mine as he dropped down next to me.

"Good God, it's massive." I ignored him, transfixed by the hulking beast galloping after us. It had the bulk of a dragon from legends, though its head was that of a mangy lion, its legs thick and stumpy as a bear's, scales covering it from neck to whipping, barbed tail.

"Dalton said it's a Tarasque," I shouted over the wind. "Whatever the hell that means."

"Fascinating. How do we stop it?"

"With this," I said, reciting another prayer in my mind. It certainly couldn't hurt. We would need more than skill and luck to keep that mountain-size lion from gobbling us up. The welts in the muddy earth it left in its wake would soon be ponds. I glanced ahead, wind stinging my eyes, the stretch of road becoming familiar as we neared Coldthistle. Dalton had raced off the road and onto the flat country land to the side, trying to divert the beast's attention, but the Tarasque remained dogged in its pursuit of our carriage. It had no interest in the fast little phaeton gliding away. The Tarasque gave another shuddering, trilling roar, and its foul breath was close enough to ruffle our hair.

There was no more time.

"With this," I repeated. "And your arm!"

Closing my eyes, I clutched the supper knife in my fist. I poured all of my concentration into it, focusing so hard on its transformation that I could hear the blood singing in my ears. My breathing raced out of control, but that only helped, the chaos and fear accelerating the dark magicks of my blood until the knife in my hand grew and grew, becoming heavier and longer until I could no longer hold it. Khent caught the idea quickly, ripping the spear out of my hand and crawling to his knees.

I craned my neck to watch him, squinting against the hard-beating rain. He lifted the spear to his shoulder and gave an experimental poke toward the Tarasque, but then he sighed and shook his head.

"Grab my feet, Louisa, and don't let go. Gods, but this is the stupidest thing I've ever done."

I did as he asked, reaching out for his boots, clamping my hands down over them and throwing myself forward to pin them better with my weight. Khent climbed shakily to his feet, balancing with the tip of the spear on the roof. Inside the carriage, I heard Mary screaming with alarm. I felt it, too. The Tarasque was gaining, tireless, perhaps spurred by seeing a living target appear so clearly. Its breath jerked the carriage forward and back, the rear wheels lifting off the ground for an instant, and its loose and flapping jowls threw spit in every direction. Some of it landed on the carriage roof by my foot, and I watched it sizzle and eat away at the canvas and then the wood, burning clear through.

"Mind your head! The drool is like acid!" I shouted. The hole drilled through and through, then hissed as it hit the cushion just beside Mary. She blinked at me through the opening, covering her mouth with both hands.

"You've got an audience, Khent! And one chance at this!"

He thrust the spear over his right shoulder a few times, preparing, the loose edges of his coat flapping behind him like a cloak. His legs were shaking from the force of staying upright, and I pressed down harder, leaning into him, my last breath catching in my throat as he gave a huge grunt of effort and used our one chance, letting the javelin fly.

Chapter Fourteen

heard the spear strike its mark before I saw it. The beast's deafening howl might be heard all the way back to London. That, more than the way it floundered—its shaggy, brown head tossing, its short, thick legs caving in—pierced me to my core. The Tarasque gave two last faltering leaps, fur and scales slick with mud, before it dove forward, jowls shoveling stone and muck, carving a ditch into the road. Khent had struck it in the left eye, but the javelin had traveled deep, only a stub of an end protruding from the bloody ruin of its socket.

Fathom slowed the horses with a cheer, and I lifted my head enough to see Niles and Dalton circle back, bringing their carriage up next to ours from the opposite direction. I pressed one hand to my heart, checking to see if indeed I still breathed. It felt as if pure lightning skittered across my skin. Then I was airborne, lifted clean off the roof and spun, Khent dancing me up and down before he threw his head back and gave his own howl of relief.

"Aha! You see that? I could have beaten the god-king any day I pleased! Any day! I hope he is watching from the Land of Two Fields!"

"It was a very fine toss," I admitted wryly, loathe to puff him up any further, laughing at his chest-pounding display. He quickly sat down, all but collapsing, resting his forehead on his knees as he drew in deep, noisy breaths.

"We made it," I murmured. The rain had matted my hair to my face, and I pushed at it uselessly. "That was very lucky."

"And *that*," he whipped his head up, purple eyes dancing, two of his fingers mimicking legs climbing a wall, "was courageous."

"Or foolhardy," I chuckled. "Though I suppose one can rarely tell the difference."

The door below us cracked open, and Mary leaned out, trying to find our faces. "How extraordinary! Did you see, Louisa? The spittle went all the way through! Down to the ground!"

Dalton jumped from his carriage and leaned back against it, running both hands through his gingery hair. "God, but we're fortunate to be alive. This isn't a good sign, Louisa. If the shepherd is desperate enough to pull the Tarasque from Nerluc, then I fear he is capable of anything."

"More retaliation for Sparrow, I suppose."

Khent leaned over the edge of the carriage and spat. "Ha. Roeh will just have to try harder. We are proving difficult to kill."

"I wouldn't encourage him," Dalton shot back with a grimace. "Because *try harder* he will." He glanced toward the Tarasque and shuddered. The thing was breathing its last, groaning as it flattened against the earth and heaved, rolling, slain, onto its scaly side. "We should press on. I don't relish the thought of being on the roads at nightfall and—what the devil?"

Mother had, without our noticing, emerged silently from the carriage and begun marching toward the Tarasque. She pulled the black veil over her eyes, taking slow, somber steps until she had climbed the mound of stone and mud heaped against the creature's face. I heard her humming something quiet and baleful, a song of mourning. Kneeling, she placed both dark purple hands on the furred snout.

"Louisa, we really should—"

"Shhh." I cut Dalton off, raising my hand, watching as the immense creature, matted and bloodied and still, gradually began to break apart, shimmering into thousands of rose-colored butterflies. I thought I heard the Tarasque give a rumbling groan as it disappeared, as if it merely dozed, and had turned over in its peaceful rest.

The butterflies scattered upward, blending almost perfectly into the hints of pink at the edges of the horizon. The rain began to abate, leaving behind the fresh wetness of the long grasses and shrubs, wildflowers bobbing their rain-laden heads along the hedge. Mother returned to us with her chin held high.

"Every creature deserves mercy," she murmured, passing between us. Before stepping into the carriage, she handed me something. A blunt, bloodied supper knife. Then she took her seat, rigid, as regal as a queen. Her eyes found mine, and hers were glistening with unspent tears. "Every creature. Even those that would hunt us."

My heart grew weighty with dread as we crested the last hill before Coldthistle House. I remembered my first visit to the place so sharply, I could almost smell the bird droppings and the cook-fire soot still clinging to Mrs. Haylam's clothes. And Lee. Lee had been there. I had thought of him frequently when summer began and I was new to London, but then city life consumed me, the months disappeared while preparing the house, and before I could even appreciate the warmer months, autumn arrived. The dizzying chaos of the past fortnight had driven him from my thoughts altogether. I wondered how I would find him, and if he would greet me warmly or as a forgotten friend. There would be no urge to blame him; I should have written. I should have kept him fondly in my thoughts more. I should have done a lot of things better.

Spoon had become knife. I tumbled that around in my head, uncomfortable with the symbolism, uneasy with the knowledge that the monster in my spirit could rage out of control at any moment and make me its unwilling tool of destruction.

I had expected to feel more conflicted about our return, but now—wet, tired, and troubled—I was eager for a hot meal and a roof over my head. What hospitality awaited us, however, remained a mystery.

Chapter Fifteen

1248, Constantinople

I had never thought to pity a demon, particularly not one as ancient and powerful as Focalor, yet the creature all but demanded my sympathy. He cowered against his cathedral of candles, brown wings half wrapped around his body as he held his wounded hands close to his middle.

"You can understand my impatience," Henry told him—a bit harshly, I thought. "We have come a very long way, and you are not being altogether cooperative."

The demon crouched, staring up at Henry and showing his teeth. "Look at me, Dark One. Look at what happened to me in the salt."

"The salt?" Henry rolled his eyes and muttered something under his breath. "What is he talking about?"

"Be kind, Henry. He's half-mad," I said.

"No," Ara said. "The salt. There's a lake of salt, massive, to the east. Tuz Gölü."

The demon hissed at that. "Go not near the salt. You will return not at all or in pieces."

Henry loosened the pack on his back and pulled out the chestnut-colored pup inside, holding it out toward Focalor, who regarded it with shifting, narrowed eyes.

"Is she right? Did you learn more of the books at Tuz Gölü?"

Shrinking, the demon wrapped its wings completely around itself, hiding. "N-No. No, there is nothing there but desolation. Desolation and pain. There are no answers. There is nothing. It is all nothing. All meaningless."

His voice was muffled but easy enough to hear.

Henry put his mouth close to the puppy's ear, murmuring, "Is he lying? Is there deceit in his heart?"

The dog, small as it was, gave a low growl and then snapped.

Henry patted it on the head fondly and then tucked it under his arm, sighing.

"I know you do not want to serve me or anyone, Focalor, but make this easy on yourself. Tell us the whole truth. Tell me what you found at Tuz Gölü. Tell me.*"*

His patience was running thin. It was rare for his temper to emerge, as most things in life, even its tribulations, were a lark to him. I had seen him laugh off the deepest insults, the most cutting criticisms, failures, mistakes, and on and on. But a red flush crept across his cheeks now, pinpricks of silver standing out in his eyes, his anger such that the charm he used to conceal his true nature wavered, his feet contorted and backward facing. I reached for the pup, taking it from him, afraid that he would squeeze the poor thing to death in his rage.

"You wouldn't want to make me beg," Henry added in a soft, almost sad whisper. "I know you wouldn't want that."

He gestured to Ara, who turned and presented her heavy embroidered bag to him, the one containing the Black Elbion. The demon's wings began to tremble, but it otherwise managed nothing coherent, muttering over and over again about the dangers of the salt.

"White sands in my wounds, white sands in my wounds, white sands . . ."

"Perhaps if we gave him more time," I suggested, watching Henry remove the black book and run a tender hand over the

symbol on the cover. "Or perhaps we should heed his warning. I like my fingers quite where they are."

"I hate to agree with the Upworlder," Ara whispered, "but here we are. I told you not to go poking around the books. Look what it did to this pitiful wretch."

"Your opinions are noted and discarded," Henry replied, brow furrowed. He cradled the book in one arm and opened it. To me, it appeared as if the choice of page was random, but I knew him better than that. His fingers drifted over rows of text, words that I could not and could never decipher. It was not a language meant for me. I held the dog close to my chest, trying to soothe its fussing and whimpering.

"I compel you," Henry stated, holding out his other hand to the demon. His fingers were steady, his arm locked, his eyes suddenly completely black. "Wayward one, reluctant servant, I compel you now: you will give me your truth, and you will serve as my guide."

The tawny wings enfolding the demon shook and shook, his babbling breaking off as Henry's voice boomed through the hollow cave. The flames of the candles danced on their wicks, threatening to extinguish. Ara closed her eyes and pressed her thin lips together, hard. A faint whisper began from the demon, but Henry ignored it, repeating his demands, each repetition growing louder and more furious.

Then, as quickly as a rope snapping under tension, the wings flew wide and the demon emerged, only he changed, rapidly, in front of our eyes. The cracks in his skin widened, no longer glowing gold but billowing black smoke. He became a thing of shadows and red eyes, still winged, but expanding until his newly horned head brushed the ceiling. The puppy shivered and shrieked, flailing until I shielded it. Henry did not waver, but the demon of smoke and eyes rolled toward us, the smell of brimstone unmistakable.

"You will give me your truth and you will serve as my guide!" Henry thundered. But the demon had broken; it had become pure defiance.

"Ai akkani, ḫalāqu. Napāṣu-akka."

"Henry. Henry. Maskim xul . . ." I had never heard Aralu Ilusha afraid before, but the tremor in her voice was clear as she warned Henry, and I slowly backed away. The creature could not be less interested in me. It had eyes only for Henry.

"You will serve as my guide," Henry shouted again, ignoring us. His outstretched hand was just about to touch the smoke, and I held on to a single breath, watching as the soot-black cloud neared . . .

"Arratu-akka! Mâzu, mâzu, MÂZU."

It was a voice straight from hell, as fell and dark as the creature itself. I felt as if I were going to vomit and dropped to my knees, closing my eyes and lapsing into prayer. I rocked back and forth with the dog in my arms, hot tears dripping down my cheeks and into his fur. He curled into me, the only small spot of comfort as the nightmare voice bled into my lungs like poisoned air, thick with ash. The whole of the cave and the hovel above quaked, and I braced for the collapse.

"Fall then, demon. I name you all that is low, all that is man."

A cold whisper chased through the room, and I opened my eyes, watching as the hand touching the Black Elbion began to resonate with glowing-red power. The power surged through Henry's arm just as his fingers disappeared into the smoke of the demon's body.

Focalor's cry of anguish died, swallowed as he diminished like steam that had burst from a cauldron being sucked instantly back inside. When the haze cleared and the echo of their dark speech had faded, all that remained was a pale and tremulous man, curled onto his side like a newborn, an oversize loincloth draped over his waist. He shook with tears, and at once I turned away. I was suffocating. I thought neither Ara nor Henry had noticed me shuffling away toward the stairs, but a moment later I heard Henry snap the book shut, and then he was at my side.

"That was cruel," I whispered, realizing my tears hadn't slowed. "You went too far."

Henry shrugged, unmoved. "He's a demon, Spicer. It's none of your affair. He will do as I ask."

When I looked at him again, something was different. He

was his same handsome self, carefree and smirking, cocky in his apparent victory, but a dark glimmer in his eye disturbed me deeply. There was an absence of light and pity there, just empty blackness.

"That isn't the point at all, Henry. How could that ever be the point?"

There would be no afternoon tea or refreshing cucumber sandwiches at Coldthistle House. My old place of employment, the house I had known as the Devil's and then briefly as my own, was smoking, in chaos, and under siege.

We stopped the carriages not far from the short drive that led up to the mansion itself. We got out and stood along the edge of the grass, which even after so much rain curled inward, yellowish and dead at the ends. The shrubberies lining the path had not been pruned in weeks. One of the pointed towers on the west side of the house had recently been on fire; the burnt wood still smoldered.

"Take Niles to Derridon," Dalton said after a stretched spell of silence. "This is no place for humans just now."

"But—"

"Please, Fathom." I could hear the exhaustion in Dalton's voice as he turned to her. His clothes were still damp from the rain, and her coat and hat were sodden, mud darkening her boots to the knees. She didn't budge, hands balled into fists at her side.

At last she relented, and nudged the owlish little Niles toward the faster, light carriage.

"Fine," she muttered as she went. "But I'll return as soon as I can."

"Take your time," Dalton called after her. "And for pity's sake, be safe."

I watched her climb back into the driver's box, wondering if that would be the last I saw of her. The wave I gave her was small, unsteady, for I was loathe to part with such a stalwart companion. She smirked and tipped her tricorn hat in return, and then she was snapping the whip, calling up the horses, and maneuvering back out into the road.

"I wish I didn't have to send her away." Dalton sounded winded, as if he had run the whole way from London to Coldthistle. "But God only knows what we're walking into."

"Now we know why Wings never returned," I replied, surveying the battered house and the unkempt lawn. Something lean and golden swooped toward the stables, wings flashing in the fading dusk light.

"One of yours?" I asked, following Dalton as he crept onto the grounds, circling away from the eastern half of the property and keeping to the shadows of the tall, forgotten shrubberies and gargoyle statues. Khent and Mary joined us, and Mother glided along behind them.

"He's called back all of his command," Dalton whispered, crouching behind a statuary. We mimicked him except Mother, who seemed simply to melt into the greenery, innately part of it.

"We must see if the others are well," Mary insisted, her big green eyes darting toward the front doors.

"Wait. We must wait and be patient. Right now we have the advantage; they have no idea we made it this far and survived the Tarasque. We mustn't spoil this chance." Dalton peered around the bush, squinting into the coming darkness. "That was an Adjudicator, but impossible to say who from here."

"Finch?" It seemed the likeliest option, given the last I had seen of him was at the house.

"Hiding is for cowards. If we have the advantage, we should use it." Khent sniffed and then prodded me in the ribs. "Make another javelin for me with that knife of yours, I'll knock that stupid bird out of the sky."

"Shhh." Mary slapped at his hands. "Look!"

The Adjudicator had ended its graceful ascent on the top of the eastern attic. It stood very still for a moment, blazing with liquid golden light, its features blending into that ever-moving surface, its spear leaning against one shoulder. Then its massive wings stretched open, and it dove toward the lawn. All of us followed it with our eyes, and as it neared the ground, a blur of brown and orange intercepted, leaping from out of nowhere. From a hole in the lawn. The Adjudicator gave a strangled cry and then wrestled free, frantic, taking flight again but this time soaring away from the grounds, disappearing somewhere over the eastern fields.

"Bartholomew!" Mary squealed, covering her mouth.

No sooner had she spoken the dog's name than it came pelting toward us, muzzle split in what looked like not just panting, but a smile. He found us easily behind the bushes and tackled Mary to the ground, plate-size paws on her shoulders as he licked her face from neck to brow.

"All right, all right, yes, I missed you, too!" She laughed and pushed at him. The dog had gotten even bigger since I left, nearly the height and strength of a lion.

"Goodness gracious," Dalton breathed with bugged eyes. "He's *huge*."

"Rather changed from the last time you saw him?" I chuckled and reached for the dog, scratching him behind the ears. Bartholomew rewarded me with a nudge of his giant head.

"He was just a pup last we met," Dalton agreed, marveling at the creature. "Could fit in two of your hands, neat as you please."

From around the yard near the stables came a soft cry, then another. It was a searching sound, singsong. Poppy.

"Doggie? Doggie! You come back here this instant! Oh, I hope that horrid meanie didn't carry him off . . ."

Her fears were swiftly abated as Bartholomew poked his shaggy head out from around a shrub, to the delighted shrieks of Poppy, his steadfast coconspirator. I heard her little footsteps on the gravel before I saw her, and then she appeared from behind a gargoyle, braided tails swinging. Dressed in a stained white frock, she seemed thinner than I remembered, though still with large, doll-like eyes and a permanent reddish-brown stain covering a large part of her face. She stopped short, understandably, finding not only her faithful hound but three familiar faces and two strangers hiding among the verge.

"I know you!" she exclaimed, pointing. "And you, and you also! Have you come to drive off the shepherd man?"

"Poppy!" Mary pushed herself up from the ground and threw her arms around the little girl, who, if pressed, could scream loud enough to pop each of our heads like an overripe melon.

"It is ever so nice to see you again, Mary," the girl said, squeezing her fast and then stepping away. "It *is* really you, Mary?"

"It's me," she replied. "I promise."

"And this is Dalton Spicer, an old friend of Mr. Morningside's," I explained, making hasty introductions. "This is . . . Well, this is Mother."

"Whose mother?" Poppy asked, scrunching up her nose.

"I'll explain more later, yes? But can you tell us, is it safe to go in the house? Are there more of those Adjudicators about?" I asked.

Poppy swung around and nodded toward the front doors,

taking Mary's hand and holding it tight. "Chijioke has the doors barred, but I know the special knock. It's quite safe inside. The shepherd's people come and go, but Mrs. Haylam says it won't be long before there are a lot and we are really and truly something that starts with an *f* but that I am not allowed to say."

"Then we should go in quickly," Dalton said, glancing nervously toward the front entrance. "All of you go ahead, I'll be along shortly. Any Adjudicators will think twice before attacking me on sight."

Khent snorted. "Is that impending betrayal I smell?"

"You have nothing to fear from me, sir, not if the shepherd is ready to send the full might of his host against Henry. Go now, and keep your heads down!"

I took Khent and Mary by the forearms and tugged them along. Mother came with us, though she looked quizzically at Poppy and then Bartholomew, as if placing them in some kind of invisible order she had sorted out. She moved with speed when she wanted to, and she matched our strides as we shouldered up to the front doors, where Poppy gave the special knock.

The Deptford safe house and its pass phrase felt hundreds of years ago. I was so bloody tired, my body aching, my hand still in dull pain, my mind eager for unbroken rest. Father's voice disturbed me less with Mother so near, and it gave me hope that she could be a soothing presence until he was removed completely. Perhaps I might never need to hear him again.

"Poppy? Is that you?"

I saw Mary practically wilt at the sound of his voice rumbling through the door.

"It's me plus a bit more, but they are all nice. I think."

"What?"

"It's us!" Mary cried, laughing with relief. "We sent word but came when you never wrote back!"

There was a soft, sworn word and then the sound of boards grinding against boards. At least six different padlocks were undone, and then, with a shuddering groan, the tall, broad doors of Coldthistle House opened to me once more. It was dark inside and musty with old air, but the sight of Chijioke there with a hopeful smile was all the welcome we needed. Mary flung herself into his arms, and we filed in behind to fill the foyer. Chijioke had just set her down lightly on her feet when someone cleared their throat from the open staircase. I knew, of course, who it would be, but my blood still ran cold at the sound of his dark, twisting voice.

"Well, it appears I was right. Fate has brought you back to Coldthistle House, Louisa, and I see you did not come alone."

Chapter Sixteen

enry Morningside, the Devil himself, did not look well.

His hair was neatly coiffed, naturally, but his dove-gray suit hung rumpled and loose on his frame. Vivid purple smudges underlined his eyes, and he had lost weight, which showed most in the too-tight skin over his hands—the flesh there looked stretched, as if he placed naked bones and not fingers on the greasy banister.

Nobody spoke, leaving the echo of Mr. Morningside's voice to dance among the dust motes until Dalton returned and stepped out from around me and presented himself, staring up at Mr. Morningside before giving a short, polite bow.

"Hello, Henry. Did you miss me?"

Mr. Morningside's nostrils flared considerably, and he stiffened, giving me a glare that said clearly *I* was somehow to blame for Dalton Spicer's appearance. Perhaps I was, but I had not forced anyone to come, and the bad blood between the two men was their own sordid business. But more and more I knew how Mr. Morningside's mind worked, and if he could find a grudge to lay at someone's feet, he would do it with pleasure. Either that, or he sensed Spicer's and my fragile allegiance to one another and wanted simply to drive a wedge in our friendship.

"Did I miss you?" Henry scoffed, and then he produced a

handkerchief, wiping idly at the neglected banister. "How long ago was Hungary? Dear me, has it already been two hundred years? Goodness, Dalton, what an extraordinary idea, that I would long for a pebble in my boot, a fly in my porridge, a bee in my—"

"Aye. We get it, you're not friendly," I muttered, rolling my eyes at his theatrics. "Be that as it may, I happened to notice a few changes since I left. Most noticeably that the house is in shambles, the doors are barricaded, and there are Upworlders attacking at random. Oh, and here's something fun for you, we were chased halfway across the county by a dragon lion the size of Whitby. Anything sound amiss there and possibly more important than an ancient spat?"

Mr. Morningside lifted his brows, retaking my measure, or more accurately, reassessing me. As an adversary, perhaps, or as a former employee with a vengeful god locked in her head. He wound his way languidly down the stairs, pausing at the bottom one to smirk.

"You haven't been paying attention, Louisa. All of this," he gestured to the floor, the ceiling, and us, "is nothing but ancient spat after ancient spat. Generally, I can't even remember what it is we're fighting about."

I strode toward him, furious, but Dalton stopped me from throttling him on the staircase. "Oh, you smug—you . . . you *liar*. You and the shepherd tried to murder all of my people, and then you had a sliver of conscience and enough spine to feel sorry about it. Now you're taking sides and still losing by the looks of it."

Mr. Morningside feigned a choking noise and pressed his palm over his heart. "Louisa, you vanquish me, have mercy. Very well, we are somewhat compromised here, but the shepherd will stop eventually. He doesn't have the stomach for direct conflict. No, he rather prefers"—and here he fixed his gaze deliberately on Dalton—"subterfuge."

"I've taken no sides, Henry," Dalton said, putting his hands up in surrender. "There is no love between you and me, but likewise I disagree with the shepherd's methods. You don't know what it's like in London. His followers are spreading everywhere; they found Louisa and attacked her right out in the open, in front of half of London society. Good God, Henry, he sent Sparrow after her."

For the first time since our return, Henry looked legitimately taken aback. "Oh? And?"

"And she's dead," I said. "We had to defend ourselves."

"Now that *is* interesting," Henry drawled. He glanced with sparkling yellow eyes at Mary and Khent, nodding. "You three make a formidable little army. Fortunately for us, you escaped the riffraff in town. Your timing is appreciated."

"Where are Lee and Mrs. Haylam?" Mary piped up, her arm linked with Chijioke's. "They're not . . . Are they well?"

Mr. Morningside took the final step off the staircase, waving away Mary's questions with his handkerchief. He had at last noticed Mother, and nothing in the world could have torn his attention away from her as he took short, slow steps in her direction.

"They're counting beans in the larder," he said. "Supplies have been scarce since the shepherd began his campaign. But who is this? That is what I want to know. *Who is this?*"

It must have been a leftover protective instinct from when she was a very small, very crushable spider, but I leapt in front of her. She did not move me aside, yet placed an infinitely caring hand on my shoulder. I knew without a glance that she was smiling over my head at Henry. With her other hand she lifted her veil, and I watched him go pale and gasp.

"Greetings, Dark One. It has been too long."

Mr. Morningside struggled to come up with a response, then swallowed hard and swept her, and I suppose *me*, a bow.

"He looks nervous," I said under my breath to Dalton.

He smirked. "Henry has been keeping Dark Fae here under contract, hasn't he? They're practically prisoners. Now Mother has returned. I would be sweating if I were him, too."

"No," I told him, still softly. "They like working here."

"Do they?" Dalton lifted a brow. "Will they still think that way when Henry shows his true colors?"

"He's fooled everyone this long . . ."

"It won't go on forever," Dalton whispered. "It can't."

Henry, meanwhile, kept a weather eye on Mother. "Gracious

me, how long has it been?" His voice was too high to be casual. "Seven hundred years? Eight?"

"Longer," she said.

"Indeed." Mr. Morningside stuffed his handkerchief away and fussed with his blue cravat. "And the nature of this . . . this visit?"

Mother's other hand landed on my shoulder, and I could feel the warmth of her skin through my cloak and dress. "I am here for Louisa. Father's twisted spirit resides in her, and there is reason to believe you or one of your kind may know how to change that. Help her, Star of the Morning, and there will be no quarrel between us."

The smallest flicker of darkness flitted across his eyes. It was there and then gone so quickly, I couldn't be certain I'd seen it at all. The corner of his mouth twitched, and his hand went still on his cravat. A plan had begun forming in his head, and if that hint of darkness was to be believed, it was nothing good.

"Of course," he said, his face splitting with a wide, white smile. "Anything for a dear, old friend."

I crept silently into the kitchens, anxious to find Lee, though decidedly less interested in running across Mrs. Haylam. She had been my introduction to the house, but she'd never warmed to me. All along she must have suspected something, that I was not just a wayward girl, recently escaped from school, but part of this world beneath the world. I was beginning to suspect that she was the "Ara" mentioned frequently in Dalton's diary. The physical description—particularly her many strange markings—fit, and so did the sour attitude.

There was no sign of Mrs. Haylam and her severe, iron-colored hair, always neatly in a bun, nor sound of her sharp voice. I heard only a rustling coming from the pantry to the left, and I rounded the tall table near the stoves, a place I had sat many, many times for meals. On good days at Coldthistle House, those meals had felt like family suppers, but now the kitchen was hollow with loneliness, the windows grimy and gray, as if the place had not heard laughter or cheer in years. A large, rough hole had been dug through the tiles near the door leading to the lawn, and when I drew closer, I could see it ran deep.

I found Lee in the pantry, his back to me, golden curls slicked back from his head with sweat as he feverishly stacked jars of dried goods. Those jars might have been far heavier, but most of them were only a quarter full. Lee whispered to himself, keeping a constant tally of what he shifted from the left side of the pantry to the right.

"Need help?" I was exhausted, but then, he seemed tired and harried, too.

Lee started, dropping the jar he was carrying, but only a few inches. Luckily, it did not shatter. I rushed forward and caught it before it could tip, righting the heavy crock of pickled green beans.

Lee blinked at me in the low light of the pantry. A single lantern had been placed on a shoulder-high shelf, making the left side of his face glow orange. "Are you often in the habit of rescuing young men and their beans?" he asked.

"Aye," I said with a sad smile. "I feel gallant now."

It had been almost two years since he swept my spoon out of the mud, but we had changed far more than two years warranted. That same spoon, I saw now—slightly bent from rough handling—was hanging around his neck, dangling out the open neck of his shirt.

Out of impulse or shock, he rocked toward me, pulling me into a tight embrace. I was glad for it and sighed with relief. Even road weary, I feared being alone with my thoughts. Father was quiet, but he could always return. There was going to be no pulling Mary and Chijioke apart for some time, and Khent had promised to keep an eye on Mother while I looked in on Lee. Dalton had agreed to apprise Mr. Morningside of all that had occurred between Sparrow's attack and the present moment, a conversation that I had little interest in joining. The chilliness between them was palpable, and I was in no rush to tell Mr. Morningside I had been reading his friend's personal accounts of their former adventures.

"I knew you would come back," Lee said, pulling away and

holding me at arm's length. "You've come just in time, Louisa. Everything has gone upside down."

"It's the same in London," I told him, taking the jar of beans and hoisting it onto his stack. "We were all but chased out of the city. I have no idea if the shepherd wanted to force us here or just to eliminate us altogether."

"Us?" His eyes widened.

"Mary and Khent have come with me," I told him. "And the spider, too, only it's not a spider anymore but Father's counterpart, and she's called, well, Mother, obviously. Mr. Morningside's old Upworlder friend has tagged along. He says he wants to help me get rid of Father's spirit inside me, but I have no idea if that's true."

Perhaps I ought to take a page out of Dalton's own diary and see if Bartholomew couldn't divine his intentions. If only I had known the dog's gift earlier, I might have saved myself a lot of trouble at Coldthistle.

"Goodness," Lee murmured. "You had a busy summer."

"So have you, from the looks of it," I said.

"It was quiet for a while after you left," he explained, sitting on the stack of jars and sighing. He ruffled his curls with one hand and leaned back. "But then it all went to hell. Birds all over the county started dropping dead. Figures started watching us from the property boundary, day and night you would see them standing there, waiting for something. Then, a fortnight ago, they began crossing over, and one almost carried Chijioke off. It's horrible, Louisa, but I'm terribly glad you're here. Mr. Morningside has not been himself . . ."

The way he gazed up at me, so expectantly, made me nauseated with fear. I couldn't crush his expectations.

"He did look a bit peaky," I said.

Lee shook his head, curls rustling. "No, no, it's more than that. He's cross with us all the time. I knew he could have a prodigious temper, but now we're the target of it, too."

"I'm sorry." It was all I could think to say. "He's in open conflict with the shepherd. He must be worried that he could lose."

"But how?" Lee scratched thoughtfully at his chin. "He has hundreds of souls trapped in birds, and he must be powerful himself. I don't understand why he hasn't fought back, why he hasn't made Mrs. Haylam raise shadows or some such."

"I couldn't possibly know his mind," I said. But Lee had a point. Why *was* he waiting to mount a proper defense? I had never known Mr. Morningside to be meek or retreating, so why the sudden change? "Listen, Lee, I don't know his mind, but I'll do what I can to help. We all will. I just need to be careful. Father's spirit is dangerous, and I frighten myself when he takes control. He's out for blood."

"Good," Lee said, furrowing his brow. When we first met, I could never have imagined him becoming bloodthirsty, but death and living as a man of shadow had changed him. It would change anybody. "Those Upworlders are more than a nuisance.

They won't hesitate to hurt us. Why should we be any different?"

He had a point, of course, and I didn't know what they had experienced in my absence, but I did know what it was like to be hounded and hunted.

"There may be a better way to solve this," I said. "You might want bloodshed now, but trust me, you will quickly tire of it. Killing, even out of pure defense, it maims your spirit. Pull the wings off a butterfly, pull off its legs, and what do you have left?"

Lee stood, glowering, and pushed his way past me out of the pantry.

"Well, if you refuse to help us, maybe Khent and Mary will."

"That's not what I meant, Lee. I'm only advising caution. I . . . was responsible for Sparrow's death. Nobody liked her, maybe, but it opened a wound in me all the same," I said.

That slowed his steps, and he hung his head, shaking it.

"She is really gone?" he whispered. "I should be relieved to hear she's gone. Just her very presence made me sick to my stomach, and she hated us, but . . . Damn it all."

"I should look in on the others," I said, walking slowly toward the open doorway to the foyer. "Mr. Morningside seems to be in a strange mood, and having another ancient god in the house with him makes me nervous."

Lee hunched, gripping his stomach, wincing and stumbling forward until he could put one hand on the high table.

"What's the matter?" I asked, going to him. His brow perspired. "Are you ill?"

"Upworlders," he said through gritted teeth. "They're near. I only feel that way when they come."

"Dalton is one of them but estranged. Maybe you sense him in the house?"

"No, no. It's too sharp to be just one of them. It feels more like when Finch and Sparrow first turned up together. They're beings of light, Louisa, and I'm a creature of shadow now. Light pierces shadow. It's torment when they're stalking us."

"Come," I said, taking him gently by the arm. "We should tell the others. You don't have to fight them on your own anymore. Our strength is yours."

Chapter Seventeen

1247. The Road East

"*What do you make of him?*"

I'd done my level best to avoid Ara when I could. Henry was arguably more powerful and more dangerous, but Henry liked me. Or loved me. It depended on the day. Sometimes the hour. But Henry's and my good-natured alliance against Ara's—shall we say—testier nature shifted once Faraday joined us. He had shaken off the name Focalor, donning human clothes and human sandals, draping himself in a sand-colored smock and a beaded belt, a hood that shadowed his face, kohl smudged across his eyes.

He kept his injured hands deep inside his sleeves and wrapped linens over the places where his fingers were missing.

"*I've had truck with shadows more solid than he is,*" *Ara said one night, crouching on a rug beside our fire. The road to Tuz Gölü was hilly but not unkind, and the passage of autumn into winter afforded us cooler climates for the journey. There was even a chill on the air that night, and I was grateful for the heat of the pup snuggled in my lap.* "*His heart is there*"—*Ara pounded her fist over her chest, leaving flecks of soot—*"*but it isn't there, do you know what I mean?*"

"*What did Henry do to him?*" *I asked.* "*Besides the obvious . . .*"

"*He's a thrall now—human, I suppose, but less than that.*

The book is what makes us, what allows and feeds our power, and maskim xul asked the Black Elbion to strip him bare." She glanced over her shoulder at the two men, who watered the horses, deep in conversation. Or rather, Henry pelted Faraday with questions, and the other man shrank and mumbled. "Once a commander of dark legions, he will now be little more than a stableboy."

I shuddered, eyes wandering to her pack and the heavy black book I knew lay within. "I hate when you call him that."

"Why?" She cackled and stirred the cauldron on the fire. "Because it reminds you of his true self? Because it reminds you why you should sleep in your own tent?"

"It's quite honestly none of your business, Ara, and it baffles me that you deign to care."

The hand stirring the pot went still. "Watch your tone, Upworlder. You're vastly outnumbered and far from home."

I shrugged, well accustomed to her empty threats. While Henry remained near, she would not attempt anything. "You seem to know much about the books. Did Henry interrogate you, too?"

Ara went back to her cooking, adding a dash of something into the cauldron. "What I know, he knows. The only difference is that I have a healthy fear of the answers he so boldly seeks."

"Focalor paid a steep price for his knowledge," I pointed out. "I can only pray we won't owe the same."

"We will, and worse," she said. "Focalor is a fool, and he paid *only a fool's price. Henry should know better than to chase this rabbit, and so he will follow it down the hole and never come back out."*

Henry's voice suddenly rose, but I could not make out the words. His brows were knit with anger, and he used his height to loom over Faraday, trapping him against a large stone outcropping. I couldn't help taking pity on the poor sod, and I shuffled Bartholomew off my lap, excused myself, and crossed the camp to where the two men stood.

"So she asked you that and you said what?"

"I . . . I could not think of the answer, and she . . . Oh, but it was horrible." Faraday shivered against the rock and stuffed his hands deeper into his sleeves.

"My word, you're simple. But then demons usually are. It's not even that hard of a riddle. Moving on. What was the next question?"

"Henry, the food is practically finished. Could you not allow him a moment to recover?"

He shot me a silencing glare and put his hand on the rock next to Faraday's head, leaning in. The poor man looked like he might tremble to pieces. "The next riddle—what was it?"

"A-Arms to embrace, yet no hands," Faraday stammered, swallowing hard. "Pinches to give, yet no fingers. Poison to wield, yet no needle."

"Please tell me you managed to get that one," Henry muttered. "Please."

"I—I did." *Faraday shook his head, turning to me with a pleading look. "At least, I thought I did. How could it be the wrong answer? She asked, and I was so sure! Then she bit me. And it went on and on. I didn't know the others, but she wouldn't stop. More questions! More . . . more biting. I think . . . Oh, I think she enjoyed watching me struggle. No. No! We are too close to the salt. We should not even be speaking of this. I mustn't speak the word."*

But Henry sighed, clucking his tongue. "Shall I fetch the book?"

"Henry. Please." *I was well beyond exasperation. This was torture, and the former demon was leading us to the salt and seemed to be cooperating with Henry's questions. It was horrid enough thinking about bringing him back to the place where he had lost so much, and Henry could not spare even an ounce of pity for the creature.*

"Tell me what you answered, and I will . . . I'll let you eat," Henry muttered, then curled his lip in my direction. "Happy?"

"Not exactly."

Faraday's sleeves rippled, and I could imagine him gripping his own arms with what remained of his fingers. At least we could stop this torment in a moment, and I vowed silently to try to protect Faraday from Henry's prodding. The irony of it—an Upworlder shielding a demon from his own master!

Though I had to admit, I was somewhat curious . . . The riddle's key seemed obvious enough to me, and I possess no aptitude for puzzles. They had been speaking in Greek for my benefit, but Faraday fell back on his native tongue, sweating as he cowered against the rock and spoke. I felt the wind come and shake the grass and trees even before he answered.

"Zuqaqīpu," he whispered.

"Scorpion," said Henry, for my benefit.

"What are you doing!?" Ara leapt up from the fire, upsetting the cauldron and sending stew cascading over the hissing coals. Her robes flowed around her as she ran toward us, still wielding the long wooden cooking spoon. "I told you to be careful. I told you."

Faraday was right. We were too close to the salt, and the scorpion's malevolent presence seemed to prove that he had indeed unearthed something monstrous there. I heard him cry out and fall to the ground as the harsh, hot wind whipped through the camp, sending sand, dust, and grit into our eyes as it all but sliced us up. The rumbling began after that, a sound like the earth belching forth the flames of a volcano. The explosion had sounded distant, but that didn't matter. I could already hear whatever the underworld had birthed moving swiftly toward us, obliterating the sands as it came.

"Abātu! Go! Now! If we are lucky, we can outrun it and lose it in the hills. It will take time for me to summon shadows, but all is not lost!" Ara looped back toward the camp, frantic, scooping up her pack and tossing Henry's to him. I grabbed Faraday by the arm and hoisted him to his feet, pulling him along while

he wept and apologized. Bartholomew paced at the ruined fire, and I took him up, too, letting Henry manage both of our packs as the four of us made for the road.

"It doesn't matter," I heard Faraday moan. "It's coming. It's already here."

We scrambled up the road, running east. The moon was obscured by heavy clouds, and without any light to see by, it was a blind retreat, but the path cut through two hilly clusters of land, thick with shrubs and trees. Ara ran ahead; even burdened by the book, she overtook us, and we followed her up the pass to the right. At last, Faraday found some strength in his limbs and climbed next to me, whispering nonsense to himself as the great rumbling strides of the creature behind us neared. It sounded like more than one enemy, but my only intent was to climb. We could face our doom when we had the high ground.

The rocks cut into my palms, and the dense shrubs, bushy and sharp with thorns, tore at my tunic. The pain was forgotten, pushed aside by the pounding in my chest. The hilltop was no mountain, but it provided ample places to hide and a vantage. Ara made it first, running only a few steps more before she dropped to her knees and hoisted the Black Elbion out of her bag. It was her turn to whisper, using the ancient language she and Henry and the demon favored. I saw the book shake on the ground as I crested the hill, its pages rustling, the bushes around us suddenly full of secretive sounds, as if the very shadows had come alive.

In fact, they had.

I herded the dog against my stomach and curled around it on the ground. Henry was not at all put off by the noises bubbling up from every direction, and instead he strode to the edge of the cliff, leaning over to watch the thing that had followed.

"It's hideous," he hissed. "Ara, darling, we have to hurry now."

She shushed him, impatient, her hands waving over the book, her voice a low, rasped music that rose and fell. The rocks under us swayed. The creature was ramming itself against the base of the hill, apparently unable to climb. Just above Ara's song, I heard the creature's eerie chattering.

"I knew not to speak of it, I knew, I knew . . ." Faraday hugged himself, rocking back and forth in the dirt beside me.

"Hush," I told him. "Let her concentrate."

I had never seen Ara at work, but it was a thing of strange beauty. As her song reached its peak, she produced a knife from inside her robes and slashed at her hand. She made a fist, as if to hold the blood there, and then threw it outward in a fan. The blood never hit the ground, hovering there in the air before the shadows seethed out of the bushes to consume the offering. Her blood gave them form, and soon a dozen or so faces of shifting black stared at her, as if the night itself had come to life to do her bidding.

"Addāniqa—ḫiṣnu, ḫiṣnu!" she commanded, waving her arms frantically.

I didn't speak the language perfectly, but I knew what she had asked—protection. Please, protection.

With dragging feet, the shadows rushed by in single file and vanished over the edge of the hill, moving with silent, unnatural speed. I crept to my knees and then stood, joining Henry at the ledge. Ara remained on the ground, holding her wounded hand to her chest and breathing deep.

"They can only be a distraction," Henry said, somber.

"What is it?" I asked him. "What pursues us?"

*His eyes gleamed even in the total darkness as he turned away from the edge. There was a guilty hunch to his shoulders. Perhaps—*finally*—he had realized the cost of this quest. "I've never seen anything like it before, love. We will need all of our courage for what is to come."*

ee's upset stomach proved prophetic. After alerting Mr. Morningside and Dalton to the possible presence of Upworlders on the property, we mustered on top of the east tower, in one of the dusty, rarely used bedrooms that had been draped with cloths to keep the moths and dirt at bay. The furniture shrouded, the floors bare of carpets, it felt like a suitably desolate setting for what we found outside.

The tall, mullioned windows faced the fields that, far in the distance, held the shepherd's house, a modest shack I had once stumbled upon by accident. Of much more pressing concern, however, was a line of Adjudicators waiting just across the rickety fence separating the two properties. Most of the fence had been knocked down, but a few narrow posts remained here and there. The yard was pocked with deep holes, and I wondered if one of those led to the other end of the tunnel I'd glimpsed through the massive gape in the kitchen floor.

"He's mad as a bag of ferrets if he thinks I'm going to take that bait," Mr. Morningside grunted. He stood with crossed arms at the window, all of his employees and visitors beside him—except Mrs. Haylam.

She arrived in a bustle of skirts and muttered complaints, then paused when she caught sight of us all amassed at the windows. Out in the hall behind her lurked two blurry black shapes. Residents. The shadows given life prowled in her wake, drifting by the open doorway but not entering. Mrs. Haylam had abandoned her apron, wearing only a sober, dark frock with a knit muffler around her neck. The spare months between now and when I'd last seen her had aged her significantly. She had previously looked like a proud but gnarled old tree, dark of skin but with a severe kind of beauty. Now she simply seemed weathered, her milky eye so pale it almost glowed in the dimly lit bedroom.

When her good eye fell on Dalton, she drew up short. It was as if someone had dropped a solid block between them, for she would go no farther.

"*Him*," she spat.

"Hullo, old girl," Dalton greeted, turning to face her, though the fabric over his eyes hid much of his expression.

"We are not so desperate that we need *your* aid," she said, sniffing. "And the problem child has returned, too? I might have known. My every bone has ached for hours, an ill omen of the fools darkening our doorstep."

"We are indeed that desperate," Mr. Morningside said. "There are Adjudicators across the fence, and the shepherd flushed this lot out of London with fires and dragons and the Pit only knows what else. It would seem he wants us all in one location. Convenient, no?"

I chewed my cheek, ignoring the searing look Mrs. Haylam tossed my way. If I needed her help to rid myself of Father, I would sweeten my tone later, but that was a problem for another moment. In the meantime, I feared Mr. Morningside was right.

"Do you suppose he knows we're here?" I asked.

"Doubtful. If he did, he would send more than that pitiful lot," Mr. Morningside replied. He leaned closer to the window, squinting. "This may just be a warning. Or scouts."

They didn't look to be in a hurry, merely pacing up and down the fence. After my battle with Sparrow, the thought of facing four Adjudicators, even with more allies of my own, lodged a lump in my throat. Mr. Morningside, for all his boasting, had to be afraid. There was no mistaking the state of Coldthistle

House—it was a wonder they were still alive with Adjudicators attacking the property at random. They would certainly need us to survive the coming storm.

"Khent," I said gently, "stay here with Lee, Mary, and Chijioke. Tell me if anything changes. I need to have a word with my former employers."

He nodded solemnly and stood still, but I could tell he itched to follow.

"What's this now?" Mr. Morningside asked, cocking a brow.

"You will see. We should talk terms somewhere more private," I added, gesturing for Mother and Dalton to accompany me.

"Terms." Mr. Morningside tasted the word and sneered; I'm sure he would have much preferred I called it a *deal*. And I would, if that was what he required. Time was too short and my need too great to worry about such details.

Mrs. Haylam remained rigid near the door, watching me closely as I strode by her and out into the corridor. The attic space down the hall, while not glamorous, would have to suffice. Residents drifted up and down in the flickering light of the sconces, then came together to follow me, so close that I could feel the cold that rolled off them like the breath of winter. The large ballroom where I had first found the black book was not far off, but I doubted the book remained there. It was only reasonable that after the events of the spring, Mr. Morningside would take greater pains to hide it.

The attic, sneezy and dark, grew dimmer still when the Residents floated in. They seemed to suck the dismal light from every corner and soak it into their blurred bodies. Mrs. Haylam entered last, carrying with her a short candelabra with fragrant yellow candles. The light held beneath her chin exaggerated every deep crack in her face.

With Adjudicators gathering at the property's edge, I dispensed with pleasantries. "I want Father's spirit out of me," I told him and Mrs. Haylam bluntly. "If Chijioke can do it, fine, but something tells me it will be more complicated than his usual ceremony."

"Far more complicated, I should think," Mr. Morningside said, propping one elbow on his hand, knuckles tucked under his chin. "But not impossible."

I glanced at Mother, and from behind her veil, she smiled back.

"I have a number of souls stored," he continued. "The birds, of course. We can choose one of the less . . . unsavory types and use their essence. Perhaps Amelia Canny, or the Italian Countess, if you're in the mood for something more dangerous. Otherwise"—and here he peered between Mother and Dalton— "we will require a volunteer, but that seems unnecessary."

"You will need to be brought to the point of death again," Mrs. Haylam said, steely. "A simple task."

And how you will enjoy that, I thought.

"Very well," I replied. "That sounds agreeable. Well, not agreeable, but possible. In return, I will ask that my companions help you defend against the shepherd's forces. You will need our help to survive."

"You will do more than that." Mr. Morningside grinned, then grinned wider when my face fell. "What you're asking is complicated and risky, Louisa, and the trouble is that you will need us for it. Therefore, we must survive. Therefore, what you are offering is the bare minimum and not at all interesting to me."

"Here we go," I heard Dalton mutter, crossing his arms.

"Or you might help Louisa because it is the kind thing to do." Mother drifted forward, removing her veil. It was always startling, how strange and beautiful she looked, with her inky purple skin and eight delicate pink eyes. Even Mr. Morningside could not tear his eyes away from her. "She is suffering greatly. Father's spirit is poison, and it is killing her with its cruelty."

"How tragic," Mrs. Haylam drawled. "She was gifted the powers of a god. That she cannot control and understand them is unfortunate but not our problem."

"It will be," I shot back, taking a step toward her. "When I pack up my toys and go home."

"Back to London? Back to the angry mobs with torches?" Mr. Morningside sighed, but it was all theatrics. "Oh, Louisa, you are in our game now, and in this game, running only takes you to the edge of the board, it does not remove you as a piece."

He had me cornered, and I knew it, but I hated losing to him this way.

"Ask what you will, then," I whispered, not afraid anymore to look him straight in the eye, to challenge the Devil himself. "But I will not agree to anything until I know exactly what you require."

"I'm afraid it involves another book." He didn't seem at all bothered by my glowering. In fact, he had turned his attention to Dalton. For some reason, that frightened me more. "Only this time, you won't be translating it," Mr. Morningside said with a wink. "You'll be *destroying* it."

Chapter Eighteen

y first thought was that Mr. Morningside meant Dalton's diary, that he wanted it gone, but of course it could not be that simple.

"You have no idea what you're asking," Dalton said, shaking his head and brushing by me, standing up to Henry. They were of equal height and similar frame, though they were different in nearly every other respect. With Mr. Morningside's dark hair and Dalton's ginger complexion, they were like ice and fire.

"On the contrary, I know just what I'm asking." Mr. Morningside dodged around him, languidly, his shoulder brushing the other man's. I saw Dalton flinch at the proximity. "What else would you have me do? The shepherd has gone plum mad. We had a nice enough arrangement going. It's a pity he had to ruin it."

"Louisa tells me you've been amassing a bloody army of souls, Henry. Perhaps *that* ruined it, mm?"

"Is all this bickering necessary?" Mrs. Haylam pinched her forehead, going to the window behind us and setting down the candelabra. "Dalton will produce the white book and see it destroyed, or he will leave, and he will take poor, *poor* Louisa with him."

She had said it with such finality that we were all silent for a moment. I could hardly believe what I was hearing. Of course, it was completely in line with Mr. Morningside's usual tricks, but even for him this seemed extreme.

"*Destroy* the book?" I breathed. "Is that even possible?"

"It is," Mr. Morningside replied breezily. "Dalton knows it, too."

I waited for Dalton to say something, rubbing my hands nervously across my skirt. "What does that do? If the book is gone, I mean, what will happen?"

"We—Upworlders, the shepherd—" He choked a little on his words and closed his eyes. "We will all cease to exist."

"Oh," I said, remembering part of the diary. "The book is what gives all of you power. Father consumed our book, which is why we Dark Fae are still here."

"Precisely." Mr. Morningside looked grim, suddenly, as if the weight of what he was asking had finally sunk in. "What would you have me do, Spicer? The shepherd is out of control. Do you see anyone else setting up cults all over London? He wants us dead."

Dalton grunted. "No, he wants you contained."

"*He wants us dead.*" Mr. Morningside rounded on him, sticking a pointed finger into his face with a sneer. "You've lived long enough and look miserable doing it. You've always hated the game, so now you're invited to leave it. Destroy the book, and I help the girl."

Nobody moved. For a moment, I was convinced Dalton

might strike him. His entire body had gone too still, frozen with rage, his cheeks dark red. His eyes were covered, but had they been visible and whole, they might have been shooting flames. A tremor began in his right leg, but he stopped it and slowly, carefully, took a step back. Mr. Morningside lowered his hand but otherwise waited, his terms given.

Mother and I watched the Upworlder go with weary steps to the door, where he paused and put one hand on the frame, leaning away from the Residents that gathered there to watch and loom.

"You didn't have to make this personal, Henry," he whispered.

"Yes," Mr. Morningside replied, adjusting his cravat. "Yes, you made certain that I did."

"You don't have to do this."

I found Dalton Spicer out on one of the narrow balconies attached to the Green Suite. Like the other rooms on that floor, its furniture had been covered and left abandoned. There were no guests at Coldthistle House, and though the people who were drawn to it had committed great evils, the place still felt emptier and colder for their absence.

He stood with his back to me, night draped around him, his palms resting on a railing still damp with rain. I watched him trace shapes into the droplets for a moment, and then he regarded the forest. The balcony faced north, toward the hidden spring and the woods where I had first encountered Khent, when he attacked me and my father, who had been masquerading as Mary.

"There must be something else he wants," I pressed. "We can find a way to bargain with him."

"No," he laughed. "You don't know him like I do. Once he sets his mind to something, he gets it, no matter the consequences."

"I've been reading the diary, and I must say it's . . . disturbing. All the riddles and violence . . . ," I said, standing half inside still for the meager warmth. "Why didn't Mr. Morningside turn back? So much pointless danger . . ."

Dalton pulled away the covering over his eyes and inhaled deeply, rubbing his face, lifting his nose to the cold night air. "When I met him, he was a different man. Not kinder, not wiser, but more malleable."

I let that hang between us for a moment, and then I said, "Mother tells me Father changed, too. That the war among all of you broke something in him."

He gave a wry smile at that and tilted his head toward me. "Yes, yes, that's it exactly. I think it broke Henry, too, but he covers it well. When I first met him, it was at a meeting between him and the shepherd. They were forging an alliance, a temporary one, to punish the Father of Trees for overreaching. Henry had this . . . this frictionless poise. I couldn't take my eyes off him. He was dangerous, yes, but he listened. He compromised."

"He *listened*?" I snorted. "Then, God, he really was different."

"You have no idea." Dalton placed the fabric back over his eyes and scrubbed one hand over his mouth, as if trying to wipe something invisible away. "After we Upworlders hunted down the Dark Fae, your people, Henry stopped listening. He stopped compromising. I think he realized he was going to live forever, and living forever with that much guilt requires a heart of stone."

"Is that why he wanted to know so much about the books?" I asked.

Dalton took my meaning and nodded. "He saw his life stretching out before him, a long, long forever of a life, always burdened by what we had done to your folk. He had tried living with that stone heart and decided it was better to shatter the thing and be done. It wasn't just knowledge he was seeking in the salt flats, it was his own annihilation."

"Did Ara know? Is that why she kept trying to stop him?"

At that, he chuckled and ran his palm flat through the rain on the banister. "No, she didn't know, not at first. Neither did I. She doesn't think that way. Mrs. Haylam would happily live forever with the death of millions on her shoulders. She's simply made of stronger stuff."

"No," I said, plunging out into the cold to stand beside him. "That isn't strength at all. I don't think there's a word for what that is."

"Anyway." He shrugged. "She's too callous, too selfish to

think Henry might endanger himself or her. Never, ever be fooled by her temperament, Louisa. She worships the ground on which he walks."

I watched him fiddle with the raindrops for a moment longer. "But he didn't ask you to destroy the black book."

"No. I think . . . I think, strange as it may be, that he's quite fond of this house and those he employs. Destroying the Elbion would be their downfall, too. Where would they go? He's protected them for so long, and you've seen how dangerous it can be."

My brows rose at that. "Awfully sentimental," I said. "For the Devil."

"Maybe they ease his loneliness. That's worth something. I imagine it's depressing, conversing with birds all day, and he long ago chased demons like Faraday out of his life. Too miserable to be around, even for demons."

It was growing too cold to stay outside, and I longed for sleep. The Adjudicators, or so it seemed, had yet to make their move. The iciness in my gut had eased, and I wondered if they had left, delaying their attack. Maybe the shepherd sensed we had come, or that Dalton had, and had chosen to restrategize.

"And Henry knows how to destroy the books? Where to go?" I asked, lingering in the door.

"Yes."

"The riddles . . . He knows the answers to them? The correct answers?"

Dalton sighed. "All but one. Finish the diary, Louisa, you will see. I lost track of Henry for so long, it wouldn't surprise me if he learned more of the riddles on his own. Or he sent Mrs. Haylam to investigate. She would do anything he asked. Somehow . . . he has that way about him, convincing others to give up everything for him. Only it's a hollow promise, and there's no reward at the end."

As I watched, he crumbled toward the balcony, holding himself upright tentatively. I wasn't welcome or needed, and I backed into the house, hugging myself.

"You're going to do it, aren't you?" I whispered.

"Yes," he said, turning his face away from the sky. "Yes, I'll help you destroy the white book."

Chapter Nineteen

1247, The Road East

Screams, hollow and damned as the void, trailed after us down the road. Ara's shadow creatures had been left to fend for themselves, but those high, terrible wails told us of their fate.

"So soon?" she whispered as we ran. "How is it possible?"

Their sacrifice was soon forgotten, as we heard the impending thunder and the quaking of the ground beneath our feet. The stretch of land beside the road was uneven and treacherous, and our lead was swiftly lost.

How the creature had circled behind the road and come back upon us before we'd even run a quarter mile soon became clear. For we traveled on two legs while our pursuer tracked us on eight. I have seen many wondrous and terrible creatures in my day, but never something so grotesque. It surged ahead, rounding, blocking our path, the size across of three men, and as tall as five. Its body—long, curved, and segmented—was that of a scorpion's, a faded-brown color translucent as parchment, the veins and organs within throbbing and red. It reeked of deep earth, with clay and bits of mud and sand still falling from its head and tail as it clacked its massive pincer arms together. A human stomach, chest, and head rose from the body, sharing the oddly thin skin, heart pulsing and pumping before our eyes.

The pointed barb of its tail swayed back and forth, preparing to strike.

I would have appealed to it but for the shock that rooted me to the ground. Even frozen, I would have begged it with my eyes, but that was no use, for it had none of its own to see me. Its pointed legs carried it backward and forward a beat, and I felt Henry's hand clasp mine, squeezing.

"Take your golden form," he breathed. "I fear this is no creature of reason."

Indeed, it was not, and before I could so much as summon the breath and will to drop my human guise, the creature dashed forward. It barreled toward us with sharp, bulbous pincers aiming for a single target. Faraday. I was still holding on to the man's wrist, but that ended abruptly, as he was torn from my grasp and carried, legs kicking, to a rocky outcropping, the one we had just used as our high ground.

We spun to face him, but I dared not follow. Not yet. The fear was too deep . . .

"We have to do something," I whispered. "We have to help him."

Without another thought, I started forward, ripping my hand out of Henry's as the creature pinned Faraday to the stone. It held him there without trouble, and for an instant Faraday fought against the massive claw, pushing and flailing, trying to land a single kick against the human stomach.

Behind me, Henry screamed something, desperate, terrified, but I would not let fear trap me into inaction. The demon had suffered enough; he did not deserve this. But even as I pumped my arms and ran as quickly as I could, the beast lowered its pale, thin lips to Faraday's face and snapped its teeth once. Then it spoke, and its voice nearly stopped me again. It was not a thing that was made to use human speech, and the words squeezed out like the gurgle of water through mud.

"What were you told in the salt?" It snapped its teeth again. "What were you told?"

"N–Never to speak of what I saw, never to repeat what I heard! Please! Upworlder! Dark One! You must help me!" Faraday shrieked and reached toward me, but even the might of my wings once unfurled couldn't carry me to him with enough speed. Snip. I will never forget the sound. The creature squeezed its pincer together once, hard, like two scythes, severing Faraday in the soft middle, his legs dropping to the ground before his torso did a moment later, his eyes wide with surprise.

I dropped to my knees, and the creature spun to face me. Whatever sight it used, I know it saw me there, and its head lowered as if it wished to say more. Then it shook out its claw, splattering me and the dirt with blood, and it gave a high, eerie cry like, "Lilililililili!" And then it was gone, vanishing into the hills, the only sign of its true departure another hot wind and the rumble of tunneled earth.

eturning to my old quarters in Coldthistle House came with a disarming wave of comfort. My little bed; my old, rickety side table; the long looking glass where I had first beheld myself in the simple frock and apron that would become my day-to-day wear . . . It felt possible to slide back into that old life, to wake each morning and see to my chores, cleaning blood out of carpets, helping Chijioke haul corpses down to the wagon, feeding the horses and buttering scones for guests—all there, just out of reach, an existence that spun in time like a dancer in a music box.

My life, but not. A future, a path, but not. I stood at the foot of the bed and touched the blankets carefully, as if this were all a mirage and might shimmer and break at the faintest touch. For a brief time, I had known the stability and routine that most young women of my station longed for, a position that ensured I would eat, that I would sleep sheltered, and that I would put a bit of money away, maybe one day to be spent upon a paltry dowry.

That was another Louisa. I went to the looking glass and smoothed down my hair. It was in a tangle from our mad dash to the house, and my gown, torn and muddied, would need replacing. Staring into my own dark eyes, I wondered, not for the first time, if like the damned guests of Coldthistle House, I, too, had been lured here by a dark promise. They were ultimately met with death, but I seemed destined for something else.

"Death will be your promise if you do not open your eyes, girl."

I watched in the mirror as the room filled from the bottom with grayish fog, the mist rising above my ankles and then to my knees. There was nothing in the reflection, but I turned toward the voice and gasped, finding myself face-to-chest with Father.

He towered above me, his image unsettled, half the fake human form of Croydon Frost, the other half his true appearance. A gruesome deer's skull protruded from the human skin, bone forcing its way through flesh. His suit was in tatters, transforming as it fell into the black rags and leaves of Father's robes. Tufts of human hair clung to the lopsided antlers that poked from his naked skull.

He smelled of death, but then that was no surprise.

I backed up against the looking glass, bracing.

"Close now," he seethed, eyes two glowing red coals. "So close now . . . My ashes, my body, the tree that sprung from my earthly leavings . . ."

"This is not a dream," I breathed. "Nor a nightmare. *How can this be?*"

Foolishly, I reached out to touch him, to know for certain that he was real and not an illusion. My palm sank through his chest as if he were made of colored smoke. But when I tried to pull my hand back it wouldn't budge—his image held me there, his hands wrapping around my wrist.

"A Binder's mark." He stared, transfixed by the now-illegible lettering on my palm. Then his crimson eyes flew to mine. "You freed Mother. You survived a Binder. You are stronger than I thought, daughter."

Daughter. Now I was not *girl* or *fool* or *child* but *daughter*.

"Release me," I whispered. "And be gone. I *am* stronger than you know, and my friends are here with me."

"Friends?" He laughed, but it was like the cackle of a raven in the gloom. "What need do you have for friends when my spirit grows powerful? Go. Go to the tree. Carve the bark, drink its sap, and there will be no dawn for the shepherd and his ilk."

No. The word was there, just on my tongue, but no matter how hard I struggled to say it, my lips clamped shut. I felt the world go blurry around the edges, and my balance trembled, flecks of red dancing across my sight. The crimson veil was dropping again, Father's influence too strong now to resist. It had been a mistake to come. I had not considered that being near to his physical form would somehow embolden his claim over me, but it did. My struggle was valiant but brief, for there was no resisting the tendrils that curled, steady and painful, into my brain.

The world went by as if imagined. Nothing seemed real. I felt my feet carry me out of the room and down the stairs, then down again, until I was turning toward the kitchens. The door leading outside was barricaded and too noisy to disturb without being noticed. So I went on hands and knees, and, like a rat in its tunnel, I crawled through the hole Bartholomew had dug under the house, a project he might have started months ago along with all the other holes he had put in the yard. Roots and dirt brushed my cheeks, but I was blind to that, though not unfeeling, the cold earth under my hands slippery, fragrant with grass and loam. Insects, free about their nighttime business, skittered over my hands and ankles, crawling up my back and into my hair, tickling my nape with their horrid little legs.

No, no, no. I could not go outside, not when the shepherd's

Adjudicators could descend at any moment. And if they did, I feared more for them than for me—Father controlled me now, and his wrath upon them would be terrible. My hands clawed and clawed, carrying me through the muddy tunnel until at last, I felt a gust of wind against my face, and the way curved upward. I scrambled out of the hole, breathing hard. I must have looked a true terror, covered in grime and insects, my eyes wide and unseeing, my every step guided by the beast in my head.

The tree was not far now. I could sense it—Father sensed it—and I trotted, then ran toward it, hurrying right for the eastern border of the property. Surely somebody in the house would notice me and help? Or would they be alerted to my presence only when Father succeeded and made war with me as his instrument?

Please, I pleaded with him as best I could in my head. *Please. Let me make my own path. How can you be so unfeeling toward your own daughter?*

But he was silent, pitiless, and I flinched, feeling suddenly the lowest boughs of the tree brush my face. Impossible. How could it have grown so fast? It had been but a sapling when I left in the spring, but now? My hands found its trunk, a full-grown tree, gifted swift life by Father's ashes.

"He should have cut this accursed thing down," I managed to whisper.

Silence, daughter. Carve the bark. Carve it.

I had only my hands, and so he forced me to use my fingernails, shards of unyielding wood splintering into my soft palms as I pawed at it like a beast gone mad. Droplets ran down my cheeks, not the cold dew off the leaves but tears, hot and steady. The pain was unimaginable, the mark on my palm pulsing with fire.

I carved and I carved, clawing, scratching with what I knew would be raw, bloody fingers come morning. If morning came. My fear redoubled when the pain stopped, numbness spreading through my fingers to my hands and wrists. Blood soaked the sleeves of my ruined gown. But Father was relentless, and I was powerless in the shade of his death-borne tree.

A mist rose around me, and I felt the stickiness of sap trickling against my skin. The sharp, herbal scent almost shocked me into control, but no, the feeling was gone, and the sap covering my hands seemed only to deepen his hold. I stumbled back from the tree, shivering, and bent to lick my fingers.

I could already hear the blood pounding in my ears like war drums. The shepherd and his folk would not see another sunrise.

Chapter Twenty

he night would come back to me in fits and starts, fragments of a dream washed red with blood.

A cry for help. Bones snapping beneath my fingers. The scent of deep forest, then the reek of fear. A body broken on the floor. Golden feathers scattered like fallen autumn leaves.

Someone was holding my hand, but when I tried to sit up I felt the bite of heavy iron chains around my chest and legs. I blinked up at the ceiling, listening to the voices around me fade. The hand in mine was familiar and small.

"She's awake! She's awake! And she doesn't look so mean now."

Poppy was sitting beside me on the bed; I had another stirring of memory, remembering the times I had woken to her face and voice before. Those times, I had not been strapped down to the bed. My head ached, and I groaned, then accepted a bit of tea from Poppy, who held my head while I sipped.

"It's very late now," she said. Mother was there, too, standing at the end of the bed watching over us. She never looked tired, as if impervious to the wear of exhaustion. "The others all got tired and went away, but I said I would stay with you. Bartholomew, too."

The dog gave a huff from somewhere next to the bed. Restrained, I could only crane my head a little. Blessedly, they had changed my gown and done what they could to clean me. At least I did not feel the wretched digging of bugs in my hair.

"Do I want to know what happened?" I murmured. My throat rasped as if filled with nettles.

"I found you before you could take too much of the sap," Mother told me gently, her hands folded in front of her. She had left her veil somewhere and stood only in a crinkled silk gown. Her bare arms had dune upon dune of muscle. "Even so, one of the Upworlders noticed you among the trees. They . . . could not withstand your fury."

"All smashed up," Poppy clarified helpfully. "Like Mrs. Haylam's mushy peas."

"It took all of us to subdue you," Mother added. Her smile was different now, sad. Mournful. "I will not leave your side. The risk of Father's influence is too great."

"The tree," I wheezed.

"I have seen to it," Mother said. "I can speak to the heart of a tree, and that one did not go quietly. It left a rotten wound in the earth. When there is more time I will purify it, and soon his ashes will be washed away by rain and wind."

That ought to have pleased me, but my unease remained. If so much as a speck of him persisted, my control over him was in doubt.

"Even if I remove his spirit," I murmured, closing my eyes and sinking down into the pillow, "I still have his blood. My father burned a field of captives alive to imprison you. That kind of darkness, that madness, will it always come out?"

Mother came around the bedpost, and Poppy made room for her, the two of them side by side, though it was Mother's turn to take my hand. There was no reason to doubt her power, but her touch proved it, inducing a soothing warmth to trickle up from my hand to my chest, releasing the tightness there.

"He once gave me a bouquet of enchanted snapdragons. When the sun shone on them, they giggled like children, and when night fell they made the dearest snoring sound," she recalled, her smile brightening for an instant. "That goodness was in him, too, and I know you have it."

"Perhaps not," I said, closing my eyes again. "I can't seem to stop killing."

"You will, Louisa. When he is gone and your mind is your own again. I can speak to the heart of trees, yes, but I can speak to the heart of my children, too." She sighed and squeezed my hand tighter. "I only fear that the Dark One will try to harness your power to fight Roeh."

Poppy leaned over and poked at one of the chains around my legs. "If we take these off, Louisa can help. I want them to go away and stop being so mean so Bartholomew and I can play in the yard again. I hate being stuck inside all day. It isn't fair! I haven't even gotten to do my screams because Mary went to stupid old London."

She pouted, sliding onto the floor to curl up with the dog.

"I may have to unleash him," I told Mother slowly. "One

more time. If it means I can see him removed, then I will do it. Please try not to be too disappointed. These are my friends, after all, and I would see them protected."

Her sad smile returned, and the warmth of her touch narrowly stayed my tears. It was hard to cry when she held my hand. I tried to remember if my own human mother had ever demonstrated such kindness, but no memories surfaced, only shouts outside my bedroom door, and my drunk of a father screaming at her while I hid beneath the blankets.

"Show mercy when you can, Louisa," Mother said, and reached for the first strand of chains, loosening them, "for the world is far too short on it."

In the morning, I was invited to take my breakfast with Mr. Morningside, though Mother refused to drift far from me. He allowed her to join us in the sitting room just off the main foyer—the place where he had first taught me to change a spoon into whatever my heart desired—but not before I caught the tail end of an argument between him and Dalton. Waiting outside the French doors, I couldn't help eavesdropping, putting a finger to my lips to keep Mother from saying anything.

"We made a pact," Henry was saying. He sounded murderous, cold. "And you broke it! In the moment when it mattered most, you broke it."

"Because you lied." Dalton, on the other hand, was passionless.

"THAT'S WHAT I DO."

The house trembled.

Dalton's voice came closer; he was just about to leave the sitting room. I backed away, pretending we had just descended the staircase and I hadn't heard the last of their row.

"I know," Dalton said, opening the doors but turning his head inward. "To my everlasting regret, I know. And I wished—and I *wish*—that you would be more than that. That's what a man is—more than his parts, more than his history and his destiny doomed him to be."

Dalton had no words for us as he marched away from the salon, turning sharply to take the stairs two at a time. I hesitated a moment, listening to his retreating steps, and then tiptoed through the doors to find Mr. Morningside gripping the edge of the breakfast table, his back to us.

"A deal over breakfast," he crowed after Mary had brought us a light meal of cheese, fresh bread, and what could be spared of the dried venison. She had resumed her role at the house almost at once, as a distraction, maybe, or habit. "Under siege and yet we're practically civilized. Do you think they ate so well while the horse was being rolled into Troy?"

"I don't think I care," I said, exhausted. Mother's peaceful presence had helped, but being chained to a bed had made sleep a near impossibility. "If you want to make a deal, then Dalton should be here, too."

We sat at one of the small tables adjacent to the pianoforte, not far from the windows facing the west. It was the farthest room in the house from the shepherd's property, likely an intentional choice. There had been no signs of activity along the fence, but that made me more nervous. It had all the makings of the calm before the storm, and my foot bounced beneath the table, giddy and alert.

"He has already agreed to recover the book," he told us, pouring sugar into his tea and stirring it with deft little circles. He was positively singing with cheer. "Your display last night pushed him over the edge. He came to me early this morning and made his offer."

My appetite was not what I expected it to be. Mother did not eat, either, but held her teacup as if simply for the pleasure of it. I choked down some of my own but took no interest in the leathery venison.

"So Dalton will find the book; then do we depart for Constantinople? How will we make the journey?" I asked.

Mr. Morningside gagged on his scone. "Louisa, you rascal, what makes you ask that?"

Ah. So Dalton had left out the small detail of the diary. I forced myself to take a drink of tea and look casual, but my hands trembled. I wanted to keep my possession of the journal a secret from him for as long as possible. There was every chance that Mr. Morningside would try to rig this deal to his advantage, and I wanted one tiny thing up my sleeve just in case. After all, he had told me himself that I was part of the game, and I needed to act accordingly. "You are in our game now, and in this game, running only takes you to the edge of the board, it does not remove you as a piece."

"The entrance, the place where the books can be destroyed . . . It's far to the east, in a salt plain. Dalton told me about it, about you and Mrs. Haylam going there when you were all much younger, just after . . ." I glanced nervously at Mother, but she didn't seem bothered. "Just after the Schism."

"Ah, so it is Dalton after all who is the rascal. No matter. Yes and no, Louisa, there is an entrance at Lake Tuz, but there are many, many entrances. I know of one much closer, in fact. You could be there by morning if you left now on horseback."

I nodded and frowned, feigning puzzlement. Yet what he said made sense. When I'd met the Binder at Cadwallader's, it had been in a space that was nowhere, and perhaps this place where Henry wanted us to go was similar, a destination between worlds, hiding somewhere in the shadows.

"He also told me there were riddles," I continued. "As part of our arrangement, I want you to give me the answers."

"Of course," Mr. Morningside said. "Dear Louisa, there's no need to look so cunning. It's my greatest desire that you should enter the Tomb of Ancients safely and fulfill our bargain."

At that, I could not hide my interest. I set down my teacup and leaned slightly toward him across the table while he nonchalantly buttered his scone again.

"So you've been inside," I said, repeating his name for the place. "The Tomb of Ancients."

"Inside? No. No, I'm afraid there are certain limitations that prevent me from entering," he said. The sigh of frustration that followed seemed genuine, but then, he was a very talented actor. "You, however, should have no trouble infiltrating, so long as you follow my instructions and use your wits. I can only help you so far, Louisa, for I do not know what awaits you inside."

"But the books can be destroyed there?"

Beside me, Mother winced. I was now a book, having Father's knowledge of ours buried in my head, and that meant I, too, could be destroyed there.

"Yes, it is where the books are created, I know that to be true," Henry said, and I could tell he was choosing his words carefully. He flecked a bit of crumb off his jacket and fixed me with one of his wide, charming smiles. A curl of black hair fell roguishly in front of his yellow eyes. "But we must not discuss it aloud in too much detail—it is a protected place, and I am not eager to call out its guardians. I will write down your instructions, the better to avoid detection."

I shuddered at the thought of anyone getting cut in half by an angry scorpion creature.

"If you insist."

Mr. Morningside studied me over his cup, perhaps divining

that I knew more than I let on. But he said no more on the subject and drank his too-sweet tea. "Then it's settled."

"I wouldn't say that. How do I know you will uphold your end of the deal? I am risking my life to destroy that book. You could simply refuse to help me once I return. No, I think you should remove Father's spirit from me now, before I fix your problems." I sat back in the comfortable chair, enjoying his brief but visible discomfort.

He tugged at the bottom of his jacket and looked at me askance. "We will put it down in writing, of course, Louisa, and I always honor my contracts."

"That doesn't satisfy me." I dug my finger into the tablecloth, holding his gaze. "If I return from the Tomb of Ancients and you do not remove Father's influence over me, there must be some penalty."

"Such as?" He leaned down toward the floor, then produced quill and ink from a leather satchel. Having arrived in the sitting room after him, I had no idea he had brought his tools along, waiting for just this moment.

"Such as . . ." I paused, but the answer occurred to me quite readily. "Such as the deed to Coldthistle House and all within it. The Black Elbion included."

"Don't be ridiculous," he snorted, smoothing out the parchment next to his breakfast. "That's hardly fair, Louisa. Be reasonable."

"Reasonable? A book for a book, it's the definition of *fair*, and the house is for my life, the one I might easily lose in the tomb. Those are my terms, Morningside, you are free to refuse me and find another way to unmake the white book."

I hated the feeling of his eyes burning into mine, and that I wanted constantly to turn away. This was a test, and I was determined to pass. He had, of course, slanted the terms of the deal to his advantage, but if this was a game, then I would not be easily played. At last, he sat back, wetting the pen and putting it to paper.

"Exactly as I said it," I added. "I won't have you worming out of this. If you do not remove Father's spirit from me when I return, having destroyed the white book, then the deed to Coldthistle House and the Black Elbion are mine. And I warn you, I will check that contract over a dozen times if I must."

"You're learning," he muttered. "I'm not sure if I should be relieved or annoyed."

"Don't push me." At that, his eyes flicked up from his work. I continued, "I know why you're making me wait, why you want Father's influence to remain as long as possible. You need me to defend against the shepherd."

"An astute observation." But he was teasing, and rolled his eyes, writing out the remainder of the contract. I could see him tacking on a clause for Dalton's part in it, and I would be studying that, too. "I know it would never occur to you that I might have somewhat-less-than-evil intentions, but my feeling is that you will want that unholy strength in you to survive the tomb. All that you have seen, all that you have survived, will be nothing like what it will demand of you."

Severed fingers. Severed *body*. Cracks in the skin that bled golden light. Madness.

I swallowed, anxious, and turned my attention to Mother.

"And you know nothing of this place? The Tomb of Ancients?" I asked.

Her eyes went soft, and she tilted her head to the side. The long pink braids of her hair were undone, the long tendrils combed out over one shoulder. She pushed her hands into that tumbling mass of hair and idly began making a plait. "My heart says I know it, long for it, like a child fresh from the womb longs to be swaddled. I know it and yet I do not; I have no memories of it, but to hear the words spoken: Tomb of Ancients . . ." She shook her head and let go of her hair. "I never thought to study such things. I never yearned to go back to the place where we began."

Mr. Morningside dashed off the final line and blew on the page, then handed it across to me, taking up his tea again. His eyes were distant. Cold. "I pray you never see it, never go near it—"

The lines I cared most about had been copied down correctly, and I put down my signature next to his, unaware that he had trailed off midthought. Then I heard Chijioke crash through the door, gasping for breath.

"They're here," he shouted, his hand pressed over his heart. "The Upworlders. They've come."

"What incredible timing they have," Mr. Morningside groused, standing. He took the contract and rolled it up tightly, then placed it in his leather satchel. "We will need all your fury, Louisa. Give them your worst. We must draw them here in great numbers and give Dalton time to recover the white book. And then? Then it will be your time to see the Tomb of Ancients."

Chapter Twenty-One

1247, West of Cappadocia

*There was nothing for it—I was never going to sleep. We burned
Faraday's body far off the road, then returned to our initial camp
to collect the horses and ride out. None of us were keen to sleep
so close to where the demon had met his doom. Nobody spoke,*

though I could feel Ara working her way up to a lecture, her mouth a tight line as we galloped through the night.

We stopped leagues from our destination, in the last vestige of hills before the land descended into a shallow valley and the salt lake began. I crawled out of my bedroll and found a place to relieve myself, then noticed I was not alone in my sleeplessness. Henry stood at the edge of our little camp, arms crossed, his eyes inscrutable as he stared out at the white valley below. The salt. I know he does not share my fear of the place, but I can think of nothing but Faraday's warnings. And that creature . . . It was not one of ours, and it apparently wasn't one of Henry's demonic friends, either.

"I'm going to say it again," I whispered. He didn't move. "I think we should pack it in and go home. This has become something else, Henry. It's more than an obsession, it's more than dangerous. It's . . ."

"All perfectly reasonable, I assure you," he finished. He ran a hand through his wild black hair and inched toward me, then laid his head on my shoulder and blew out a breath. "Do you ever think about it? Eternity?"

"Occasionally." Leave it to Henry to distract me with philosophy.

"I think about it all the time," he said. "I don't want to be old. How long will it take to be old? I already feel ancient, and by our standards I'm a child. It's ghastly."

"Oh hush, you will never look old," I chuckled.

"Not on the outside. But on the inside? I feel it already on the inside. Like I'm breathing coffin dust. Like I'm already entombed. But it just goes on for us. I don't know if I can bear it. What will I do? Take up needlepoint?"

No answer would suit him, but I had to try. He was inconsolable when he descended into one of his melancholic moods. I wrapped my arm around his waist and held him close and hoped that touch would bring him back to himself. "You'll be wise and powerful. You can . . . I don't know, live up a mountaintop and dispense wisdom to any who dare make the climb."

"Don't be ridiculous. There's no jellied lamb up a mountain."

"But you will be wise," I said. "You could be wise now and listen to us. Ara agrees—this is a fool's errand. I have no idea what you will be like when you're old, but by God, I should like to see it."

He kissed my chin and then turned away, unwinding himself from my grasp. "I love you, you spicy imp, but you're wrong. I know what I'm doing. I know . . . what I can look forward to. I think I know what eternity looks like." Only a few steps from me, he stopped and then turned, hurling one more question my way. "Honestly, Dal, can you live with what we did to them? We all but snuffed out a flame, simply because it dared to burn before us. Will you promise me something?"

"Yes," I replied, meaning it. "Anything."

"Promise me you'll come with me when I find the Binders. If

I can find where the books are made, promise me you'll come see the place."

Something itched at the back of my mind, but stupidly, I agreed.

"I promise," I said. "I'll come with you."

In the morning, Henry woke us at an ungodly hour. The horses had already been saddled, the packs readied, and Bartholomew fed. A traveler's breakfast of hard biscuits, nuts, and stewed greens had been prepared, and Henry paced impatiently while I bolted down my share. Then we were riding, all of it happening so fast that neither Ara nor myself had time to stop him. That was the idea, of course, because he knew we were tired of playing along.

"Look there," he called as we descended toward the plains. A few nomads dotted the edge of the lake. "They won't go near the center. We must be close."

"Henry—"

Ara and I had called out to him in unison, but he raced ahead, spurring his horse with flashing heels, the brown-and-black-spotted beast dashing down the embankment. I had spent plenty of hours in the saddle, but Henry was the vastly superior horseman. We gave chase, and now Ara did not appear angry but concerned. Her brows were permanently knit, her lower lip trembling.

"We'll stop him," I yelled to her over the whip of the wind.

"I don't know that we can." Ara's hood fell back, her iron-gray and black hair flying free of its ribbon, streaming behind her like a pennant as we pursued Henry down to the salt.

Tuz Gölü. The sea of crystalline white stretching out before us made my breath catch and my heart throb—it was a beautiful place, unearthly, a flat glistening dish of diamonds so vast its edges could not be seen once we descended. The sky seemed bluer here, the horizon just a suggestion, almost as if we had stumbled upon the edge of the world. And there was Henry, riding right into it, the top crust of salt breaking, water splashing the knobby knees of his horse.

The nomads scattered at his approach, and by the time Ara and I caught up to him, we three and Bartholomew were alone. The place was emptiness itself, the salt and water making tricks of the light, rainbows cascading across the ground, rippling at the slightest touch.

Henry swore and jumped down from his mount, letting it go. He wandered forward into the desert of eerie white, pressing his hand to his forehead against the sun.

"Where is it?" he whispered. "This is the salt. It has to be here."

Ara and I watched as he cut a line through the center of the salt flat, shallow water sloshing around his sandals. He trudged on, impervious to the sun and glare, determined to make his pilgrimage.

"What do we do?" I twisted in the saddle, holding Bartholomew, my hands shaking with powerlessness.

"Nothing will stop him. We can only protect him now."

Ara dismounted, grunting under the weight of the book and the pack. I joined her, and together we trailed behind, retracing Henry's path through the salt. When we reached him, his face glowed red with fury.

"If that idiot demon lied to me . . ."

"There," Ara said, pointing. "Old tracks. They lead deeper into the salt."

Henry hurried in that direction, the shallow water deepening as we traveled toward the center of the salt flat, his tracks swallowed up. His robes were soaked to his knees, but he ignored it, fixated on the unbroken crust and the strange imprints that were too delicate to have cracked it. He stopped a hand's breadth from the intact salt and reached out, running his fingers lightly over the shapes. As I neared, I saw that they looked remarkably like giant paws.

"I'm willing," he muttered, almost feverish. "I'm willing, damn you, where are you?"

There came a deep rumbling from beneath the earth. I stumbled, grabbing onto Ara as she grabbed onto me. Bartholomew whined and burrowed under my robe, hiding his muzzle under my armpit. The sun flashed off the mirror of salt, blinding me, then the brightness exploded outward, sending a hot wave across *the desert. The salt under and around us softened and then sank, becoming hard and flat, until we stood on a perfect alabaster disk.*

The blast had knocked Henry to his knees, where he stayed, all of us silent and watchful as the tracks in the salt shook, then lowered, a gradual ramp cutting itself into the ground. I had seen such things in Egypt, smooth, glittering architecture cut neatly into limestone. At the very bottom, perhaps half a kilometer into the earth, a door appeared. Under my robes, I had begun to sweat badly, and I nudged Ara, who wouldn't take her eyes from the door.

It was too late now, I thought, to forget this madness and go home. A simultaneous loathing and curiosity rooted me to the spot, for I wondered what might emerge from that door, and what lay beyond it.

Something moved in the darkness, a figure stepping through the square-cut door. At first I thought it was another of the scorpion creatures, but as it climbed the ramp toward us, it became clear that it was half woman, its lower half that of a lioness. That explained the paw prints. More than that, she had not two human arms but six all told, the extra two pairs folded back slightly, like wings at rest. She approached slowly, and I couldn't help wondering if that was to give us time to change our minds and flee.

And I longed to do just that. The sun vanished, and the desert was plunged instantly into night. Gasping, I watched the darkness light up with more stars than one sky ought to hold. Not just stars, shapes. I did not fancy myself an astronomer, but even I knew these were not ordinary constellations and that no stars in the firmament glowed so brilliantly. The moon, perfect as a pearl, hung full and fat and too close to us, nearer than I had ever seen it.

The creature finished her journey up the ramp and observed us, her eyes catlike, her skin a buttery gold, like that of her lioness half. A blue, beaded curtain hung from her neck, chiming softly when she moved. Around her neck and shoulders lay a snake, draped there, as white as the salt, though its head held no eyes and its mouth ever opened, a toothless tube that sucked at the air.

Henry stared up at her, marveling, still on his knees.

"I am Malatriss," she said. The stars burned clearer when she spoke. "One Who Opens the Door. Who is willing?"

"I am," Henry jumped to his feet. "I'm willing."

"And these others?" she asked.

He turned and stretched out his hands, pleading with his eyes. I had never seen Henry look so helpless before. "Please," he mouthed.

"I am willing, too," Ara spoke up, taking a step forward.

I gazed into the doorkeeper's eyes, and what I found there frightened me. She would know if I lied. I thought of Faraday— Focalor—the demon, and of his madness, his wounds, his horrible descent. Had he been truly willing? Or had he passed that first test only to fail the next? Sometimes to protect the people we love, we have to disappoint them.

"I'm sorry, Henry," I said, holding Bartholomew close to my chest.

"Dalton. Dalton. *Don't you dare do this, don't you dare . . ."*
He advanced toward me, yellow eyes flaring wide. "You spineless shit. *Did you come all this way just to betray me? Is this amusing to you? Did the shepherd put you up to this?"*

"I don't need to answer that." I stepped back. "Just listen to yourself, and you will know exactly what I'm doing."

"No." Henry flung himself toward Ara, spinning her around. He tore the Black Elbion out of the bag and shook it in my face. "There must be something else. There must be a way, a way to be free. Free from this book, free from this . . . this . . ."

Guilt.

He wilted, hugging the book and falling again to his knees. The journey was ending—he could feel it, and so could I—but it was not the ending he'd hoped for. Not for the first time, he changed in front of my eyes, pitiful now. Unmoored.

"You promised," he spat. "You promised."

"I didn't see it then." I backed away, slowly, backed away from him, from it all. "I didn't know your purpose, and I won't help you destroy that book. Damn it, I won't lose you."

Henry scrambled to his knees, a spark of hope in his eyes, one I already knew I would be responsible for stamping out. "Go to Judgment. Bring back the white book, bring it here, we can free ourselves together. I know there's something else, Dalton, I know it. Trust me."

"I'm sorry," I said again, watching that light flicker and die. "I won't help you do this. Forgive me."

"No." He swiveled back toward Ara and Malatriss, leaving me behind in the salt. "No, Dalton, I don't forgive you. I never will."

The field lay before us, pocked with holes, the already damaged fence on the border now a dwindling fire. I had never known whether the Residents could actually leave the confines of Coldthistle House, but now I had my answer as they hovered in wait, no longer with any walls between us, an army of floating black shapes. Mrs. Haylam stood at the center of the mass.

"Now's your big chance, Poppy," Chijioke was saying. His eyes glowed red, standing out sharply from his dark skin. "With Mary here again, you can scream your little heart out."

It was odd, going into battle with a child at my side, but she had helped save my life once before, and I knew better than to question her power.

"I have so many bundled up," Poppy said, grinning. "But I hope it is enough."

The only one among us missing from the east lawn was Mr. Morningside. He hadn't emerged yet from the house, and there was no telling what plan he might be concocting. Mary and Lee stood next to Chijioke, though Lee was wobbly with illness, the presence of so many Adjudicators making him green in the face. And there *were* many. Dalton had called it a host, but with their golden bodies filling the sky, the glare made it difficult to count them.

Moonless, Khent was forced to stay by my side, as I had an entire drawer of cutlery ready to transform for him. There were a few stray pistols and a hunting rifle in the house that were brought along, too, though I doubted they would do much against this motley arrangement of foes.

"Bah, Nephilim," Khent muttered, spitting in the grass. "I thought I killed the last of those ugly fiends in Giza."

I had hoped only to ever read of them in Bennu's journal, but Khent was right—the huge, misshapen giants with their faces full of wasps lumbered toward the charred remains of the fence. I could hear the steady humming of the bees above their heavy footsteps. The six-winged, sword-wielding warriors above them were familiar, too, as were the cries of "sanctus" as they charged toward the house.

"It isn't at all like reading a book," I murmured, hoarse. Khent reached for my hand and squeezed it.

"You wouldn't happen to be hiding a Sky Snake under those skirts?"

"Just petticoats," I lamented. Then I turned a hard look toward the advancing enemies, too numerous even to contemplate. This had to be the bulk of the shepherd's army, and our last stand against them would have to be enough of a distraction to let Dalton slip by. There was no sign of the shepherd, but then, Mr. Morningside was still absent, too. "Khent, if I need to let Father take over . . ."

"I will draw you back when the time comes," he said, pressing my hand again. I had expected him to relish this chance for war and bloodshed, but his eyes were sad. "You make the javelins, I throw them. Father is only if we find ourselves overrun, yes?"

"Of course." But what I really meant was, *I shall try*. And also, *Are we not already overrun?* The shepherd's resistance was far beyond what I had expected or imagined, and for a brief moment I understood Henry's dark motivations. This was what he feared when collecting his souls—this annihilation at the hands of former allies. Maybe it was always going to come to this; maybe peace between folk so different simply could not be.

"What is it, *eyachou?*" Khent asked.

"I was only thinking, this is all such foolishness. Do we not all inhabit this place within a place? We should be friends."

"Yes." He nodded, rubbing his jaw. "But these servants of Roeh, they do not look very friendly today."

I strained to hear him above the noisy buzzing of the wasps and the beating of so many golden wings. We waited, silent, Bartholomew pawing listlessly at the ground, Mary and

Chijioke holding hands while the Residents drifted back and forth at our flank. They all might be hurt. They might be *killed*.

"Mary—" I called out, intending to say something, anything, that might express my gratitude, my relief, that I had wished her into being all those years ago, trapped in a cupboard while my parents argued, desperate for one true friend to distract me from the misery.

She had just turned toward me when the first Adjudicator dropped out of the sky, hurtling toward us with two golden axes raised high. Finch had to be among them, I thought, but it was impossible to sort them out from the giant, floating phalanx of gold. That was the signal that broke the restless peace, and soon giants swarming with bees and screaming six-winged demons surged toward us across the field.

For an instant, it was so startling, so terrifying, that I froze. But then there was Father. *Blood*, he helpfully reminded me. *More blood.* No, came my answer, less blood shed by my friends. The only way to get through this was to protect my companions, no matter the cost. Mother had at first refused to assist, but at my nudging, she'd agreed to do what defensive spells she could. She stood closest to the house, in the shade of the overhang outside the kitchens. The ground all around us trembled and shook, then hundreds of hidden roots burst from below, rising high into the air before twining themselves together, forming a thick fence.

I heard the Nephilim giants rush up against the roots, fists striking, little wasp wings a symphony of furious frustration. The root fence did little against the winged enemies that soared above and then quickly dipped back below. They came a hundred across, a golden lance *thwipping* into the ground beside me. The lances. Of course.

At once I fell to work, feeling the anxious blood gather in my face as I took up knife after knife and closed my eyes, a short reprieve from the chaos while I transformed the cutlery with my Changeling powers. Khent handily took the lances from me as they formed, hurling them at any Adjudicator or Seraphim that flew too close. His aim was good but not perfect; a few slipped by his assault, and a long-haired female made of liquid gold landed not ten paces away.

"Ahhes, ahhes, ahhes." Khent held out his hand to me and flexed his fingers. *Hurry, hurry, hurry.*

I panicked and felt the knife in my grasp slip, tumbling to the grass. Shrieking, I knelt to find it, feeling a rush of air over my head as Bartholomew leapt cleanly above my back, colliding with the Upworlder and taking her hard to the ground. Her screams were quickly silenced, but my eyes were closed in concentration, transforming another knife for Khent and telling myself I could not afford to slip up again.

Chijioke did his best with a hunting rifle, his aim skilled but the reload slow. Mary's bright, glittering shield surrounded us, deflecting javelins hurled from every direction as the shepherd's winged forces circled above, swarming. I could see Poppy jumping up and down, jittery with excitement, waiting for the right moment to unleash hell. The Residents slipped along our sides, no more than swift black blurs, and then they drifted up through Mary's shield, high enough to reach the golden Adjudicators that controlled the air. Reaching for a fork to transform, I glanced upward, watching as a Resident overtook one of the host, enveloping it as if it were swallowing the creature whole. But it merely stripped the Adjudicator's shining energy away, leaving the enemy in their mundane and decidedly flightless state. Startled, shouting, the poor thing plunged to the ground, reaching behind for wings that had disappeared.

That same Resident shimmered into nothingness afterward, breaking apart as the light it had swallowed dissolved the shadow. There were perhaps a dozen more Residents lifting into the air, but that was all Mrs. Haylam had brought. I was getting down to the spoons, exhausted, every transformed piece of silverware taking a little more out of me. Falling to my knees, I tried to catch my breath, finding the air devilishly hard to swallow.

"Breathe," Khent reminded me. He had broken a heavy sweat from the effort, black hair matted back on his forehead, shirtsleeves soaked. "We may just make it through this."

I glanced behind, watching Mother chant wordlessly while

she kept the root barrier strong and stable. Mrs. Haylam, however, looked far worse. She had run out of shadow servants and endeavored to make more, slicing at her hands to make her minions, pulling from the meager shadows around the edge of the mansion. Had we battled at night, she might have instantly produced another dozen reinforcements. The few she managed to create, their strange, fat heads blossoming out from the shade of a crate or a flowerpot, birthed themselves into the ether, then immediately shot into the sky. Blood stained the front of her skirts, and she was beginning to look alarmingly pale.

The clamor against the root wall increased. Six of the wasp-faced giants crashed against it in unison with their shoulders. They were serviceable-enough battering rams, and soon the wood began to splinter, then give. I gasped, watching a single, thick arm punch through the fence. Not long after, the menace had torn open space enough to crawl through.

"Poppy, get ready!" I cried, then made another lance for Khent, dashing toward Mrs. Haylam. I skidded to a stop next to her and reached for my own skirts, tearing strips of fabric from the bottom and using them to bind her badly bleeding arms.

"Stop, girl, I know what I'm doing," she muttered, her voice more rasping than usual.

"You'll bleed to death, you stubborn old witch, let me help."

She gnashed her teeth but allowed it, and I at least managed to staunch the bleeding on her forearms and near her elbows. But as soon as I bound a wound, she made another, the knife flashing as she cut into her skin through the frock.

"That's enough now," Mrs. Haylam whispered. "Go do something *useful.*"

Useful. Of course. She wanted me to dip in to Father's powers and end the battle early. But I couldn't, not when we might win without his help. I feared too much what it would mean for me if I relied on him. Every moment of greater influence seemed to stitch some piece of him to my brain permanently.

I returned to Khent's side, handing off another lance, my hands shaking from lack of strength. His throws were weakening, too, and he grunted loudly with each toss. I had no stomach for it, I knew, cringing whenever my eyes fell on another fallen body on the grass. It was a relief, of course, that we were holding them off, but I felt no real animus toward the shepherd's people—Sparrow had been the one thorn in my side, and now she was gone. These deaths felt utterly meaningless, wasteful, and they piled up, one after another, beautiful golden forms falling out of the sky, spinning lazily downward like some grotesque hunting party gone awry.

The numbers in the sky dwindled, but the fight before us on the field had only just begun. The Nephilim, buzzing and angry, lumbered toward us, picking up speed.

The spoon in my hand refused to change. I closed my eyes, I squeezed hard, and I channeled the last drips of will in my body toward the bloody thing, but nothing happened. I could sense Khent's hand waving in front of me, but there was nothing I could do.

"I'm sorry," I whispered, feeling tears slip down my face. "I have nothing left!"

The thunder of the giants' feet masked a different kind of rumbling. To my right, from around the front of the house, came a spray of grass and gravel. The cavalry, so to speak, had arrived. Fathom, Giles, and Niles rode onto the field, Fathom screaming bloody murder as she cocked her pistol and fired at speed. They each managed a shot off toward the giants before circling back around to us, slowing their horses and fishing out their small arsenal of pistols and rifles.

"Just like the old days at Auntie Glinna's, shooting pheasant in Somerset!" Giles called. He and his brother had come in matching hunting flannels done in the most fashionable purple-and-green plaids. "Good to see you again, Miss Louisa, though I do wish it were under less calamitous circumstances."

"No time for pleasantries," I called back, managing a weary smile. "But your aid is most welcome!"

"Where is Morningside?" Chijioke muttered, trying to unjam his rifle before giving up and accepting a fresh gun from Niles.

I shared his curiosity and glanced toward the house. Inside, I saw Dalton briefly at the kitchen window, and then he was gone, disappeared, a sharp popping sound reaching us even through the walls. That still didn't account for Mr. Morningside's tardiness. Had he left us? Had the bastard really abandoned us to fight his war while he retreated to safety?

Mary dropped her shield for a moment to rest and recover while Mother tried in vain to repair her wall. Smaller bursts of roots shot from the earth, but they did little more than trip up the giants, who collected themselves and pressed on. They would be upon us any moment.

There was no more I could do for Khent. I scrambled to my feet and went to Poppy, putting a tremulous hand on her shoulder. "As soon as you can make out the wasps on their faces, give it your all."

"I am so ready, Louisa, I have not done a scream in a very long time, and it hurts so to be bottled up." Bartholomew came to stand in front of the girl, guarding her, licking the copious blood from his paws. The melee had changed him, and he had never looked more like a hellhound, with a rigid spine of dark fur and slavering jaws.

Out of the corner of my eye, I watched Mrs. Haylam collapse to the ground. Before I could go to aid her, a flood of gold brightened the horizon. More Adjudicators. As many or more than had come before.

"Stars," Mary cried, covering her mouth. "He must have called back his folk from every corner of the earth!"

"Now, do you think, Louisa?" Poppy asked.

"Aye," I told her, my heart sinking to my toes. "Now. Do it now."

While Poppy readied herself, I disappeared to tend to Mrs. Haylam, trusting the little girl to know when her power would help us most. She looked almost proud, like a soldier, and I wished that it was not so, that she was not a child forced into this war, that she could be somewhere at play, holding her dog and singing songs, not using her voice for bloody mayhem.

Chapter Twenty-Two

"I never disliked you."

The bedlam behind me twisted her words into nonsense. It took me a moment to untangle them, just as I untangled another torn strip of skirt to tie around her thigh. There was no pretense of housekeeper and serving girl now, no stations, no polite barriers—Mrs. Haylam's wiry leg was stuck out toward me, propped in my lap while I wrapped it with coarse cloth.

"Did I accuse you of such things?" I asked, shaking my head. Before, I had seen just glimpses of the tattoos on her arms, always peeking out from her sleeve, but now I came to realize that underneath the sober, high-necked gown, she was covered in markings. Having suffered one such agony on my palm, I couldn't imagine what she had endured to become that way.

"The way you look at me, girl. Always fleeting. Nervous. I was hard because I sensed the cleverness in you. The strength." She coughed, a trickle of blood running down her chin, and I flinched. "Even before your father came. I wasn't hard enough on Henry and look how he turned out. I'm one of the last of his true allies. He was never soft, never kind, and it forced them all away. We could use a couple of demons right about now."

"I'm going to tell him you said that, you know," I teased, hoping it would bolster her spirits.

"Do it. I won't be around to suffer his complaints."

"I won't have you speaking that way. Where is Mr. Morningside? Why isn't he helping us?" I pressed.

"He's"—*hack, hack*—"making preparations. But like always, he will be fashionably late."

Tragically late, more like. I thought more about what she had said, about Henry never being soft or kind. He had been, in my eyes, for a time—to her and Dalton, at least. He had taken in many of my kind out of guilt, but now . . . Stopping briefly, I glanced around, looking at us all battling against the Upworlders. Fighting *for* him. And where was he? Why was he absent at his own fight? I felt suddenly angry, furious, dangerously furious, so much so that I felt Father flash against the weak membrane holding him at bay. These weren't demons like Faraday putting their lives on the line for Henry's house and livelihood, it was *us*. The cruel unfairness of it cut, and I wondered if maybe this was what Dalton wanted me to see in his diary. That it would always come to this, Henry hiding and scheming, while everyone else did the dirty work for him.

Even his one and only true friend lay bleeding and suffering.

I finished tying off her upper leg and sat back on my haunches, then turned at the sound of a gun volley. The bullets did next to nothing against the giants. Mary's barrier extended outward again, enshrouding us, the noise of the battle growing dimmer for a moment. Then Poppy stepped forward and threw back her head, balled up her fists, and let loose one of her bone-piercing shrieks. The nearest wave of Adjudicators fell, gripping their heads in agony, distracted enough to become easy targets for our crack shooters. Poppy had weakened our foes, leaving them far more vulnerable to gunfire. I watched the Nephilim fall back, deterred, but only briefly.

Her scream, no matter how powerful, was not enough to turn the tide.

When it was done, I saw Chijioke go to comfort Poppy, who began crying, disappointed and afraid.

"Where is Morningside?" Chijioke shouted, clutching Poppy. "Damn him. We need his help!"

"Are you prepared to watch them die?" Mrs. Haylam whispered. More blood poured from her mouth. "Are you ready to have that on your shoulders?"

The thunder of the giants' feet neared, deafening. A hail of javelins fell against Mary's barrier, which itself would fall soon as she grew tired. Khent could do nothing, for I had no spears to give him and he had but a rudimentary knowledge of rifles. I sighed and stood, knowing what had to be done, however much I dreaded it.

"Louisa . . . ," Mother pleaded with me softly, but I turned my back on her.

"Let the child do what she must," Mrs. Haylam said. "Let her choose."

I took a deep breath, smelled the gore and gunpowder all around us, felt the quaking of the ground . . . It would be easy enough to summon Father. This was his chosen arena, his natural element. He craved bloodshed, and now, at last, I would give him as much as he could stomach. For my part, I had already seen more than enough. In my head, Father's soul snapped and snarled and raged, denied his feast.

Then the glass behind us shattered. It seemed as if the whole of the house had imploded, but it was only the windows. I covered my head, shrieking as shards of glass rained down on us, and then, with the fluttering of a thousand wings, birds gushed from the mansion. They were a riot of color and sounds, their cast-off feathers joining the shower of glass from the windows. Brushing debris off my shoulders, I marveled at their speed, following their trajectory as they all but erased the sky. Whenever a bird found a target, be it winged foe or giant, it would burst in a cascade of feathers that flowed into wisps of silver. Those blobs coalesced, then formed ghostly figures.

The souls. He had at last released the army of souls he had reaped and stored in his birds.

Mr. Morningside appeared directly after, loping out from the kitchen with a cup of tea. He downed it in one gulp and threw the porcelain against the nearest wall.

"Fashionably late!" I screamed at him, exasperated.

Mr. Morningside shrugged and strode past me, tending to Mrs. Haylam. "But *still* fashionable. Still want the deed? Sorry, I seem to have made a mess."

"I hate you," I seethed back.

"That's allowed." He shot a look over his shoulder, just in time for Dalton to appear, a heavy bag strapped to his back, also departing through the open kitchen door. "You can hate me later. It appears it is time for you to go."

The souls shrieked as they regained their forms, and I had to lean closer to Henry just to divine a single word. Gunfire. Screaming. The dull thud of javelins hitting Mary's barrier . . . It was all too much, and I had only just pulled myself back from the mental brink. Khent sprinted to meet us, putting himself between me and the field of battle.

"What's going on?" he demanded.

"You're going," Mr. Morningside said. "Leave this bit of bother to us, you have work to do. He's got the book, Louisa. Now it's time for you to do as you promised. Take the dog man, he's useless without a moon around."

"Mother is coming, too," I told him. "She isn't meant for this kind of bloodshed."

The tide seemed to be turning, with Mr. Morningside's birds allowing our side to gain more ground. That didn't erase my concern completely, and I hated the thought of leaving even one of my friends behind.

Mr. Morningside sighed and rolled his eyes, then gestured to Mother. "I'm only agreeing because she's apparently useless. Now go! We'll keep them busy while you four depart."

"So sudden," I murmured, feeling as if the ground had been knocked out from under me. "Where are we going?"

"Helmsley Castle. It isn't far. Dalton has your instructions." Mr. Morningside clasped me by the arm, and not for the first time, I wondered if this would be our final meeting. He was suddenly serious, oblivious to the violence bearing down. "And Louisa? Good luck. I know you won't let me down."

There was no time to say goodbye, a fact that would haunt me for the entirety of the ride.

"I just don't know what to expect," I told Khent and Mother, who sat across from me in the carriage. We had taken the roughshod carriage Chijioke used for errands, with Dalton in the driver's box, a cloak wrapped around the book on his lap. "And I couldn't say a word to Mary or Chijioke. Or, God, Lee and Poppy! How will I explain any of this to them?"

"They will understand," Mother assured me. She had recovered quicker than I expected, sitting upright and calm, her veil draped over her face. The mourning garb seemed appropriate. "You are walking into the unknown, child. There will be time for apologies later."

Khent, however, had climbed into the seat next to me, watching through the back window as the house disappeared in the distance. Helmsley Castle lay not far from Malton, which also struck me as fitting, going to the start to reach the end. Malton was nothing like Constantinople, and I hoped this wasn't some kind of trick. But it wouldn't surprise me in the least if this mysterious place—the unknown, as Mother had called it—had many doors. After all, the one Mr. Morningside had found in the diary had appeared out of thin air.

"Something is wrong." Khent pointed out the window, grumbling.

"What is it?" I asked.

"They should be following. They should sack their strategist. A chariot leaves the battle, you follow. No matter how empty it looks, you follow. Either they are very stupid or we are riding into a trap."

"Stay alert," I told him. "I have a bad feeling in my stomach."

Mother watched me closely, the carriage rocking us all as Dalton spurred the horses and we flew down the road. I nestled down into the seat, exhausted, trying to recover some of my strength for the trials to come. Whatever we faced, it would require more than just following a few directions. Which reminded me . . .

I pulled out the small scroll Mr. Morningside had provided. Dalton had handed it off to me before we departed the house and suggested that I memorize it. There wasn't much to it, and most of it I already knew.

"There will be riddles," I told them. "And there must be something different about me . . . Morningside said he wasn't allowed inside, but that I should be able to pass. I cannot say too much about it just now, even speaking of the ritual can summon horrid things to punish you."

"*Perou huer hubesou,*" Khent muttered, his nose still up to the rear window. *More deceptions.*

But I shook my head at him. "No . . . We're quite different, he and I."

"That is an understatement."

"Maybe . . . ," I mused aloud, rubbing my forehead, "maybe only women can enter. Or perhaps only those with Dark Fae blood are allowed. If he tried to enter the tomb with Dalton and Ara then that wouldn't work. Oh, I don't know, it's pointless to speculate."

Mother leaned over and touched my knee, then lifted her veil and patted the seat next to her. I climbed across and settled down, then felt a warm, soothing sensation rush over me as she touched the side of her head to mine. "Read the scroll. Recover yourself."

I did, and it was far easier with her there. Just her touch had a way of obliterating my fears, a balm for the battle we had just endured and the battle no doubt to come. My thoughts eased, and though I still felt heavyhearted from the bloodshed and from leaving behind so many of my friends, it did not feel so hopeless with her there.

Flattening the parchment across my knee, I read over the brief lines, written in Mr. Morningside's exceedingly elegant hand. They were what I expected—the riddles he had discovered, the answers he thought to be correct, and even the words to speak to call out the door. My eyes caught on one line in particular, and I felt a pang of sorrow deep in my chest. Now I was infinitely grateful that I had read the entirety of Dalton's diary; without it, I would be in awful peril.

For Mr. Morningside had lied. I read over his recounting of the riddle again and again, hoping it was a simple misspelling or error. But no, there was no way he had written the wrong answer by mistake. Either he wanted me to suffer, or he wanted me to fail. Or perhaps he was simply too dim-witted to count and realize that Faraday had been missing three fingers. Three. He had gotten every single riddle wrong, which meant . . . which meant . . .

Something inside me hardened, a cluster of nerves that had been soft became steel, and I knew then that I would do what he could not: I would enter the Tomb of Ancients and behold all that he had wanted so badly to see and been denied.

"Arms to embrace, yet no hands. Pinches to give, yet no fingers. Poison to wield, yet no needle."

Betrayers betrayed. Liars lied. The Devil deceived. Or else Mr. Morningside was not as clever as he thought.

Scorpion was not the answer, but I knew what was.

Chapter
Twenty-Three

1247. Tuz Gölü

I was about to mount my horse when I heard Ara's screams.

The dog nestled in my robes fussed and poked his head out of the collar, leaning into the sound of her agony. I tracked it, too, then, powerless to stop myself, I trotted back toward the center of the salt. Malatriss presided over a gruesome sight. Ara was on the ground, writhing, holding both hands over her eyes, her legs kicking at the diamond-hard ground.

"What did you do to her?" Henry shouted, falling to her side.

"I can see into her heart, as I see into yours, Dark One," the lion creature said. A droplet of blood, perfect and red, clung to the open mouth of her strange white snake. "You are truly willing to enter the tomb. She is not."

"That's hardly cause to attack!" I said, out of breath from sprinting to reach them.

Malatriss, eyes glowing and gold, smiled at me, displaying pointed, regular teeth, all of them sharpened to gleaming daggers. "This is not a game for little children," she whispered, her smile never failing. "Through that door, you play with cards of flesh and dice of bone, you wager in blood and sinew. Your friend the demon learned that the hard way. He did not take it well when Nira sucked the fingers from his hands."

The pale snake around Malatriss's neck bobbed its head and coiled more tightly around its mistress.

Ara's hands dropped away long enough for me to see that one eye was shut, blood weeping down her cheek. I had never heard her cry that way, in such childlike anguish, raw and helpless.

"Come away with me, Henry," I whispered, kneeling with them and taking him by the arm. "Have you not seen enough? This place is cursed. Come away."

"No." He wiped furiously at the tears on his face, tilting his head up to the doorkeeper. "No. The book must be destroyed. I have not come this far for nothing. I want answers, do you hear me, wretch? I want answers."

"That is my desire, too," Malatriss purred, unmoved by his shouting. It occurred to me that many had probably discovered clues to the Binders and made this journey, making similar appeals. Any who encountered the books would want to understand their power and know how such things could be made. How many bumbling adventurers had she tortured and turned away? "I make a meal of answers, or flesh, as the case may be. I harvest them. Riddles are the tool with which I till the field."

"Yes, the riddles." Henry was in a constant state of weeping, trying not to weep more, and wiping at his mouth with sloppy, desperate pawing. "I will answer your riddles, witch. Proceed."

She laughed. The constellations above us spun and surged, so bright it hurt to look up.

"Bold. Bold and arrogant. I almost like you; your flesh would taste of pride," Malatriss whispered, lightly petting the body of her pet snake. "You would do well to listen to your friend. You may be willing, Dark One, but this place is not for you. Only the dead may enter here, and you have so very much longer to live."

Malatriss showed us her teeth again, and then, as if the whole sordid scene had been a nightmare, we woke, and she was gone. The salt crust broke under us and we sank into the shallow water, daylight returned, the sun beaming over a cloudless sky. But the wound Ara had suffered was real, and though her hysterics had calmed, Henry's had not.

"No!" He beat at his chest, standing, turning in every direction. Slicking both wet hands through his hair, he giggled, a deeply mad sound. "No, it . . . it cannot be. The book." He stared at it, soaking in the salt lake. "The book . . . I was so close. No."

Henry didn't notice that I had helped Ara to her feet. That she leaned against me, that she had taken up the book to carry back to the horses. He did not notice Bartholomew trying to lick at his hand, the only consolation he was likely to receive.

elmsley Castle, a fawn-colored spike reaching up from a low hill, stood abandoned. Someone had maintained the grounds, but I heard no farmers or townsfolk from Malton out for a stroll. The grass was slick still from the rains as we climbed toward the structure, and I felt compelled to stare holes into the back of Dalton's head.

The medieval ruin towered above us, just one lingering facade, the rest of it long since crumbled away. Which made it look, upon reflection, rather like a gate.

"Why didn't they follow us?" I asked. Khent and Mother flanked me, though I could sense them watching Dalton, too. "It seems foolish to just let us go."

"Henry told me he would create a distraction," Dalton said, stopping. He put one foot up on the higher level of the hill and twisted, resting his hands on his raised thigh. The fabric over his eyes was damp with sweat. "He had to, or I never would have been able to go to Judgment and steal the book."

"Judgment," I repeated. "Is that where you take people to be Judged? Sparrow took me there once. It's another realm of some kind?"

"Yes. Only accessible by us. You could only see it because Sparrow forced you to go."

"Was the book difficult to take?" I asked. He wasn't volunteering much, and that only made me more nervous. I now knew Mr. Morningside was inadvertently or intentionally trying to sabotage me; I didn't need his old lover doing the same.

"To be frank with you . . ." Sighing, Dalton shook his head and then began his way up the hill again. "It was unguarded. There was no one there at all."

"Well, *that's* not suspicious." Khent picked up the pace, overtaking me and then Dalton, charging his way ahead. I was not going to let them beat me to the ruins, so I ran to catch up, hoping Mother would do the same.

"Wait!" I managed to maneuver around the two men. I stooped and put my hands on my knees, still weak and out of breath from using my powers so recently. "I want to trust you, Dalton, but why would you do this? You will be annihilating all of your own people, and for what?"

He crossed his arms over his suit and lifted his chin to the wind, letting it catch his hair and the bandage around his eyes. Breathing deep, he let it go through his nose. "I will miss this place, but I'm tired. I'm tired of this fighting, this war. I'm tired of Henry. He thinks destroying us is revenge, but it is not so."

I waited, giving Khent a dark look to keep him quiet.

"There will be no one left to blame when I'm gone," Dalton said, more to himself than to us. "Now, how does that go? Ah, yes—'I tasted too what was called the sweet of revenge—but it was transient, it expired even with the object, that provoked it.'"

With that, he walked off across the green, toward the remains of the castle, the rising gusts across the hills tearing at his coat. I followed, but Khent hesitated, and I was forced to nudge him along.

"No man that melancholy has betrayal on the mind. Come on," I said softly. "He need not have brought the book. He need not have returned from Judgment at all."

We made a silent procession into the ruins, passing through the door and into the cool, shaded area beyond, which almost felt like a courtyard, but with no high walls to hem it in. Mother went to sit on one of the fallen chunks of wall, gazing up at the height of the castle front. I had memorized the scroll Mr. Morningside had given me, and I knew how to proceed; my only doubts lingered over whether or not to tell Dalton of his friend's deception. Or error.

Stand in the very middle of the door, take twenty paces, then turn back and speak the words.

Those were the instructions in the journal, and I did exactly that, holding on to one breath all the while, my heart pounding faster with each step. Khent stood rigidly to the side, alert, his purple eyes following me so intently they felt like physical pressure against my cheek. Dalton, however, seemed relaxed, or perhaps resigned, hands in pockets as he admired the ruins.

When I had gone twenty paces, I paused and swiveled back toward the door. Even though I knew what might come next, it felt like jumping off a cliff, hoping to find water at the bottom but feeling just as strongly that I might find stone. Dalton approached me silently, pulling the pack from his shoulders and handing it to me. It was unbelievably heavy, the canvas top shifting aside, showing me the gleaming white book within.

"Don't touch it," he warned with a gentle smile. "It will burn."

"I have some experience there," I said. "I'm going to begin now."

He nodded.

"Are you certain this is what you want? It isn't too late," I said.

"You need to be rid of Father, and Henry needs to be rid of me. It will all be wrapped up neatly, I think. You'll see."

I didn't see, but I decided to trust him, pulling on the bag and inhaling one last time, telling myself that I could face the trials, telling myself that I could achieve what Mr. Morningside could not.

"I'm willing."

The effect was instantaneous. Night fell, the sky lighting up with a thousand gleaming constellations—alligators and snakes, rams and spiders, stags and rabbits. The moon appeared, a circular white beacon that felt close enough to touch. Then the ramp appeared, cutting its way into the grass, the square black door appearing just under the door into the castle. Just as the diary described, Malatriss emerged shortly after, climbing the ramp with the almost-bored air of someone going about their daily tedium. She might have been feeding the chickens or going to the baker's for bread.

Dalton had failed to describe her beauty, or the way the sudden constellations reflected in her feline eyes. She studied him first, in fact, grinning as if stumbling upon a long-lost friend. But I had been the one to call her, and she swiftly turned back to me. Mother and Khent sidled close, protectively so.

"I am Malatriss," she said, bowing her head just a little. "One Who—"

"Opens the Door," I interrupted. "Yes, yes, can we move this along? We're in a bit of a rush."

That startled her, which felt good, honestly, and she gave another wide smile, recovering with a laugh. "You are impatient," she said, licking her teeth. "And willing. And these others?" she asked.

I saw Khent open his mouth to answer, but Mother stepped in front of him, pushing him away. Her smile matched that of Malatriss, though it contained far less contempt. "I am willing."

My eyes followed the horrid white snake as it traveled in a slow circle around Malatriss's shoulders. It had the same open, gaping mouth as the Binder's fingers.

Malatriss closed her eyes, the smile vanishing, and for a moment I was sure we had done something wrong. Mother was unwilling, or maybe *I* was unwilling. But then the doorkeeper blinked and sniffed, nodding her satisfaction. "Two willing hearts. Two hearts that have known death."

So that was what had kept Mr. Morningside from gaining entrance to the tomb. I had died briefly, just long enough for Father's soul to be guided into me, and Mother had been drained to the point of death for the ritual that bound her in that spider. Glancing up at her, her eight pink eyes staring straight ahead, I wondered if she had known, or if she simply wanted to be there with me to face the challenges ahead. Whatever the explanation, she took my hand, and I felt better for it.

"Willing hearts. Immortal hearts. But are they wise?" Malatriss mused. "What falls but never breaks? And what breaks but never falls?"

"Night and day," I said at once.

Malatriss inclined her head, a flicker of irritation tightening her right eyelid. "My leaves don't change, but turn, what am I?"

That was the one puzzle Mr. Morningside had never managed to solve. He had written directly into the instructions that there would be one riddle that I must solve on my own. The answer seemed apparent to me right away, however, given the excruciating weight strapped to my back.

"A book," I answered.

Malatriss bobbed her head, as did the snake, and then she folded her hands out in front of her; the other four hands remained tucked still behind her back. The beads on her collar twinkled gently, and then she gave me the final question. I swallowed, more nervous for this than for the unknown riddle. The answer provided by Mr. Morningside was wrong, I felt sure of that, but I was not at all convinced that I had the right clue. Or perhaps I had been confident, but now, faced with that hungry little eel around her neck, I wanted very much to be right and keep my fingers.

With another vicious smile, Malatriss offered the final test. "Arms to embrace, yet no hands. Pinches to give, yet no fingers.

Poison to wield, yet no needle. What am I?"

I couldn't help it—I glanced at Dalton, who had abandoned his casual posture, watching me with his fingernails between his lips. His eyes were hidden, of course, but I knew all of his thoughts, all of his prayers were bent toward me. The demon Focalor had failed, Henry had never gotten the opportunity, but still I summoned the courage to believe in my own wits.

For I did not know the word for an ancient scorpion creature with the chest and head of a man, but Father did. He spoke the ancient language of Khent, of Ara, of every tree and insect and man. No language escaped him. I shook, fearing what it might do to use his knowledge, but I wasn't going to lose my fingers.

"*Girtablilû,*" I said, my voice ringing out, all my hopes going with it.

Chapter Twenty-Four

very inch of me froze with fear. I watched the snake, waiting for it to strike. Mother's grip on my hand tightened and then relaxed, and Malatriss squinted as if seeing me anew.

"Willing hearts. Immortal hearts . . ." She extended all six of her golden hands to us. "Wise hearts. You have passed the first trial, but further tests await you within. I will be personally interested to see how you fare, little one. The door is open to you—all that remains is to walk through it."

A hard, cold wind blew through the ruins, and a moment later I heard a rustle of wings. Malatriss had begun to walk back down the ramp, but we were no longer alone in the castle. I turned, tucking my hands protectively over the straps of the pack, finding that the shepherd had come, and Finch, proving Khent's suspicions that our absence was noticed.

"Go through that door if you must, child," the shepherd said, hobbling toward me with a cane, his blind eyes finding me easily. "But you will not take that book with you."

Finch rushed toward me, the gold of his body fading as he reverted to his human form. He was not to reach me, as Khent stepped between us, his lip curling into a snarl.

"Louisa, please," Finch implored, his huge, brown eyes—wet with tears—searching me out over Khent's shoulder. "You don't know what you're doing. We were friends once, and though different, you always showed me kindness. Would you see us all killed?"

"There's more to this than you know," I told him. "I'm sorry, it's too late, I won't be persuaded."

"How did you find us?" Dalton stepped up next to Khent, and I began backing away, knowing I may soon need to run and run swiftly.

"Oh, brother, I can sense you. I can always sense you. You may have turned away from us, but that does not mean our bond is broken," Finch told him, shaking his head of dark hair and glancing away, disgusted. "I knew you were changed, but to take the book? To work for *him*?"

Guilt and doubt tugged at the edges of my mind, but not for long. The sharp sting of a headache seared across my forehead, and I gasped, nearly felled by the pain. Sometimes I could feel Father's influence building gradually, but this came on with the quickness of a summer lightning storm. Father had sensed the shepherd's proximity and clawed his way through my mind until I could hardly hear a word being said around me.

Let me face him, let me rend him with teeth and claw.

Mother's hands curled around my shoulders, urging me away from the arguing. We stumbled toward the ramp, fragments of the shouting breaking through the bloody mist filling my head.

"It isn't for me," Dalton was saying. "It's for everyone. You have them cornered, your entire host against a handful of *children*. This isn't a war, it's another massacre. Henry's released those souls, his strength is spent. What more do you want?"

"To live, brother! And to punish you for killing my sister."

But that was me.

More bickering, more dark laughter from the corrupted recesses of my mind. The ground sloped, and I let Mother guide me, finding my feet as we descended the ramp.

"I won't let her take it!" Finch was screaming now, all pretense of civility gone, and I heard a deafening clash of steel. "You turned away from us, brother. You've diminished. I will take no pleasure in defeating you, but I *will* defeat you. Louisa! Louisa, please! She's getting away . . . We shall spare your friends, Louisa, if you only listen to us. Listen to reason!"

They are feeble, alone. Let us end this, daughter, let us have our revenge.

I gritted my teeth. *No.* Not now. Not when we were so close . . .

"Khent," I managed to whisper. "The moon . . ."

"I see it. Go, *eyachou*, go! We will not let them advance."

But I leaned hard against Mother, hissing. It was wrong to go, to leave them like that, to let others fight my battles. And yet I feared what would happen if I stayed, if Father emerged and used me for his ancient revenge. I blinked hard, concentrating on Mother's presence, hoping that if I stayed near to her his influence would fade away. It did, but only a little, and I had time to open my eyes and see her and Khent staring down into my face with twin expressions of concern. How could I leave? A hundred possibilities flashed before my eyes, none of them encouraging. What if we emerged from the tomb to find Khent slain? What if I might have bargained for mercy and found some way to save us all? And those bleeding and dying for us at Coldthistle House, what if it was all for nothing?

"Go," Khent said again, pressing his hand between my shoulder blades, "and take my courage when you do."

Dalton flared gold behind him, wielding a staff with blades flashing on both ends. He blazed like fire, and through the flames I could see the shepherd advancing toward us, the kindness of his face wiped clean by rage. As Khent turned away from me I saw the first ripples of tension beneath his arms, a spray of gray fur clustering at his nape as he took his power from the moon and came to our defense. Malatriss was almost at the door. It was time to go, time to carry the weight of the book down the ramp and into the tomb beyond.

Even with Mother there, my skin prickled with cold. We were entering a tomb, after all, and a whispering voice of dread reminded me that only the dead belonged in such places. Willing hearts. Wise hearts. *Immortal* hearts.

God help me, I did not feel so immortal anymore.

Amazed, relieved, I stepped through the door and into my dream. No, not a dream this time, but the place itself. Another realm. I had seen the realm of one Binder, but this was something else completely, not just a void of nothingness and impenetrable shadows. An incredible vision, so otherworldly that no simple mortal could be meant to see it, and I stopped short, gazing up at the endless glass hall of stars and night, standing in a tunnel with no walls but infinite constellations rotating slowly around it. Yet I was there. Not a simple mortal, perhaps, but a reluctant god bearer that still felt like a serving maid.

"I've . . . I've been here before," I whispered.

Malatriss continued through the corridor at her unwaveringly languid pace. "Many dream of the Hall of Gods and Glass. Few ever see it with true eyes."

"How many have come before?" I murmured. We at last seemed to have found something that amazed Mother. She, too, cast her eyes in every direction, reaching out for a walled boundary that was not there. Yet her fingers touched something solid, even if it could not be seen.

"Akantha the Seeking, Romulus the Founder, Miigwan, Hereward, Valens, Nochtli the Thorned, Ying Yue, Owain . . ." Malatriss had tucked her second and third pair of arms back behind her shoulders again and gestured to us with her right hand. The snake around her neck appeared to be sleeping. "Now your names will be added to that list."

"And how many of them escaped the tomb alive?" I asked. The corridor was endless, but Malatriss led us forward, more constellations sparking to life above and below.

"Oh," she replied lightly. "None."

We followed Malatriss five paces behind, and already I felt weary from carrying the white book. It was heavier than I could have imagined, and my back ached. Mother glided along beside me, her veil long since removed, and she touched my shoulder.

"Shall I carry it?" she asked.

"No, I think I should be the one to do it. This is my wretched mess," I said. "Do you think this is what Mr. Morningside wanted? To trap us in here forever?"

She considered that with pursed lips, then glanced ahead to Malatriss.

"It certainly would make life easier for him, wouldn't it? If we destroy the book, then that's the shepherd sorted, and if we never leave this place then he has all of England to himself." I thought of the instructions, the word *scorpion* standing out in my mind as if it had been written in fire. "He gave me the wrong answer to one of the riddles, Mother. I don't think he really knew what he was sending us into. He must have suspected this might be where we meet our end."

My heart sank. I had never really trusted him, but I had hoped at least that my terms were fair enough to tempt him into decency. But even that was beyond him. I had helped him against the shepherd, against Father, and for what? Now he had trapped us in the Tomb of Ancients, a place nobody had survived. Could he have known that, too?

"We have to get out of here," I murmured. "If only to throw it in his horrid face."

"The Dark One has shown kindness to you before, yes? Perhaps there is more here that we cannot see."

Her optimism deepened my despair. Mother was ancient and wise, but I had known Mr. Morningside long enough to understand that his motives were always selfish. He had led Dalton and Mrs. Haylam to the tomb's entrance once, content enough to put them in the worst kind of danger for his own plot. If that was how he treated friends, what would he be willing to do to me?

The hall stretched on and on, but I could not concentrate on its beauty. Panic rose in my chest. I looked behind us, but there was no door. Courage. There were trials to come, and the promise of death to face, but I needed to find a way to take that knotted ball of panic and transform it into determination. I was a Changeling, after all, such a feat ought to be possible. Above all, I wanted to see Mary, Khent, Chijioke, Lee, and Poppy again. And I wanted answers, real ones, from Mr. Morningside. I would get the answers I sought, no matter what I needed to endure.

How very like Mr. Morningside himself.

I noted a gradual slope to the floor now, a descent that grew steeper as we went. The Hall of Gods and Glass was conspicuously absent of scent. Not even dust touched this place.

"Where are we?" I asked Malatriss as we went. "Certainly not Yorkshire."

I heard the amusement in her voice as we went deeper and

deeper into the tomb. "We are nowhere, suspended in time. There is no description I could offer that would tell you *where* we are. We simply are here."

"But it is possible to return?" I pressed. "If we pass your tests, I mean."

"It is possible. Difficult. But possible."

The corridor turned and twisted, still leading us down. Above, below, and all around us, the constellations began to fade, the tunnel becoming solid black and then, brick by brick, embossed yellow brick. A carpet spread out under our feet, narrow and blue, running along a floor of that same embellished brickwork. This place *did* smell. I knew the odor well and drank deep of it, the comforting scent of parchment, old ink, and leather reminding me at once of Cadwallader's. Books. Of course. We had entered a library of sorts, though it had no end. Instead of books in shelves lining the walls, there stood innumerable cases made of glass.

I slowed and veered to the right, approaching one of the cases. No, not a case, a sarcophagus. A body was suspended within, eyes closed, floating, seemingly asleep. It was a beautiful dark-skinned woman with long hair and feathery wings for arms. The next case held a man so wide and muscular he seemed almost to burst from the sparkling glass confines.

My hand smoothed across the glass, but the figure within did not wake.

"What are they?" I breathed. Mother stared at my hand and

then at the man entombed beyond it, her eight eyes filling with tears.

"Gods," she answered for Malatriss. "Ancients. Those that came before and were made to surrender."

"Some have yet to be," Malatriss added. "Many decided to return here to sleep."

"This . . . This is where I was born." Mother walked to an empty tomb, spreading her palms across it. There were other cases like it, abandoned or waiting to be filled. "I have memories of this place. I have dreamt of it, too."

"That's why I could see it," I said. "Because Father remembered it." The library, rectangular but with a ceiling so tall it simply became darkness, stretched on and on, perhaps into eternity. This place, as she had said, existed out of time. I felt compelled to speak only in a whisper, as if afraid to disturb the slumber of so many dreamers. Mother began to cry, and I went to her side, ignoring the pain of carrying the book to wrap an arm around her waist in comfort.

"I'm sorry," I told her. "I should not have brought you to this place."

"No," she said, smiling through her tears. "It is beautiful to see it again."

"When you have had your fill, you may approach the Binder," Malatriss announced, standing apart from us and petting her snake. "Time is meaningless here, and I am in no rush to watch you die. If you have made it this far, you deserve to mark the tomb's splendor."

And mark it I did, wandering down the endless line of coffins to see the array of gods and goddesses within, all unique but for the peaceful, blank expression they shared. Mother remained slumped against her own empty case, and my curiosity soon curdled as my feet brushed something brittle on the ground. Bones. I had stepped directly onto a skeleton, its arm turning to dust under my foot.

"But . . . I thought one had to be immortal to enter," I whispered, jumping back in horror. It was not my intent to desecrate the dead, and the empty sockets of the fallen skull stared at me accusingly. "To have known death and returned . . ."

"There are many ways to taste death," Malatriss replied. "You two are the first truly immortal beings to enter the tomb."

The bones had shaken me, and I stumbled back toward Mother, hefting the pack higher on my shoulders before turning to Malatriss. "Mother, I know you are overcome, but I must hurry. My friends are in danger."

"Of course," Mother said, pressing her forehead to the glass sarcophagus. "Of course. Go on, let us see this Binder."

I returned to Malatriss, a lump in my throat. Now I needed all of my courage. I had met a Binder before, and every inch of me recoiled at the thought of seeing another. The thing had brought me only pain and torment, but then, it had also given

Mother back to us. And my purpose in the tomb was not to admire all the gods that had been and could be, but to destroy the white book and earn the ritual that would sever Father from me for good.

"Tell me, then," I said to Malatriss, with great trepidation but also great urgency, for time might not have had meaning in this place, but it undoubtedly did in Yorkshire. I watched her cat eyes dance with excitement. "Tell me what comes next. I came to unmake the white book, and then I will be leaving this place."

"The Binder comes," she hissed, showing me her demon's smile. "The unbinding begins. You will ask of it one boon, it will take from you two. You ask of it two favors, it will require three. Choose your words carefully, little one. Nothing in this place is free."

Chapter
Twenty-Five

nce, delinquent as usual at my old school, Pitney, I had sneaked out of my bed to enjoy the pleasure of nighttime solitude. To be at a boarding school was to endure constant noise. Even when the candles were snuffed out and we were put to bed, somebody snored or coughed through the night, and I, ever a light sleeper, would spend another restless spell counting the days until our lessons broke and we received a brief respite. Not that anyone would visit me or that I would be allowed to leave—my grandparents wanted nothing to do with me, thinking me a broken bird with a wing that never mended. That injured wing, naturally, being my contrary nature, my strange black eyes, and my bothersome habit of speaking my mind.

But still, when those days arrived, I might spend all my ungoverned hours hiding up a tree with a book, and then throwing rocks at squirrels with my one friend, Jenny. Her family never visited or invited her home, either, her father gambling away their money, her mother ever abed with some real or invented frailness.

And so, desperate for those easier days, but knowing they were far off, I tiptoed past the sleeping teachers at the door that night, over the threadbare carpets, down one set of stairs, and across the left side of the second-floor gallery to the library. Nobody thought to guard the library, since the dozing sentries outside the bunk room were considered vigilance enough. The wood floors of the library were icy cold on my bare feet. Francine Musgrove, the person, at the time, whom I considered the worst person in England, had stolen my socks and hidden them in a chamber pot. Nothing, not even warmth, was worth the price of fishing around in someone's piss bucket.

The books, however—the lovely, lovely books—and the quiet banished the misery of the cold. I found a nook near the window and read by moonlight, rousing myself with pinches so as not to be caught sleeping there come morning.

Now I stood once again in a darkened library, and I felt strangely similar—cold, alone, delinquent, choosing to put myself in a place where I did not belong.

God, I thought, blinded for a moment as all the light in the Tomb of Ancients went out, what would Jenny think of me now? My greatest adversary was no longer Francine Musgrove and her penchant for thieving my undergarments; my adversaries were gods, creatures of ancient myth, vengeful spirits, and the unquestionably evil thing descending from the ceiling now. I shivered, realizing that it had been hovering in the darkness all along, watching us. Waiting.

Even Francine Musgrove did not deserve to be faced with this.

Instinctively, I reached for Mother's hand. She watched the Binder drift down toward us with narrowed eyes. The fine, purple hairs on her arms stood on end, and she whispered something, a prayer, in a language far older than English. The true language of the Dark Fae.

This Binder looked nothing like the last. Indeed, it was hard to consider it one thing at all, for it was primarily a collection of arms, each dangling from the end of a glistening string. I did not need to step closer to know those strings were living, more like tendons than twine. The hands at the ends of those arms, perhaps thirty in all, held quills and inkpots, blotters and pouches of sand, wax, brands, and various jars filled with colored liquids, most too thick to be ink. One hand juggled a pair of dice, one cube red and the other black, each side mottled and carved with odd symbols.

And at the center of this pale and fleshy array hung an overlarge head, attached to a withering white torso. The Binder had no legs, and it appeared sexless; it was bulbous and smooth, the color and quality of an egg. Its odd, round body, floating amid the detached arms, gave it the vague appearance of an insect with many legs, yet it defied even that comparison, for its "body" was at least the size of a wagon.

The only resemblance it bore to the other Binder was its slit-like nostrils and unsteady mouth, which flapped and jostled as it floated there above us.

"This one carries two of my creations." Its voice reminded me of a workman who drank in the alley outside my childhood home. Buoyant, nasal, jolly. But then, he had gone on to stab his wife in a drunken rage, so maybe not so jolly after all.

"The white book," I said, dredging up my voice from a chest fluttering with fear. "I . . . I would see it destroyed." I removed the pack from my shoulders and dropped it. Malatriss swooped out of the darkness and took it up, then carried it closer to the Binder.

The Binder's face careened toward mine, so close it shocked

the breath out of me. I gasped and closed my eyes, then forced myself to open them slowly. Its loose mouth chewed, passing spittle from cheek to cheek, as it studied me from an inch away.

"A mark upon this one's hand. The mark of a Binder," it whispered.

"Yes. I—I met one of the Eight before, the one that binds souls."

"Then this one has met Six. I am Seven." It gradually eased away from me, and one of its arms dropped down on its sinew to fish the white book out of the bag. Then it looked back at me. "And what of the book inside this one? What is to be done?"

Wringing my hands, I looked up at Mother, who nodded gently. "You carry it, Louisa, it is yours to do with as you please. I would not be myself if I imposed my will."

"But it's part of you, too," I said. "It's the only reason they gave me Father's soul, to keep the book of the Dark Fae from being lost." Seven had grabbed the white book and begun flipping through it, one disembodied hand holding the spine while another floated down to flick the pages. I cleared my throat. "Malatriss said I should choose my requests carefully. So I am. I only want the white book to be destroyed, and then we should like very much to leave."

Seven laughed at that, again reminding me of a drunk. It swayed as it laughed, bumping into several of its arms. "To leave. Yes, good. To leave. Then this one will have what she asks, but only after I receive my due."

Two boons. I had no doubt the cost would be steep, and I braced to hear it, thinking of the pile of crumbling bones in the corner.

"Balance or chaos, balance or chaos?" The Binder's pale hand holding the dice began to shake them, and I gulped, but I had no idea which outcome to hope for. All of its other arms went still as the hand threw the dice, the two little squares landing directly in front of me, held aloft by some unseen force. They both landed to display tiny scale symbols. Balance.

"The white book is unwritten." The hand paging through the book glided away, another, holding a black quill, took its place and began tracing over the words. As each illegible letter was written over, it vanished from the parchment. "Story becomes memory. Memory becomes rumor. Rumor becomes legend. Legend fades."

It hurt, unexpectedly, to watch the book being undone. With each disappearing word, I thought of an Upworlder going with it. Their lives, their very essence, erased from the world. And I thought of Dalton, whom I had come to admire, and the sad longing in his voice when he'd insisted I destroy the book. "There will be no one left to blame when I'm gone." Perhaps that wasn't true. Perhaps there would be someone quite obvious to blame. Me.

Or Mr. Morningside, as it was at his request that I had

come. My heart filled with regret and my eyes with tears. The choice could not be unmade, but I wondered if I might have been strong enough to live with Father's influence, to run far, far away, up a mountain, to the depths of a desert, and find some way to quiet his voice. Now I would be left trusting the Devil in the world to remove the Devil inside, and all of his mistakes and his lies told me I had erred when I chose sides.

I peered into the darkness. Somewhere, an empty case waited, and soon it would hold the shepherd. Would another soon hold Father? Father, who was uncharacteristically passive while the white book was wiped clean. Perhaps, finally, I had done something to win his approval.

Seven closed its round black eyes, quiet and thoughtful, mouth slack as the Binder swayed back and forth. I glanced at Malatriss after minutes of this strange silence. Had the Binder . . . Had it gone to sleep?

"What happens now?" I asked, clearing my throat.

"The unbinding will take time, and the Binder must choose your sacrifices."

Sacrifices. We had traveled the windy road from boon to favor to *sacrifice*. Not that I was unduly surprised—a wrong answer to a riddle lost a finger. This was not a place of light conversation and idle threats.

"Sacrifices?" Mother asked. She apparently shared my unease.

Malatriss moved across the single pool of light remaining in the tomb, reaching out to touch my cheek. I recoiled and she chuckled.

"What do you think the Binder uses to make the books? Air and wishes? Nochtli the Thorned provided the leather for your book, though it may now reside in living flesh." Malatriss took great pleasure in my horrified look, that much was obvious. Her chuckle drew out into a laugh, and she regarded her pet snake with a tilt of her head, chucking the thing under its head. "She found the gate at the mouth of three rivers and brought her pretty bird inside. Willing, wise, she tasted death in disease, but a shaman cured her before she went to the true night. Nochtli brought her pretty bird inside the tomb, and when the Binder commanded she kill it, she refused."

"Barbaric," I whispered. "Why the bird? What could it possibly have done?"

The Binder continued its work and its contemplation.

Malatriss glanced up from the snake, sneering. "It was a truly awful bird. I could tell it didn't like Nira."

I stoppered the ugly things I wanted to say about that—if the doorkeeper could look into a heart and divine its willingness, perhaps she could also sense my dislike for her pet.

The Binder worked faster now, pages flying, the words disappearing so quickly the quill seemed only a blur. We waited for Seven to make its decision, and each passing moment filled me with greater anxiety. My palms were slick with sweat. I could hardly bear to stand still, knowing some impossible pronouncement was soon to be made. I scrubbed my face with both hands and sighed, wanting the whole ordeal to be over at last, wanting to at least know what I must do to escape the Tomb of Ancients.

"All of this over a silly book," I said.

Malatriss jerked her head up at that, scowling. "The Binders make the world, the Binders make the books, the books make the gods."

"Would that not make the Binders the gods?" I murmured. Mother brushed my hand. She was right, I was pressing this creature too hard and being foolish in my frustration and impatience.

"No, it makes them Binders, and it makes you all but insignificant."

Seven woke up. Its fathomless black eyes gazed down at us, glassy and momentarily unseeing. Then it seemed to find us, *see* us, and I took Mother's hand once more. She leaned her head toward mine, her soft pink hair touching my shoulder.

"Do not forget," she told me. "Courage."

The Binder's voice boomed through the hall, echoing into the endless shadows around us. The mark on my hand burned and burned. Willing. But was I? I stared into the more-than-a-god's eyes and hoped that it knew what I wanted. Mercy, and the chance to see my friends outside the tomb once more. Had I not done enough? But then, could a thing like the creature before me care?

"This one's book will be bound again," Seven proclaimed, nodding toward me. "I will claim this rebound book of the Dark Fae, Daughter of Trees, and remake it with your very essence."

Chapter Twenty-Six

ather did not like that at all. For his spirit knew, just as I did, just as Mother did, that to remove him was to remove the one thing keeping me alive. Then something shifted, and with it, my understanding, too. Father was no longer angry but excited. Elated. This ritual would take him from me, and without my body to hold him, give him the chance to be completely free. Resurrected. Whoever won, I lost. The Binder had handed down a death sentence, and for a long, painful moment I could not breathe.

Inside my mind, Father smiled. Then the screaming began.

My screams. The first time Father overpowered my will, it had been a gradual thing, the slow creep of a negative thought twisted into something more dangerous. A thorn that became a barb that became a knife. The drip, drip, drip of confusion, of not knowing whether a thought was mine or his. First, I stopped taking my tea with cream and sugar, until I began preferring a strong herbal brew that could only be found at one shop in the neighborhood. Then each tree began to have its own unique and alluring perfume, and insects, if I skewered them with a look, would retreat, leaving me in peace.

And that was when it was all still manageable. When it felt not like being captive but like putting up with an odd relative come to stay.

Needless to say, it had gotten worse.

A single thought survived the heat now exploding through my skull: I had done the right thing, for whatever I could do to rip this monster from my mind was, indeed, what must be done.

I felt my knees collide with the ground, and somewhere, in the distance, a cry from Mother. What a response to the Binder's demands, though this was not my own. Father had waited, letting me grow comfortable, letting me lower my guard. And now he'd struck, with all his pent-up rage, not just red before my eyes but bright crimson-and-black spangles, and a steady sound like the drums of war pounding in my head, louder and louder, until I felt sure my eyes would pop and my teeth would slice through my tongue.

Here it came, his wrath. I had worn a pin once, gifted to me by Mr. Morningside. *"I am Wrath,"* it said. But I had never been this, never been the last desperate attempt at living by a god cornered into death. Was this what Khent and Dalton faced back outside the door? Did the shepherd sense his time was close and find terrible power and pain in his imminent end?

Every word of the book inside of me was whispered by the Binder at once, and though my eyes were no longer my own, I felt the searing in my fingers as they elongated into claws, felt the tightness in my skin, my legs, my arms, my spine, as the twisted deer of Father's nightmares surged through me. Even Malatriss shouted something obscene and afraid, in a language that was lost, in the tongue I had used in the stranger's ritual at

Cadwallader's and that was now branded into my palm.

"Do not whisper your elder speak before me, doorkeeper. The gods may sleep in your tomb, but you have never woken one to challenge it."

Father's voice through my lips. He spread outward like smoke, and Mother's warm hands fell on my arm, but Father threw her off, into the darkness. I cried out but was instantly silenced. He had pushed me to the bottom of the sea, and though I sensed a light high above me, no amount of thrashing and kicking brought me near the surface. I drowned in his black-blooded fury and tasted the sourness of revenge on my tongue. It was all he craved, blood and revenge, his spirit impervious to Mother's pleas for understanding. For patience.

"You would rip me from this fleshling, and once I would have welcomed it," he roared, and his arm—mine—swiped with razor claws toward Malatriss. He was going to get us all killed. "She has proven herself somewhat useful, but I can take many forms. You may unmake the white book, but you will never unmake *me*. I am the Dark Father of the Trees, Caller of Night, the Stag in the Sky, and I will carry the book within me from this place, and I will not be stopped."

Mother no longer pleaded with him, but with Malatriss. How long would they put up with this insubordination? Father had to be mad to think he could overpower those that had created him in the first place. I had read Dalton's diary, which meant he'd read it, too. Only a madman would take such warnings, such violence, lightly. But yes, of course. Of course he was utterly, irredeemably mad.

"I see now." The Binder spoke, unperturbed. *Intrigued.* "This one is not one, but two. This, too, like all things, can be undone."

Father roared, undeterred, and lashed out against Malatriss. She hissed, as did her snake, the white serpent striking fast, batted away with a swift riposte from Father, and then Malatriss unfurled all of her arms, moving lightning fast, dodging each swipe of claws until at last she managed to hook Father by the arm. One, then two, then three hands clamped down, yanking him—*us*—hard to the ground.

"Two will be one," Seven said, more somber now. Father's panic, his pain, filled my head and flowed through my screams, tears pouring down my face as Malatriss twisted hard, snapping the bones. "Two will be one, and from one emerges the book. A new book. A new beginning for the children of the Fae."

And then we were floating, lifted into the air by four of the Binder's pale hands. My arm throbbed, hot with agony, but my thoughts and feelings gradually became my own. Then I would sense Father again, as if a flimsy wall existed now between us and he spent his remaining will, bashing against the barrier.

"No! Please!" Mother knelt below us, reaching up with both hands. "It will kill her! If you take his spirit, she will die!"

"THEN SHE WILL DIE." Malatriss whirled on her, brandishing her six powerful hands.

The first time I died, it had been a quick thing. This was slow torture, the ripping of a fresh scab still hard-sealed to the skin. Father did not want to go, and he dug in, each of his deep and tearing claws removed with precision but not mercy.

I began to feel cold, first in my feet and then in my hands. The iciness spread fast, like the first frost rushing to kill the last tenacious wildflowers of autumn. So, too, did my spirit cling on in Father, resistant to the frost but not invincible. I heard his cries as my own, and for one brief instant I pitied us in equal measure. He had made me suffer in life, and now he made me suffer in death, but I felt his twin pain and wished it upon no one.

Cold. So cold. A silvery puff of air left me, crystalizing with ice, and I watched it dance away toward the Binder's smooth, white face.

Was that my last breath? I did not think it would be so very cold.

"Balance." Seven did not cease its torture, tearing Father's spirit from me steadily until it was a thing made real, a ghostly rendering of his form, skull, antlers, robes, and all. It floated apart from me, helpless, seeing its former home and reaching for it. "One favor, two sacrifices. Balance, said the dice, and balance there will be. One book is unmade, another rebound. One creature undone, another reborn. Two souls again in one body. The Mother replaces the Father."

Wait. I tried to speak, but nothing happened. My voice

was lost somewhere, spinning there in the darkness, trapped in Father's soul. *Wait, no, this isn't right.* I couldn't know what exactly the Binder meant, but how could it be kindness when all I knew of this place was pain?

It was too late. Seven had made its decision. I saw a flash of understanding in Mother's eight eyes, her arms still lifted in pleading and prayer, and then she, too, was hoisted into the air with us, held by the Binder's unnaturally strong hands.

Father's screams were unending, but I didn't look at him. I could only stare at Mother, hoping she could see in my dying eyes that this was not what I wanted, that none of this was balanced. That none of this was fair.

Then Father's spirit thinned, turning slowly to smoke, smoke that was caught in one of the Binder's jars, settling there to mix with some inky liquid within. A quill was dipped into the vessel and a blank book was produced from the shadowy nothingness above us. At least, I thought, helpless and hurting, it would not be Mother's skin used to make that new cover, as it was already bound in something smooth and pale. Whose it was, I would never know, but I saw the beginning of the binding, of the writing—Father's spirit, his knowledge of the Dark Fae book, rewritten in his own essence.

One of the thin, pale hands of the Binder wrapped around Mother's neck and began to squeeze. I was frozen, dying, and soon she would be, too. Her arms stretched out toward me, her lips twisted in a lost, sad smile. I watched her tears disappear into the void around us and heard Malatriss cackle with satisfaction from somewhere beneath our feet.

"Courage, Louisa, daughter," she whispered. "Your feet are on the path. I'll be going with you."

Chapter
Twenty-Seven

t did not feel as if my feet were on the path. I felt . . . nothing. What a strange sensation, nothing. No pain and no fear, no understanding if I had become hot or cold, or if my body was scattered in a million pieces. Instead, I existed only in my mind, in a place, like the tomb, out of time. I was dead, that much I understood, or soon to be dead, suspended by the Binder's will, not in my body and not yet laid to rest.

When sound and light and feeling returned, it was all too much. I cried, as a baby must cry, forced through darkness and uncertainty, entering the world reluctant and confused. The place of not feeling or knowing was better than this. Here, back on the floor of the Tomb of Ancients, there was only more pain. Dust. The smell of wet leaves and earth, as if I had not been born but sprouted from the ground. My arm remained useless, broken, limp, and aching at my side.

The Binder waited above, Malatriss hovering close, and Mother, sprawled and empty on the stones, dead at the place of her birth.

I pulled myself toward Mother, heedless of the Binder, of its arms like slender white birds flying through the air as they prepared the new book and unwrote another. Mother looked as if she could be sleeping, with her lips slightly parted, as if the last breath pulled from her had been a sweet one. She didn't smile, but her eyes were closed, her hair pooled around her like a pillow of camellias.

"After all that I did to save you, it wasn't enough," I whispered, finding that touching her hand did not give the same soothing comfort. "I failed you. I should never have brought you to this place. You were nothing but peace and light, no soul so undeserving."

A shadow fell over us. Malatriss.

"Are you quite finished?"

"You." Refusing to leave Mother's side, I twisted toward her on the floor, wincing as my injured arm took some of my weight, then collapsed. "I won't let you keep her body," I whispered fiercely, covering Mother with my arms. "It was not one of your demands."

Malatriss glared down at me with her yellow eyes. One single scratch bled across her shoulder. Father's doing. Her snake had not suffered, still wound faithfully around her neck. "It would not be wise for you to return here, little one, no matter how great your need. I grow weary of your tone."

"What is this all for?" I sighed, lifting Mother's hand and clutching it. "The books, the gods, the Binders. Why keep them here? Why not just give the world all of these creations?"

It was not Malatriss who answered me but Seven. I had not expected to be worthy of its notice now that it had passed judgment, but the egg-round head and soft white torso dipped low, regarding me with a curious smile.

"This one sees so much yet understands so little. Chaos, Daughter of Trees. Because *chaos*. The humans wander. They squabble. They battle. All so amusing. And if the humans do it, why shouldn't the gods? It is one more game to watch, one more match to observe."

Chaos and balance. I shook my head, outraged, knowing that many a wicked and wayward schoolgirl had proposed to me that there truly was no God above, and that all our mortal toiling was meaningless. But to hear it, plainly, from one that might actually know . . .

"So it . . . it's all a game," I murmured. "You create the books, these gods, just to see which one will *win*?"

The Binder stared at me as if I were simple and perhaps a bit pathetic. "Well. Yes."

"A game. A *game*. My friends, the shepherd's people, Father, Mother, all of us bashing against one another just for your amusement?" A voice within me said to be still. A voice within me said that nothing more could be done, that to die here would accomplish nothing. I held my tongue for one moment longer, then took a long breath and said, "And if I refuse to play this hateful game?"

All the Binder's free hands, perhaps twenty in total, spread wide. "What this one does when it leaves this place is not for me to say. But I will watch this one." And here Seven smiled for the first time, and it shook me to my bones. "I will watch this one with great interest."

"You will be disappointed," I said.

The scribbling above us stopped; the quill rewriting our book had finished its task. It had all happened so quickly, but then, to these strange and otherworldly beings, our lives—our game—was probably a play readily consumed. Our human lives, no doubt, passed but in the blink of an eye, and the eternal ones like the shepherd and Mr. Morningside warranted only marginally more attention. *We cannot be killed*, Father had told me, *only be made to surrender*. Only . . . That was no longer true of me. I sensed not even the smallest trace of Father's influence in my mind. I forced myself to think of the shepherd, and about him, my feelings were blessedly my own.

That was the one good thing to come of all this . . . loss.

I dragged myself up and watched as Malatriss accepted the finished book from Seven. She received it reverently enough, then placed it into the bag I had discarded. Returning to me, she waited until I offered my back and then slipped the shoulder straps over my arms, surprisingly cautious of my broken right arm.

"How will you take her from this place?" she taunted, hissing in my ear, so close that I felt the beads of her collar brush my good arm. "We do not waste a single part. You may leave her knowing she will resume her place in the world as a future book, as pages, as another story to tell. You will never see it, but she will not be wasted. You may take her spirit with you, but you cannot take her body from the tomb. You haven't the strength."

"Watch me."

The book was not heavy this time, but light. I supposed that only the words of another or other gods weighted one down. Mother was still sprawled beneath the Binder, and I turned from Malatriss, crouching and slipping one arm under her soft, feathered gown. It did not matter how difficult the burden, I would carry her back with me.

Malatriss observed, then smiled as I gained my feet again, grunting, struggling, but still managing to slide Mother along with me as I approached the doorkeeper.

"She should be in that case," I spat. "She should be at rest."

Her eyes widened, the snake around her neck drawing back. "She is at rest, little one. In you."

I blinked. "Like . . . Father was? Her whole mind and will was given to me, not just her spirit?"

"I am sure you will hear her," Malatriss said with a nod, "when she is ready to speak."

Mother did not speak as Malatriss led me away from the single pool of light in the tomb. And she remained silent as the Binder retreated to its nesting place, its body and legs receding into the deep shadows of the vast, perhaps endless top of the tomb. This had been a place of my dreams once, and with Mother within me, I wondered if I would see it again. I wondered if it would return only as a nightmare, after all this.

Mother remained silent as I limped along, dragging her body because I could not properly carry her. Over and over again I looked at her lips, realizing each time that they would be still. The tomb never brightened, but I sensed the sleeping forms of all those gods around us, waiting to be pawns again in the Binders' games.

A door appeared, much like the one that we had entered through at the castle, but instead of blackness beyond there was the promise of something else. I saw green and sunlight, a hint of ancient stone. There was nothing to feel but persistence. Need. The way out lay before me. Mother had to come along, and no matter how long it took to drag her out, I would huff and sweat and grunt and struggle. She would not be fodder for another book. She deserved to have the sun's kiss and the fields' embrace one more time.

Malatriss waited next to the door, her head drawn back, chin high. She lifted one dark brown brow in expectation as I sidled toward freedom. Her snake, Nira, danced its head back and forth, sizing me up for a meal.

"Do not trouble yourself," I told her, sensing the cold, fresh air of our world. "I will never come here again. I wouldn't be *willing.*"

She froze, but the snake darted forward, wrapping itself around me, Malatriss holding her tail while the snake squeezed, forcing the breath out of me. In my shock, Mother's body slid out of my grasp.

"You were the first to survive the dice and the Binder in this place," Malatriss whispered, her eyes as cold as the void. She flashed her razor-sharp teeth. "Maybe you should die instead. Maybe it would be better if nobody escaped, not even when fortune and fate have their way."

"Please." My hands wrapped around the snake, and I found Mother's strength, pressing hard, digging my fingers into the soft, fleshy middle of the creature. "Let me go, or your pet dies with me."

"Nira!"

It was a call to attack. But I could attack, too, with what little strength I still possessed. I had come too far, lost too much, to give up on the threshold of survival. My hands crushed down before the snake could strike, and it gave a strangled hiss. Malatriss screamed in fury, and I felt the creature's grasp loosen around my neck. With the last of my breath, I pulled, hard, flinging the broken snake at her mistress, crouching, grabbing Mother by the shoulders and dragging until every muscle screamed. The door was open only a crack, and it closed, slowly, but I forced us through, listening to Malatriss weep and curse as we landed on the other side, my last glimpse of the Binder's realm a mouth full of teeth and sorrow.

I collected myself on the other side with a gasp, falling to my knees under the dead weight of Mother's body. At first, I was greeted with silence, then intermittent bird song, then a long, groaning *harooh* that I knew could belong only to a dog.

That spurred me to my feet, and I ignored the blinding pain

in my arm, staggering under my burden, taking one slow step after another away from the castle door. There was no ramp this time; I had simply been dumped out where I had begun, like so much unwanted refuse. A low sprawl of bodies lay across the courtyard, each more covered in blood than the last.

Khent was closest to the door, lying in a heap, panting, lingering in his moon-touched form. But the moon was gone now, the sun returned once we emerged from the door. I watched the magic fade from him until he was but a man again, slashed with deep wounds, his eye and jaw badly bruised. Mother slid from my arms gently, and I joined him on the ground, pressing the blood-soaked fringe from his eyes and breathing a sigh of relief as he swore, spat blood, and slicked the sweat from his face.

"Did we win?" he asked, head lolling back on his shoulders.

"In a fashion," I said at first. Then, "No, not really. But stars, I'm so happy to see you alive."

"Me, too," he teased, then twisted on his side. "That one was about to finish me off," Khent explained, pointing at Finch. "But then . . . but then . . ."

"The book," I told him. "It's gone. I cannot say what will happen to them now."

"*Teyou*, they dropped all at once," he said. "Like leaves floating one by one down to a river." He noticed me favoring my left arm and frowned, getting onto his knees and gingerly taking my right wrist. I hissed through my teeth, clamping a hand down on his shoulder.

"Broken. No idea what it looks like. Frankly, I'm not ready to see."

"We must find a physician then." Khent stood, shaky, and lifted me up by my waist. "Or Mother could try to heal you, but—"

"But she's gone," I finished. We had only a moment to look at her, for there was movement among the other bodies. Their need was more urgent, and I accepted Khent's help as he guided me over toward the three men flat in the dirt.

"Did you do it?" Dalton gasped. He did not appear terribly hurt, but he clasped his chest, gulping air, harder and harder, and it was clear he could not breathe. "Is it gone?"

"I destroyed it. I'm so sorry, I don't know if it was right . . ." I lowered myself next to him, and took the hand that he offered, letting him place it back on his fluttering chest. "You're dying."

"Now that it comes to it," he whispered. "I'm not afraid. Tell Henry . . . Tell him I was wrong. He can be more than he is. There's still time." Blood trickled from his lips, and I reached under him to support his head. He wasn't finished, and I wasn't leaving until he had said all he wanted to say. "What was it like?" Dalton asked. The bandage had fallen away from his eyes, and I gently wiped the blood and perspiration from his forehead, looking down into the darkened red pits where his eyes had been. "Was it astounding?"

"Yes," I nodded. "But terrible, too. I wish I could tell you all about it."

"My dreams of it will be better," he said. "They always are. But this feeling . . . I think it's time for me to go now. I think I have no choice."

I pressed my eyes shut and tried not to let it hurt so much. "I've killed you," I said. "I'm so sorry."

"You saved your folk, gave them a chance," Dalton wheezed, a thick clot of blood dribbling down his chin. "That's what I wanted. We never let them have that before. You will say goodbye to Fathom? The safe house," he said at last, "I want it to be hers."

A muddled groan came from behind us, and Dalton's head turned toward the sound. "Father—"

But there was no more, the last word pulled everything out of him. There were no eyes to stare or close, but I felt him go, felt the last shuddering breath that rustled the grass. Gently, I let his head fall back into the green carpet of the courtyard, and then laid the bandage once more over his face, folding his arms one at a time across his chest.

Mother had not spoken until then, but her spirit whispered to me now.

One kiss to the moon, one bow to the sun
A gift of flowers to where the wild deer run
That is all that is asked, when our day is done

I repeated the prayer to Dalton, knowing it was what Mother had used to send restless souls to their repose. And then it seemed the wind took him, and all at once he was a riot of yellow butterflies and light.

Chapter Twenty-Eight

wren fell out of the nest once outside my dormitory window at Pitney. Jenny and I puzzled over what to make of it, neglecting our mandatory exercises. Neither of us cared much for taking turns about the lawn to keep the bloom in our cheeks, and so instead we hid behind a solid oak and debated what to do with the dazed bird.

"We could knock it on the head and put it in Francine's bed," Jenny suggested.

It was creative but nonetheless cruel. To the bird, obviously. Francine could go soak. "I'm not sure I can bring myself to kill it."

"The nest is awfully high. We might fall and break a leg trying to put it back."

Jenny was reasonable *and* creative. It was part of why I liked her, and why we had become fast friends. Perhaps also we had become friends because we were the only two girls at Pitney who would spend time considering whether or not to shove dead birds into a rival's bedclothes. Francine and the rest would never consider something so vulgar, but they had not grown up in the shit-stained slums. Their distant family still wanted them in some regard, and they simply awaited their return to place them as a governess or to offer them off to some random lad as marriage material.

"If we leave it, then a fox will come," Jenny added.

"But isn't that what would have happened if we had never found it?" I asked. I dropped the stick that might have been used as a tool of execution. The wren twitched, little feet kicking helplessly. "We never notice the bird. The fox comes. The fox eats the bird. If we cannot decide anything productive, then I believe we should let nature take its course."

Jenny presented no compelling alternative, and so we left the bird behind the tree and returned to our vigorous walking. The next day, alone, I looked behind the oak. Nothing remained but a tuft of feathers. The fox had found its meal, or the bird had regained itself and hopped away. I think I always knew the answer, but I told myself the wren escaped unscathed.

The fallen wren lying before me today was not so lucky. The fox had found this bird, and I could only wonder if anything would remain of him after.

I knelt next to the shepherd, amazed at his smallness. He was not a large man, but in dying he seemed to shrink more; his arms were very short, and his oversize flannels made him look childlike. Pitiable. Dark blood ran from his lips as I knelt beside him. Khent stood a ways off, perhaps aware that he was not invited to the exchange. Or perhaps he did not trust that our battle was truly over.

"Are you the fox," I murmured, watching as his milky eyes found me. "Or are you the wren?"

"I took you in once, girl, and this is my reward?" he sputtered.

He coughed, hard, and I fished the handkerchief out of his pocket, holding it to his stained lips. "Courtesy? Now? I shall never understand it."

"You murdered my folk," I said. The words came easily, as if practiced. I blinked, gazing a little to the right of him. Something inside me felt warm and ready, perhaps what a mother experienced when she knew 'twas time the babe came. "You were the fox. We were but stunned birds. Now we are naught but a tuft of feathers."

He shook his head slowly. "You aren't making sense, girl. You're mad. You've killed us, killed us because you are mad."

The warmth in me spread, up and out, but it was not troubling—quite the opposite. I didn't know what was happening, why I could feel so much at the sight of Dalton's death and nothing at all as this weakened old man lay expiring on the ground. His worn gray cap had fallen off his balding head, and it lay in the mud. "I am the fox now, only when I make a meal of you and yours, there will be nothing left. Not a feather. Not a foot. Not a trace of you on the land or in the air."

"There you go," he sighed, hacking into the cloth I held to his mouth. "Sounding as damned crazed as your father. That's your problem, you have so much of your father in you, lass. It's put you down a path from which there's no"—*hack*—"return."

The smile I gave him was sad, but perhaps vacant, too. I took the handkerchief away and flattened it next to his head. The blood on it had made a pattern like a fallen leaf.

"My father is all gone now," I told him. "Our book is rewritten. Our story starts anew. Father is nothing. I carry something else. Do you know?" I watched his brow furrow, terror in his eyes even as they were filmed with blindness. "Mother told me that what you and Henry did to us broke Father, watching so many of his children die. It scorched his heart to ash. But I walked through the fire with her in the Tomb of Ancients, and the fire did not break us, it did not char us to dust, no—we walked through the fire and it forged us anew."

He let his head fall back against his cap, though his mouth never closed. "I should have asked forgiveness for what we did. I should have made amends. I never . . . never thought this would be the way it ended. God help me. God help Henry."

"We're well beyond that," I said, watching his eyelids flutter and then close. I waited, thinking perhaps I should say the prayer Mother had gifted to me through her spirit. But then I thought better of it and stood. Finch, however, had tried to show me gentility once and might have become a friend had things been otherwise. I held no real animosity toward him in my heart, and he looked almost frail, crumpled on the ground. He had already left, probably before I had even emerged from the tomb.

I knelt and crossed his arms, closed his eyes with a soft touch of fingers, then spoke the words and watched him dissolve into wings and lift again high into the sky.

Khent waited for me at the castle door, leaning against it, his wounds making him slump with fatigue, all the more because he had taken up Mother's body and now carried it across both shoulders. Together we left the ruins behind, walking in silence down the grassy hill to the road, where the carriage and horses waited to take us back to Coldthistle House.

It would take time, I knew, for this new dark will in me to settle. But it was nothing like Father's influence, jarring and foreign; this new voice, new perspective, felt entwined with me naturally, as if it had been there all along, a dormant fire waiting to be stoked. Mother's spirit had changed when it became mine, and briefly I considered that, just like Father, she really was, in some sense, broken. That gave me pause, but then I sat with it, joining Khent in the driver's box, the wind harshly cool against my face as he took us back, and I decided that yes, Mother *was* broken.

And so was I. So were we all. Death had changed her. Her peace had turned to passion, and now that ardor was mine to bear. If we had left the tomb unchanged, then why enter it at all? Our story was the only one to survive the tomb. I had looked into the face of the one that made us all and found only contempt, and I knew that I could not let my own folk, my own friends, look into my face and see the same.

I would play the Binders' sordid game of lives and loss, but I would—must—change the rules. Mother taught me that. My dear, dear friends taught me that, too.

"How do you feel?" Khent asked, his voice lost amid the

thunder of hooves and whistling winds.

I took the pack from my back and laid it across my lap as we chewed the ground, making haste back toward the mansion. "I only feel . . . hollow."

"Hollow? I had meant your arm, but very well. Yes, hollow. That is all right, to be hollow. That can be filled up with hope. Or with grief."

"Grief. Hope." I puzzled over those words, then smiled into bracing cold. "Instead I shall choose resolve."

Chapter
Twenty-Nine

1247, Unknown

There are things best left unsaid in the hours after defeat. The heart is weaker in those hours, when a vague sense of consequence becomes truth. Becomes life. Henry has asked me to try once more, to join as they travel east, following the jade caravans along the Silk Road. There are rumors—and there are always rumors—of a woman in Si-ngan who has heard the remaining riddle.

But I will not be going east. I will not be going anywhere. I cannot watch Ara bandage her eye once more while Henry writes obsessive notes and insists, first to himself, then to us, that this journey has only just begun. When I refused, he called me a coward, but this time it did not sting.

Henry, if time or circumstance or some foolish trick of luck ever brings this diary into your possession, I would have you know something. There is, in fact, one more riddle, and it goes like this:

What is a tree that needs the sun but bends and grows away from it? What is a flower that craves rain but only blooms in the desert?

You can run to the ends of this world, Henry, search in every dusty corner, ask every passing merchant, and chase down every idle rumor, but you will not find what you seek. The answers to your questions are not in a hidden tomb or an ancient book, and while my sight dims as I turn away from Roeh and my people, your sight failed a long time ago.

Your riddle is not at the end of a long road. The riddle lay before you all this time. Why live? Why go on? Why choose creation over destruction? I am glad to leave the dog with you, because perhaps, dear friend, you will one day see it in his eyes. Why choose to go on? Because that which is unconditional is eternal. You were made to be eternal, and I love you for it, if only you loved yourself with my same true heart.

As you travel east, I will go west. I think I will seek out poets and sit in their presence and listen to their sad rhymes, wondering always what cutting critique you would offer them. One day Roeh will call me back to service, and I shall go, and I will lament, over and over again, that the request has not come from you.

The house, not in turmoil but in silence, looked shattered against the fields. Not a single window remained intact, and the east tower, that closest to the border with the shepherd's property, had collapsed. When the carriage stopped and I was on the drive again, I at last felt the extent of the damage to my body. I was bruised in places I had never been bruised before. My arm vacillated between stinging needles and numbness.

Khent lifted Mother's body out of the carriage proper and carried her along beside me as we circled back toward the site of the battle. Corpses littered the lawn, but not our friends'. I wondered if they would stay there and rot, and I thought with weary resignation that it would fall to me to see them all on. It would do everyone good to see a display of butterflies after so much blood.

"They're back!" Poppy, who had been resting on the ground with Bartholomew, jumped up and ran to us. "But you are hurt, Louisa, and the purple lady, too."

I saw no sign of Niles or Giles. Or Mr. Morningside and Mrs. Haylam, for that matter.

"Oh dear!" Mary, Lee, and Chijioke emerged from the kitchen at the sound of Poppy's shouts. They rushed over and helped Khent lay Mother down on an unstained patch of grass under the kitchen awning. Mary's eyes drifted to the bag on my back.

"It's our book," I told her. "The shepherd is gone and the white book destroyed."

"Aye, they all dropped out of the sky the moment it happened," Chijioke said. His hands were burned from the rifle muzzle, and his shirt was stained with soot. "I can't believe you did it, that it . . . that it could even be done."

"I saw the place where the books are made," I explained. "There were . . . complications. To destroy the book, ours had to be remade, which meant my spirit had to be removed, which meant—"

"Another soul was needed," Chijioke finished. It was his area of expertise, after all, and he bowed his head, sighing. "That cannot have been easy."

"Easy!?" Mary cried. "Look at her arm! We should get you inside, and Khent, too. We can see to all your injuries and find you something to eat. Giles was badly wounded. He's upstairs with Fathom and his brother. I do so hope he survives."

"In a moment," I said. "Only, is there something I could use to bind my arm up? It hurts to let it swing so."

Chijioke patted Mary on the shoulder and then trotted into the kitchen. He returned shortly with two white sheets from the pantry and carefully lifted my arm, bracing it against my middle before using the sheets to wrap it and then swaddle me diagonally across the shoulders to keep it firmly in place.

"Thank you. Where is Mr. Morningside?"

"Behind the house," Lee said, pointing. He stood straighter now that the Upworlders were no longer a problem. "He took Mrs. Haylam behind the house."

"Walk with me and show me," I said.

There was no rush now to deal with Mother's body, and I knew Mary and Chijioke would take good care of Khent and find something for his wounds. Finding Morningside was my most urgent task, and Lee's eyes widened in surprise at my suggestion, but he agreed, falling into step next to me as we picked our way across the hole-ridden ground and fallen Upworlders. I whistled and tapped my thigh with my good hand, and Bartholomew lifted his head, then heaved an immense doggy sigh and loped over to join us.

"Why him?" Lee asked, reaching out to stroke the dog's head.

"You will see," I said. "But first I must ask you something."

We walked slowly, for we were both sapped from the fighting.

His knuckles and forearms showed a boxer's welts, and with his strange, unnatural new strength I could easily imagine how he had made himself useful in the final push of the battle. We had come so very far from nervous flirting in the library.

"Something is changed about you," Lee observed. "I suppose anybody would be changed, after what you must have seen."

"It's more than that," I admitted. The walk was not long, but I took my time. As we rounded the house, I saw across the north lawn that Mr. Morningside was indeed there, and he was finishing building a pyre, stripped of his coat and down to his shirtsleeves. The sight of him doing menial labor was like watching a hedgehog dance a gavotte. "Father is gone. Mother is with my spirit now. I'm still learning what that means, and I know you were not there to see what I became when Father took control. It was ugly, violent, wild in a way that frightened me."

"Mary told me something of it," Lee replied. "I couldn't understand why you would make a deal with Mr. Morningside again, but she said it must be done."

"Aye, and she spoke truly. It had to be done." I paused then, watching Mr. Morningside carefully lift Mrs. Haylam's lifeless body onto the piled wood. She had given her all to protect the house. Just like the others. It was a miracle she and Giles were the only casualties. "Do you know, I once saw a farmer burning his field. I never understood why until now. He was cleaning away the useless stuff so that new and better plants might grow. That's how I feel now, Lee. Father was an inferno, unbridled, but Mother is quite different. This is a fire I want to set. A fire I can control."

Lee stared at me, unblinking. "Then . . . you're happy?"

"I didn't say that." I offered him a thin smile and nodded toward the pyre. "Mrs. Haylam is gone, but you're still here. Is her magic not needed to sustain you?"

He scratched his chin at that; a bit of whiskers had started to grow there. "Chijioke thinks I might be tied more to the book than to her. I don't feel any different now that she is dead."

"Good," I said softly, thinking. "That's good. Because I own the black book now, so you are in no near danger of disappearing."

Chapter Thirty

r. Morningside had just lit the kindling beneath the pyre when Lee, Bartholomew, and I reached the clearing.

He stood back from the crackle as it sparked, spread, and grew into a blaze. The flames leapt upward, chewing the too-wet wood that smoked and sent a pillar of black smoke straight up into the air, as if signaling to some distant army. With arms crossed, he watched as the fire neared Mrs. Haylam's still body. Without Dalton's diary, I might never have known how long they had been together, or how closely their lives were linked. I couldn't help thinking of what she had told me as the battle against the Upworlders raged around us, that she should've been firmer with him, as if she were a mother and not his devoted follower.

Maybe, in a sense, she had been his guardian. And now, with all of his ancient friends gone, he was adrift, unanchored.

We did not make a stealthy approach, and he twisted at the hips, perhaps simply expecting employees of the house. His whole manner changed when he saw me there with the Dark Fae book still strapped to my back. He dropped his arms and frowned, then smiled, then frowned again as I advanced.

"I'm deeply sorry about Mrs. Haylam, about your friend," I said.

"Me, too. She was a loyal companion to the end, and such a feature of my life that her demise seemed impossible." Mr. Morningside looked away and back into the fire. "But you've returned and the battle has ended, which means—"

His brows lifted in anticipation.

"Yes," I told him. "The white book is no more."

"Then . . . it's over," he said, staring off into the forest. "It's over."

"I am sorry about your friend. *Friends*," I continued. "Or rather, I'm sorry that you lost them this way. That they tried to help you, believed you, and all along you were just using them. And I'm sorry about the house. I know it will be difficult for you to lose it."

"Lose it?" he repeated. It wasn't until that moment that Mr. Morningside took note of Lee's presence. He stepped away from the pyre and toward us, studying Lee with more interest, golden eyes aglow. "My dear Louisa, you haven't even given me the chance to fulfill my end of the deal. It will be more difficult, surely, with Mrs. Haylam gone, but not impossible."

"Indeed. The contract, do you have it?" I asked, then continued on before he could answer. "There's no need. I remember the wording precisely. You were to remove Father's spirit from me. You. If that did not come to pass, then Coldthistle House and the Black Elbion would be mine."

In his eagerness to respond, he smiled, then crooked one finger under his jaw and hesitated. "I'm sure you're just itching to explain your reasoning."

"You cannot remove what is already gone," I said, advancing on him. He looked startled, truly startled, and perhaps it was not until that moment that he realized how unlikely it was for me to have returned at all. Swallowing hard, he then also noticed Bartholomew. His mouth opened and closed a few times, but nothing came out. That was well enough, for I wasn't yet interested in what he had to say. He was at his most dangerous when he poured honeyed words into one's ears. "Mother is dead. All of the Upworlders are dead. And I would be dead, too, were it not for luck and strange coincidence. This is what you wanted, isn't it? Centuries of planning and plotting, moving us—the pieces in your little game—with promises and lies. Now that we've come to the end of your game, will you answer a riddle for me, Devil?"

His lip curled into a sneer, and he glanced toward the pyre as if to shame me for causing a scene in front of the dead. "Go on."

"Arms to embrace, yet no hands. Pinches to give, yet no fingers. Poison to wield, yet no needle." I put my hand lightly on Bartholomew's furry head and scratched. "What am I?"

Had I eyes that penetrated his skull, I might have seen all the wheels turning, all the quick calculations as he stewed over his answer. And were he a teakettle, steam would have clotted his ears, everything suddenly too hot. Mr. Morningside shifted his weight and crossed his arms again, tipping back his chin in an imperious manner that reminded me instantly of Malatriss. That didn't go in his favor, either.

"A scorpion," he said.

"Lying or inept, I hardly know if it matters anymore." I nudged the giant shaggy dog at my side, snapping my fingers in Mr. Morningside's direction. "Go on, Bartholomew. Is he telling the truth? Does he really think that's the answer? Or did he hope, secretly, that I would lose a finger for his error, that I would fail or die and become one less mess to sweep up?"

"It isn't so, Louisa. If I told you something in error, it was not intentional. I wanted dearly for you to succeed!"

Bartholomew glanced up at me with his seeking eyes, puppyish, while Morningside snorted, then stumbled backward, his own gaze widening with shock as the dog leapt toward him. He knocked Mr. Morningside off his feet, startling all of us, and then crawled over his body, the stiffer fur along the dog's spine standing up, rigid. His lips peeled back, showing finger-length teeth, and his eyes, normally so sweet, had gone feral with purpose.

"Louisa—" I heard Lee murmur.

"Just watch."

This was when I would know. Mr. Morningside's scheme would be revealed, his plot to end Mother and me, including the unlikely but certainly not unwanted possibility of Dalton and all the other Upworlders being wiped completely away. No matter what, there would be fewer to stand against him. I saw Mr. Morningside paw lightly at the dog's shoulders, a small, whimpering sound escaping him before Bartholomew lunged forward and . . . did nothing. The dog neither growled nor licked him. Bartholomew seemed only confused. Maybe it meant that there was no lie and no truth. That Mr. Morningside had not himself known what to expect when I approached the tomb.

"Satisfied?" Mr. Morningside grunted. He shoved his way to his feet and brushed the fur off his trousers. "I told you what I knew, and you did what I could not. Would you indulge an old fool and describe what it all was like?"

"It was . . . it was . . . beauty and then sorrow, amazement and then pain." I pushed my hand through my snarled hair in frustration and winced, even that movement upsetting the other arm in its sling. Was I wrong about him? Had he sent me out in ignorance and not with malice? In the end, it mattered less to me than the knowledge that he had waited until the last moment to sacrifice his beloved birds, long after his friends and employees had jumped in to defend the house. "You have no idea what you asked of me, what that place *was*. There were no answers there, only misery. I saw the place where the gods are born and where they go to sleep. I met a Binder, and it ripped my soul in half, then used an innocent to repair what was wounded. I only survived because of what Dalton told me, because of what I read in his diary."

I spun away, feeling the tears coming on. But the voice inside me, Mother's voice, emerged, gently at first and then with an insistence that could not be ignored.

"I'm sorry, Louisa." Mr. Morningside went quiet for a moment, and I could imagine him staring contemplatively into the flames. "I have no idea how you could stomach reading about us. The whole affair was, well, rather Byzantine, to be honest. My kind and his were never meant to mingle, for obvious reasons. Though I suppose I *must* be honest, eh? You have me at a disadvantage, knowing, as you now do, my intimate secrets."

It struck me as vain and sad that he would worry about such things when so many lives had been lost that day. "You will find that I am the last soul likely to pass judgment," I assured him. "I can . . . see, quite naturally, how one could fall hopelessly for Dalton. He was very genuine. Nothing but accommodating."

"Oh yes," he chuckled. "Dalton Spicer was certainly accommodating. He accommodated me right into his grave."

I turned around to see that he was not looking at the fire, but at me. "We are all of us thralls to our better nature."

"No," Mr. Morningside said drily. "No, not all of us are, Louisa."

"Indeed?" It was time to take what was owed, to move on. To bury Mother and find a place to start again. I had an idea for that, of course, or perhaps Mother did. "Indeed. Well, then you will not be surprised when I ask for the house and the book. You did not remove Father's spirit from me, and thus I want what was promised."

Lee shifted uncomfortably, and Bartholomew padded over to him, nuzzling into the young man's hip.

Mr. Morningside laughed again and smiled, but it never reached his eyes. "You cannot be serious, Louisa. It was I who sent you into that place, so in essence I was responsible for—"

"Do I look to be in a bargaining mood?" It came out in a deadly whisper, one that snatched his smile away handily. "I would sincerely advise against taking full responsibility for what occurred in that tomb. You who sees all ends and plans for all possibilities, even you could not prepare for what I learned, what I endured. And I doubt you could have survived it. I'm already feeling rather irritable, and you will hear now the extent of my mercy."

He stared back at me, fuming, his hands falling to his sides where they balled into fists.

"Louisa—"

The sound of a coughing fit drew my attention, and I turned briefly to see that its source was Poppy. We had amassed an audience, the remainder of the house staff as well as Khent and Fathom having gathered to watch us from a safe distance. I whirled back to face Mr. Morningside.

"You will abandon this place, and it will be torn down," I said, nodding toward the house. "I don't want it. Nobody should want it. As for the book . . ." Turning to Lee, I softened my tone, for he was innocent in all of this. "Lee, should you like to go on living as you are?"

"I . . . believe so, yes. Yes, I should like to go on, even if it is a strange new existence."

"Then keep your book," I said to Morningside. "But you will tear one page from it, and it will go to Lee. What he does with it, where he takes it, will be his business. If the book's power has sustained so many Residents over the years, then a page should prove more than enough."

I hooked my arm through Lee's and coaxed him away from the pyre. The wood had started to burn in earnest, igniting Mrs. Haylam's stained frock and the bandages I had tied over her arms and legs. The black, black smoke funneled into the air, forming a cloud that hung heavy over Coldthistle House.

"And me?" Mr. Morningside called after me. He sounded ragged, desperate. "What becomes of me?"

"You?" I spared him a single glance over my shoulder. "I never want to see you again."

Chapter Thirty-One

We buried Mother's body at sunset, in a hollowed-out cave beneath the house. I hoped that when the mansion was torn down, her roots and branches would spread through the foundation and become something lovely on the site of so much pain.

I left Mr. Morningside the diary, placing it just outside the green door in the foyer, the one that marked the entrance to his subterranean domain. Inside the cover, I had inscribed Dalton's final message for him.

Tell him I was wrong. He can be more than he is. There's still time.

"What will you do now?"

Lee had finished packing his things, which fit neatly into the small case he had arrived with when he came to Coldthistle House with his uncle. We stood outside in the late autumn air, the day after the battle. Chijioke and Fathom worked to load Giles's body, wrapped tightly in a sheet, into the wagon that would carry Niles back to Derridon. The undertaker had not survived the night, and a somber, still mood had fallen upon the house. Nobody spoke in tones above a whisper. No meals were served. We found our tea and sustenance on our own and ate in silence, for nobody knew quite what to say.

"I thought I might go home," Lee said, sitting down on the

gray stone stoop. The spoon necklace had been tucked under his shirt, and he wore a fine coat that he had saved from his initial travel to Yorkshire. "Things will feel much different there, now that I am, well, as I am. But more than that"—he looked into the middle distance and breathed deep—"now that I know that I was not the cause of my guardian's death, it might be easier to be at peace. Oh, I don't know. I've been in this strange, new form for so long now, it will be difficult to be only among normal humans again. I have no idea if I can inherit anymore, but I should like very much to see my family again."

"It won't be easy," I told him. "I never really found my way in London. When you've seen all that we have seen, the mundane world begins to lose its shine. I hope you fare better than I did, and I hope your family accepts you just as you are."

Family. The word did indeed have its draw. I gazed around at the assembled friends and former colleagues, who had all changed into shawls and cloaks for travel. Nobody fancied staying any longer at Coldthistle House, not when it was empty and even more dreary, the windows blown out, the turrets crooked and charred. No more Residents prowled the corridors. No more birdsong greeted one when dawn came.

"You know you are more than welcome to join us," I told him. I had bathed and changed into a simple black frock, one of my old uniforms, but chose to keep the pack with the remade book close to me at all times. It felt like a talisman, or perhaps, a charge. "It will be a long ride north, but there are places to stop along the way. Might be a pleasant ride, you know, if taken with friends."

Lee nodded, his blond curls bouncing, and he gave me a good-natured smirk. "Will the post reach you if I try to write? Perhaps when I have had my fill of family I can come and see what your world is like."

"There will always be room for you," I said, pressing his hand. "And about the post . . . Well, why don't you put down your address, and I will see what can be done about it."

Chuckling, Lee dug into his bag, bringing out a bit of parchment. Inside, I saw a flash of yellowed paper, rolled up. The page from the Black Elbion. He would need it with him always, but at least it would allow him some sense of freedom.

"There you are." He stood, handing me the slip of parchment. "Now it looks like they are ready to depart. I thought I should go with Niles as far as Derridon, and from there I will find my way home."

We clasped hands, and then he pulled me into an embrace, mindful of my arm. But I knew it would not be the last time we met. I longed for him to see home, as I had never imagined it might happen again, but he was now a creature of shadow and magic, and one day he would need a place where that was not shocking at all. Standing on the stoop, I watched as he said his goodbyes to the others, then climbed into the wagon with Niles. The two men turned in the driver's box and waved, and my heart clenched a little in loss or regret as they rumbled out of the drive, making their way to different homes, both shrouded in sadness.

"And you?" I followed the rut of the wheel left in the gravel, tracing it to Fathom, who watched the wagon disappear with one hand tucked above her eyes, just under her dashing tricorn hat. "Will you be accompanying us or taking up the safe house in Deptford?" I asked.

"Neither." Fathom shook her head, picking thoughtfully at a bandage on her hand. Of all of us, she seemed to have escaped the battle mostly unscathed, which was quite the feat for a human. "I'm off, I think. Somewhere far. Too many memories back in Deptford. Too raw. I have a friend in Massachusetts, Lucy, whom I should look in on. She'll put up with me for a while, at least." She chuckled and knocked me gently on the good shoulder. "Come see America, Louisa. Plenty of spooky nonsense there, and I don't just mean the politics."

She had procured a horse from the stables, and she jumped up onto it with practiced ease.

"I'm sorry for what happened to Dalton," I told her, glancing away. "He spoke fondly of you at the end."

Fathom gave another bawdy laugh and tipped her hat to me, wrangling the horse toward the road. "Of course he did. Crazy ginger always did have a thing for me. And he was one of the rare good ones. The good ones don't last long in this world, and he lasted longer than most. Living in that safe house, I saw a lot of folks come and go, but Dalton was always there, always dependable. It just wouldn't be the same there now that he's on his own adventure."

With that, she was gone, dust covering her departure as she sped out of the drive and south, toward distant London.

And there was, of course, the looming question of where Poppy, Mary, and Chijioke would go. Bartholomew would follow wherever the little girl went, and they, along with Khent, waited expectantly by the final two carriages, one riddled with holes from the Tarasque, the other the light and fast phaeton Niles and Dalton had driven up from St. Albans.

"You're packed," I said, with some surprise, finding that while I'd said goodbye to Lee and Fathom, Mary had carried out a number of overstuffed bags, including one filled with silver and trinkets, no doubt to sell. I had considered that they might want to join me, but after so many broken families, I never allowed myself to truly believe it. "I thought . . ."

I had no idea how to even begin. "But in the spring, when I bargained for your contracts to be severed . . . Well, I thought you all wanted to stay."

"We did. *Then.*" Chijioke took Mary's hand and picked up one of the bags. "There isn't anything left for us here, and Mr. Morningside . . . Well, he almost got us all killed, and I might not love the Upworlders, but it was ugly business. If he thought he could make us fight his battles for him and do his bidding forever, then he had things seriously twisted around. I don't want to stay here another minute and watch him put you or Mary in danger again."

"And you're right," Mary added with a sheepish smile. "With how hard it's all been, we thought it best to stick together. Family-like, you see. We're all eager to be away from here."

Poppy nodded, but then seemed to change her mind, glancing back at the house. She frowned, and marched up to me, tugging hard on my skirts. "Bartholomew comes, too! He comes with, or I won't go at all."

The dog howled in agreement.

"Of course," I said, tossing Khent a glance. "Canines are welcome in this family."

Khent rolled his eyes, grabbing two of the packed cases and taking them toward the larger carriage. "I am much cleaner than that thing. And better behaved."

"But this is what you want?" I asked again, looking at each of them in turn. "It will be a long road north, and I have no idea what to expect when we reach the First City. This was never how I thought it would go."

"That makes five of us," Mary said with a sigh.

"*Six*," Poppy insisted, grabbing Bartholomew by the ear.

That seemed to settle it. We would all go north together and find what we could find along the way to the First City. There was room enough for us all in the carriages, and Chijioke knew the surrounding roads well. I expected no ambushes on the road, not now that the Upworlders were no more. Poppy hauled a bag far too big for her toward the carriage, and Bartholomew picked up the slack, grabbing the drooping end in his jaws and trotting along. While the final preparations were made, I found myself drifting back toward the house.

It had looked more foreboding the first time I laid eyes upon it. Now it was merely empty, gutted, the cold hearth and home of only one man. One man who watched us like a fleeting shadow from a high-above window. Gazing up at him, I wondered at his sad eyes, at the confusion and betrayal I saw there. His help had served him faithfully, to the last, but even loyalty had its limits. Perhaps, I thought, he would one day understand why he lived now in abandoned infamy, having gotten his way and finding it wanting.

"Do you think he will try something?" Khent asked, startling me.

He put a hand on my back, where he had before, to give me courage.

"No," I said honestly, watching the Devil turn away from me to haunt other empty rooms. "No, I don't think he will."

We returned to the carriages to find the others bickering over who would ride where. Bartholomew had already claimed a spot in the lighter box, perhaps desirous of the wind in his face. Poppy's choice then, was made for her, and Chijioke helped her scamper up to settle in next to the hound.

"Where do you think he will go when the house is gone?" I

asked Chijioke. He knew at once who I meant.

"Where all devils go," he replied with a shrug. "Where he is most needed and least expected. Here," he said, opening his hands to me. "Let me help you with that."

He was implying the pack on my shoulders. I removed it carefully, wincing when it grazed my arm, then stopped him, stooping to pull out the book, which weighed no more than a normal volume. It was larger, however, and far more fantastical, bright green with purple vines scrolling across it, a stag and spider stamped in the middle.

I ran a hand across the leather with a shiver, knowing it was some poor adventurer's hide. A voice shimmered up to me from the pages, deep and relieved, a man's voice. Father. But it did not sound like any memory of him I had. It sounded like a man unbroken, a man made whole.

Released from the agony of anger . . . At last.

The others had frozen, watching me. I looked at them gathered there, Mary with her tousled brown hair and dainty freckles, Chijioke still waiting to take the bag with outstretched hands, the dark skin of his forearms bandaged heavily from the fight. And Poppy with her beloved dog, both of them leaning out of the phaeton, the little girl with the mark on her face twining one braid expectantly around her finger. Khent leaned against the carriage, lavender eyes inscrutable, his smile kind as he waited and I tarried.

"Courage," he mouthed to me and I nodded.

"We are creatures of darkness and curiosity but there is good in this book, and goodness is powerful. It has always been powerful, only that has been forgotten." I did not know if I spoke Mother's words or my own, but they came freely and with a confidence I had not felt before. "This book, *our* book, will help the world to remember. And goodness . . . Goodness does not always mean peace. It does not mean weakness. What goodness is in this book and in us will see us through to the north, and then beyond, into our lives."

I took a deep breath and let Chijioke take the pack and book, watching it go into his arms with tears filming my eyes. "They tried to snuff us out. This was their age, of angels and shadows and demons. Now comes our chance, our age, the age of our fury."

"Hear, hear!" Chijioke shouted, giving me a wink. "Now say that all back again when we get to the pub. It demands a toast, eh, lass?"

"Aye," I said with a laugh. "I promise not to forget a word."

Then the book was put into the carriage, and Mary came to take me by the arm, and we took the last few steps together.

But after I had taken the step up, I lingered in the open door of the carriage, looking back at Coldthistle House once more, expecting—perhaps hoping—to catch one last glimpse of its former master. On the topmost floor on the most easterly turret, there was a glimmer of yellow eyes. But as soon as they appeared they were gone, a pair of curtains shutting up tight, as if to say the play had ended, as if to say no more. As if to close the place off forever, a lone, forgotten tomb.

Epilogue

walked out one day across County Leitrim and County Sligo, taking not the road but the fields and woods, finding I wanted to be a hidden thing. The mists on the emerald carpets of grass hung low, a fairy twinkle in the dawn light. The pack on my back, heavier than it had ever been, had long since carved ruts in my shoulders. 'Twas all but part of me now, that bag with that book, but I would never be separated from it, it being my eternal burden to bear.

A devil walked out in the early morning, across rolling, rolling hills, wildflowers thick along the stone walls, so bright they seemed almost artificial, hothouse perfect, dazzling rows of blue and yellow heads. They marked the way and I followed. Many times I had tried to walk this path, and each time something stopped me. But not this time. My heart, set in stone, would see the journey through. The hissing song of night gave way to the softer morning chatter of distant roosters and closer wrens. There were dunnocks, too, and singing thrush, blackbirds, and doves, all a-warble with the promise of a new day.

A sad, old creature, decrepit as only the ancient and regretful can be, walked until his feet ached and were bloody. This is how it happened:

Night had been blessedly cool, but now it turned to day, and so came the heat, and I stopped for a while to rest on a toppled stone ruin. The lake, undisturbed as glass, spread out behind me, the mountainous woods and my destination to the east. I watched the sun break over the water and fished out a canteen, helping myself to last night's beer. It was sour but cold enough, and I drank deep, flinching as a buzz began over the horizon, then grew, a pointed white object soaring over the lake toward me, low enough to make my bones thrum. I would never get used to those things shooting overhead. Once, it would have been a

Sky Snake protecting those skies; now it was only machines.

"Are you lost?"

It was a tiny voice, and from a girl. I turned to my right, resting the canteen against my side to find a lass no higher than my knee watching me from the hedges. She seemed a part of the place, wild, with tiny flowers dotting her very dark hair. Her eyes, huge and amethyst, watched me with such intelligence that I nearly laughed. Was this a girl or a little fairy creature? Impossible to know.

"I might be," I said kindly, reaching into my pack again and coming up with a bit of chocolate I had bought in the last village. "I might be. Do you like sweets?"

"Mother says I must never take things from strangers," the girl replied. "And you seem awfully strange."

"Strange, yes, but also harmless." I ate the chocolate myself, noticing the flash of envy in her eyes. "Do you have a name, little sprite?"

"Dahlia."

I nodded and finished the chocolate, wiping off my hands on already-stained trousers. "You know, Dahlia, you must be careful who you give your name to, for names have power."

Her eyes, already so large, grew bigger. "My mother says that, also. What's your name?"

"Henry," I said, then pointed to the wooded plateau to the east, miles and miles away. "Do you live there, by any chance?"

"Near." Ah, a smart child. She took a few steps forward,

putting her hands into two big pockets on her floral-patterned shirt. She wore wide trousers and round, brown shoes. I watched her take a spoon from her pocket and hold it at her side.

"I see," I said, nodding toward her hand. "And what is that spoon for?"

"Nothing," the girl replied. "I just like to have it."

"I'll bet it keeps you safe. But don't you worry, I won't harm you." I would never harm you. "Won't you keep an old man company? We might walk together, for I am bound for that hill, too."

"Really? Have you come to visit?"

Her innocent, high voice pierced my heart, and I hefted the pack, sliding it onto my shoulders before starting toward her through the grass. Another plane whirred overhead, low, and she dropped into the hedge with practiced skill. I knelt and parted the branches, offering a kind smile.

"I hate them, too. They make my ears ring."

Her nose wrinkled as if she could sniff out my intentions. Perhaps she could. Dahlia climbed out of the brush and dusted herself off, then reached for my hand, tugging me along the path of wildflowers and stones.

"You will get lost without help," she said. "The woods are very twisty. How do you know to visit? Nobody is allowed."

"I think I know your mother." I grinned. "You have her hair and her eyes, though the color is all wrong."

"Everyone says I have my father's eyes," Dahlia informed me.

"Do you know him, too?"

"Perhaps. And what do you think of the moon, fair one?"

She put the spoon back in her pocket and toddled along more confidently. "I like it. I like it very much. But why are you here? Nobody is allowed, so it must be very important."

We broke away from the lake, heading directly into dense, hilly country. The mist grew thicker, rising until only Dahlia's head poked above it. A tiny blossom fell out of her hair, but I caught it and tucked it away.

"I need your mother's help. The world has gotten ugly and dark, people are hurting each other."

"Father says it's because humans are awful and don't know how to behave," Dahlia told me. She wasn't wrong, but I had to chuckle. A child's view was simple, full of conviction, and I had no evidence to contradict her. She had also, apparently, divined that I was not human and therefore worthy of trust.

"He isn't wrong, but that's why I need help. We must . . ." How to explain war to a child? How to explain the unfettered crisis tearing the world to pieces? I sighed and moved a branch out of the way. "We must help them remember how to be good. Your folk were always full of goodness and light, and if we do nothing, all those human problems will find you, too."

"Nobody finds us," she declared.

"They can," I said. "They will. But we can help them. Your mother can help them. I know she wanted to go away, to protect you all, but now she's needed again. When something terrible happens you must do something, Dahlia, you must never do nothing. I did nothing once, and I regret it every day of my life."

She considered that for a moment, a bullfrog taking its time to move out of the way as we tromped through the forest. Normally I would have taken pains to be more discreet, but then, I had a guide.

"Mother is quite stubborn, but you may try."

Yes, I thought, she was the most stubborn person I had ever known. It seemed impossible that we should meet again, and yet, the paths of the gods had a way of crossing. I was only ever made to bring darkness to the world. Now more than ever, we needed light.

"Then I will try. You know, it is important, Dahlia, that we try. Tell me something, dear," I said, helping her across a narrow, trickling brook. "Do you fancy birds?"

The End

Acknowledgments

This series would not exist without the patience, thoughtfulness, and guidance of Andrew Eliopulos. The team at HarperCollins worked so, so hard on these books, and I'm grateful for their creativity and persistence. Iris Compiet brought the magic of this world to life, and I've been so lucky to have her art side by side with my words. Thanks as well to Olivia Russo for publicity help, and Brooke Shaden for her gorgeous cover work. A sincere thanks to Kate McKean for always being such a rock and giving excellent advice. Additional thanks to the Association Assyrophile de France and Amanda Raths for translation assistance.

And lastly to my family, friends, and fans for coming along on this twisty journey and helping me realize the dream of these books. It has been the most gratifying adventure of my career.

Image Credits

Victorian border on pages ii, iii, vi, vii, 1, 5, 17, 29, 39, 52, 68, 75, 89, 105, 119, 130, 139, 154, 166, 171, 186, 198, 214, 222, 232, 245, 267, 277, 289, 301, 312, 320, 332, 339, 347, 356, 367 © 2019 by iStock / Getty Images.

Wall texture on pages ii, iii, vi, vii, 1, 5, 17, 29, 39, 52, 68, 75, 89, 105, 119, 130, 139, 154, 166, 171, 186, 198, 214, 222, 232, 245, 267, 277, 289, 301, 312, 320, 332, 339, 347, 356, 367 © 2019 by iStock / Getty Images.

Rusty wall on pages 4, 51, 88, 129, 165, 185, 213, 266, 288 © 2019 by iStock / Getty Images.

Photographs on pages 4, 51, 88, 129, 165, 185, 213, 266, 288 © 2019 by Shutterstock.

Illustrations on pages 40, 76, 120, 172, 223, 246, 302, 340, 368 by Iris Compiet.